Shadows of Power

The Shadows Series
Book 2

Jennifer Carr

JCarr
WRITES

Published by JCarr Writes (jcarrwrites.com)

ISBN-13: 978-1969792014 (paperback)

ASIN: B0F1Y84VJS (digital)

Prologue

Alessandra

The cold weight of the gun still lingered in my hand, a phantom sensation that refused to fade even after I had discarded the weapon. The echo of the gunshot reverberated in my mind, drowning out everything else—the sound of his body hitting the floor, the sharp intake of breath from those who witnessed it, and the suffocating silence that followed as the reality of what I had done settled over us all.

I had killed my father.

I walked through the darkened halls of the estate, the place that had been my home for as long as I could remember, now a prison of ghosts and memories. Every corner seemed to whisper reminders of my father's presence—of the lessons he had drilled into me, of the woman I had once been before his shadow consumed me. My footsteps echoed softly on the marble floors, a reminder that I was still here, still breathing, even though it felt like a part of me had died alongside him.

The Navarra legacy was mine now, but instead of power, all I felt was the crushing weight of responsibility. The grand rooms of the mansion, once alive with my father's commands and calculated plans, now felt hollow, like a tomb where even the air carried the weight of what I had done.

In the distance, the low hum of voices drifted through the halls—men discussing deals, strategies, alliances, all now under my control. I paused outside the study, the room where my father had built his empire piece by piece, a place that had always felt more like a war room than a sanctuary. But today, it was silent, abandoned, as if the house itself mourned his death.

I felt the presence before I heard his voice.

"Alessandra."

I turned to see Nico standing behind me, concern etched in every line of his face. "The men are waiting," he said gently. "They need direction. They need to see that you're in control."

Control. The word sounded foreign, as if I were grasping for something slippery and unstable. But Nico was right. The men needed to see strength, and I couldn't let them see the cracks beneath the surface. My father's death had left a vacuum, and if I didn't fill it with unwavering authority, they would devour me like wolves.

"They'll get their direction," I replied, forcing steel into my voice. "But first, I need a moment."

Nico hesitated, then nodded, stepping back into the shadows. As he disappeared, I continued my slow journey through the mansion, each step heavy with the knowledge of what lay ahead.

I stopped outside my father's private quarters, the place where he had once ruled over his empire. The room was untouched—his books still neatly arranged, his desk cluttered with papers he would never finish. The old leather chair where he had sat for hours on end was empty now, and the room felt colder for it.

I approached the large mirror that hung on the wall, and for the first time, I forced myself to look.

The woman staring back at me was not the woman I remembered. Her eyes were hollow, her face hardened, her expression a mixture of grief and determination. My father's bloodline ran through my veins, but it was the blood on my hands that defined me now.

I reached out, touching the cool glass, as if I could pull the woman I used to be back from the depths. But that woman was gone, buried beneath the choices I had made.

A memory flashed through my mind—Steven's face just before I pulled the trigger, his voice pleading with me to choose love over loyalty. I had made my choice. I had killed my father to save him, and now, there was no turning back.

The crushing loneliness pressed down on me like a suffocating weight. But alongside it, something else began to grow—a flicker of resolve, a determination to see this through. I had taken the first step, and now I would have to live with the consequences.

I couldn't afford to mourn the man who had shaped me. I couldn't afford to let guilt consume me.

The family was mine to lead. Steven was mine to protect.

With one last glance at the woman in the mirror, I turned away, steeling myself for what was to come.

There would be no room for doubt, no room for hesitation. The wolves were watching, waiting for a sign of weakness. I wouldn't give them one.

As I walked down the hall, the weight of the crown my father had left behind pressed against me like a vice. But I would wear it. Even if it crushed me.

Because I had made my choice, and there was no turning back.

That was the price of survival in a world that didn't allow for innocence.

Part One

Chapter 1

A Captive Audience

Steven

I woke up groggy, my mind swimming through layers of darkness that clung to me like a heavy fog. The first thing I noticed was the faint, metallic taste in my mouth, the kind that comes from being drugged. I'd been in enough situations during my career that I knew this to be true but right now it was hard to make sense of my thoughts to even grasp at those memories. My head throbbed with a dull ache, and I struggled to remember how I had ended up here, wherever *here* was.

I blinked, trying to focus as my surroundings slowly came into view. The room was dimly lit, the soft glow of a lamp casting long shadows across the walls. I pushed myself up into a sitting position, the sheets sliding off me as I took in the unfamiliar space. The last clear memory I had was of Alessandra, standing in front of me, her eyes filled with a mixture of regret and something far darker. She had been holding a gun.

A cold chill ran down my spine as the memories started to piece themselves together, coming in disjointed flashes. The confrontation.

The barrel of the gun aimed directly at me. Her voice, trembling with emotion, saying, "I'm sorry." The gunshot. And then... nothing. Just darkness.

I glanced down at myself, half-expecting to find a wound, but there was nothing—no blood, no pain. I was physically unharmed, but that did little to ease the panic building in my chest. I had no idea how long I had been unconscious, no sense of time passing. Had it been hours? Days?

And why did it feel like I had died and come back wrong?

I threw off the covers and swung my legs over the side of the bed, the room tilting slightly as I stood. My head spun, and I had to grip the bedpost to steady myself. The weight of the drug still lingered in my system, slowing my thoughts, making it hard to focus.

As I steadied myself, I forced my mind to work through the haze, to make sense of what had happened. The last thing I remembered clearly was the gunshot, the sound deafening in my ears, and Alessandra's face—her expression one of devastation. But if she had pulled the trigger, why was I still alive?

I took a deep breath and began to explore the room, the need for answers driving me forward. The furniture was ornate, the kind of stuff you'd find in an old estate, with heavy wooden pieces and intricate carvings. There was a faint scent of lavender in the air, a small vase of flowers on a table near the window. It was almost too perfect, as if someone had gone out of their way to make me comfortable in the space.

I spotted my phone on the dresser and rushed over to it, my hands shaking as I picked it up. The screen flickered to life, but my hope quickly faded when I saw the signal—no bars, nothing. I was cut off, isolated, with no way to reach the outside world. The reality of my situation began to settle in, heavy and oppressive.

I tried the door next, testing the handle. It was locked. Of course.

So I'm a prisoner.

I sank into a nearby chair, the events of the last few days crashing down on me. The last conversation with Alessandra replayed in my mind, her words haunting me. She had been pointing the gun at me. I was supposed to be the victim. But something had changed. She'd hesitated, and in that hesitation, things had spiraled out of my control.

I buried my face in my hands, the weight of it all pressing down on me. The love I had once felt for her was now tangled up with fear, confusion, and anger. How could she do this to me? How could she bring me into her world, knowing the danger, knowing what it had cost?

But even as those thoughts churned in my mind, there was a deeper, more troubling question gnawing at me: *Why was I still alive and what was going to happen next?*

The gunshot echoed in my mind, over and over, as if it were happening again. I remembered the way her hands had trembled, the tears in her eyes. Had she missed on purpose? Had someone intervened? Or had she saved me in the only way she could by pulling that trigger and rewriting the script at the last second?

The questions circled like vultures, picking at my thoughts.

The uncertainty was suffocating, the not knowing worse than any physical pain. I wanted answers, needed them, but there was no one here to give them to me. No one to explain what was going on, or why I was still alive when, by all rights, I should be dead.

Just then, I heard the faint sound of footsteps outside the door. My heart leaped into my throat, the adrenaline flooding my system as I tensed, every muscle in my body on high alert. The footsteps grew louder, closer, the steady rhythm matching the thud of my pulse.

I forced myself to stand, my legs trembling as I moved toward the door. I had no idea what I would find on the other side, but I couldn't just sit here and wait. Somebody had to have answers.

The footsteps stopped just outside the door, and I held my breath, the anticipation nearly unbearable. Then, the handle turned slowly, and I braced myself for whatever—or whoever—was about to come through that door.

Chapter 2

The Shadows We Live In

Alessandra

I stood outside Steven's door, my hand hovering over the handle, unable to bring myself to turn it. My heartbeat thudded in my ears, loud enough that it drowned out the faint sound of footsteps passing somewhere down the hall. I clenched my fingers into a fist, willing them to stop shaking, but the tremor wouldn't go away. Inside that room was the man I had risked everything to protect—the man I had betrayed, trapped, and lied to.

Steven.

Just his name sent a pang through my chest, a reminder of everything we'd had and everything I'd destroyed. The last time we stood face to face, I'd been holding a gun. I'd chosen to kill my father to save him, and still, here we were, in this cold reality where no choice was without consequence.

Taking a deep breath, I turned the handle and pushed open the door. The hinges creaked softly, the sound unnaturally loud in the silence of the room. Steven stood near the chair in the middle of the room, his posture rigid, shoulders squared like he was ready for a fight. His gaze met mine, cold and sharp, his jaw clenched so tightly that the muscle twitched. His fists hung at his sides, knuckles white, and I could tell he was barely holding himself together.

When he saw me, a mix of emotions flashed across his face—anger, betrayal, confusion. But above all, there was a cold distance that made my heart ache. I could feel the tension between us, so thick it was almost suffocating, the air heavy with everything that had been left unsaid.

"Steven," I said softly, my voice barely above a whisper. It was all I could manage, the name feeling like both a plea and a confession on my lips.

He didn't respond right away, his eyes narrowing as he studied me. I could see the anger simmering beneath the surface, held back by a thin thread of control that could snap at any moment. "Why am I here, Alessandra?" he finally asked, his voice cold, laced with bitterness that cut me to the core.

I flinched at the harshness in his tone, but I couldn't blame him. He had every right to be angry, every right to demand answers. But how could I explain? How could I make him understand that I'd done this to protect him—that keeping him here was the only way to keep him safe?

"You're here because it's the only way I can protect you," I said, taking a tentative step closer, even though every instinct told me to stay back.

He laughed, but there was no humor in it, just a hollow, bitter sound that made my heart ache.

"Protect me?" he echoed, his tone laced with incredulous anger. "By making me a prisoner in your family's web? Is that what love is to you—control, Alessandra?"

He took a step forward, and I flinched involuntarily, guilt prickling under my skin like a rash.

"It's not like that, Steven," I said, desperately trying to make him see. "I'm trying to save your life."

"Save my life?" He scoffed, as if the very idea was a cruel joke.

"Let me guess, this is the part where you convince yourself that your act was noble."

"I don't expect you to understand," I whispered, but my voice broke under the weight of the truth.

His words struck like blows, each one hitting with more force than the last. I felt my resolve wavering, but I knew I couldn't let it falter. "I didn't want it to be like this," I said, keeping my voice steady. "But I didn't have a choice. You don't know what my family is capable of. You don't know how far they'll go to protect their secrets."

"And you're just like them, aren't you?" he said, his voice razor-sharp. "Willing to destroy anything that gets in the way."

His words stung, but what hurt more was the memory they brought with them—a warm spring day on the NYU campus, sitting on the library steps with his arm slung lazily around my shoulder. "Promise me one thing," he had whispered back then, his lips brushing my ear. "No matter what happens, we never hurt each other. Deal?"

"Deal," I had whispered back.

But that promise had shattered. I had shattered it. And now, here we were, with that memory turning into a knife twisting in my chest.

His accusations hung in the air, and for a moment, I couldn't find the words to respond. Because the truth was, he wasn't wrong. I had become like them—cold, ruthless, willing to sacrifice anything and anyone to protect what I loved. But it wasn't for power, or money, or the legacy my father had left behind. It was for him.

"Maybe I am," I admitted, my voice firmer. "Maybe I've become the very thing I've always feared. But I did it for you, Steven. Because I love you, and I couldn't let them take you away from me."

He shook his head, turning slightly as if he couldn't bear to look at me. "This isn't love, Alessandra," he said quietly. "Love doesn't do this. Love doesn't destroy everything in its path."

The pain in his voice cut through me like a knife, but I forced myself to stand tall, to not let his words break me. "I didn't know what else to do," I confessed. "I couldn't lose you, Steven. I couldn't let him kill you. I know you're angry, and I know I've hurt you, but please... understand that I did this because I didn't see any other way."

He remained silent, his posture rigid, and the distance between us felt insurmountable. I had feared this moment, feared what would happen when he finally learned the truth about me, about my family. But no matter how many times I had imagined it, nothing could have prepared me for the reality of seeing the love in his eyes replaced by something I couldn't bear to name.

The silence stretched on, heavy and suffocating, until finally, Steven spoke again, his voice so quiet I almost didn't hear it. "I don't know who you are anymore, Alessandra. And I don't know if I ever really did."

His words hit me like a physical blow, and I took a step back, the full weight of his rejection settling over me. He was right. He had never truly known me, because I had never allowed him to. I had kept my secrets, hidden the darkest parts of myself, thinking I could protect him from the truth. But all I had done was push him further away.

I wanted to reach out to him, to close the distance between us, but I couldn't move. I was paralyzed by the fear that any attempt to bridge the gap would only drive him further away. So, I did the only thing I could—I let him go.

"If you hate me," I said, my voice steady, "I understand. But you can't leave. I need time to fix this."

For a long moment, there was only silence. Then, slowly, Steven turned his head, just enough for me to see the pain etched into his features. He didn't say anything, but the way he looked at me—like I was a stranger, like I was someone he'd never seen before—tore me apart.

Finally, he turned back to the chair, sinking into it heavily as if the weight of the world was pressing down on him. The conversation was over. He clearly had nothing left to say to me.

I stood there for a moment longer, the silence echoing in my ears, my heart breaking in ways I didn't think were possible. My fingers tightened around the door handle, nails digging into my palm as I fought back the tears threatening to escape.

As I closed the door behind me, I felt more isolated than ever, the weight of the choices I had made threatening to crush me. But even as I walked away, I knew one thing for certain—I wouldn't let him go. I couldn't. Not after everything we had been through, everything we had lost.

No matter what it took, I would find a way to protect him, to make this right. Even if it meant sacrificing everything else, even if it meant losing myself completely in the process.

Because without Steven, there was nothing left of me worth saving.

Chapter 3

The Gilded Cage

Steven

I didn't know how long I sat in the chair, staring at the door that Alessandra had just walked through. My thoughts were a tangled mess of emotions—anger, betrayal, confusion, and a familiar sense of loss. It was as if the woman I loved had been replaced by someone I didn't recognize, someone who could look me in the eyes and justify everything she had done.

The weight of the situation pressed down on me, making it hard to breathe. I had never felt so powerless, so completely at the mercy of forces beyond my control. My life, once dictated by my own choices, now ruled by someone else's decisions—someone who had decided that keeping me here, locked away in this gilded prison, was the only way to protect me.

I glanced around the room, trying to distract myself from the turmoil inside. It was a beautiful space, tastefully decorated with rich fabrics and expensive furniture, but it felt oppressive, like the walls were closing in on me. The opulence of the room only served to remind me of how far removed I was from my own life—from the freedom I had taken for granted.

The light outside the window had dimmed, the sun sinking low on the horizon, casting shadows across the floor and walls. I had no sense of time, no idea how long I had been unconscious or what day it even was. Everything felt disjointed, as if I were living in a dream—or a nightmare—I couldn't wake up from.

I stood up, pacing the length of the room in an attempt to clear my head, but the thoughts kept circling back to the same questions. What was I supposed to do now? How was I supposed to get out of this? The anger surged again, a hot, burning sensation that settled deep in my gut. I needed to move, to do something, anything that would make me feel less like a caged animal.

But just as I was about to cross to the door, it swung open, and a young woman in a crisp uniform stepped inside. She carried a tray, the clatter of dishes the only sound in the room as she set it down on the small table by the window.

"Dinner, sir," she said, her voice polite, but there was an edge of caution in her tone. "Ms. Navarra wanted to make sure you had everything you need."

I stared at the tray for a moment, the sight of the food making my stomach churn. The last thing I wanted was to eat. "I'm not hungry," I said, my voice rough.

The woman hesitated, her hands fidgeting with the edge of her apron. "Are you sure, sir? Ms. Navarra was very insistent that you take care of yourself."

I almost laughed at that—take care of myself? In this place? But the look in the woman's eyes stopped me. She wasn't just here to bring me food. She was here to check on me, to see if I was going to cause any trouble. I could see the fear in her eyes, the fear of what might happen if she went back and told Alessandra that I had refused.

I stared at the tray, the scent of roasted chicken and garlic filling the room, but my stomach twisted at the sight of it. Alessandra drugged me once before. What was stopping her from doing it again?

"I'm sure," I said, softening my tone slightly. "I'm not hungry. But maybe you can answer something for me."

The woman nodded quickly, eager to help. "Of course, sir. Anything you need."

"What am I allowed to do here?" I asked, folding my arms across my chest. "Am I free to leave this room, or am I expected to stay here?"

She blinked, clearly surprised by the question. "You're not a prisoner, sir. You're free to move about the estate as you wish. But..." She hesitated, her eyes flicking toward the door. "There will be someone with you at all times, for your protection."

"For my protection," I repeated, the bitterness creeping back into my voice. "Of course."

The woman nodded again, clearly uncomfortable. "Ms. Navarra just wants to make sure you're safe, sir. The estate can be... a bit overwhelming for someone who's not used to it."

I couldn't help but scoff at that. "Overwhelming is one way to put it, I'm sure." I looked back at the tray, the smell of the food turning my stomach. "Thank you for the dinner, but I'll pass."

She hesitated, clearly torn between doing her job and respecting my wishes. Finally, she gave a small nod and began to gather the tray, her movements quick and efficient. As she reached the door, she paused, turning back to look at me.

"If you need anything, sir, please don't hesitate to ask," she said, her voice soft.

I didn't respond, watching as she slipped out of the room, leaving me alone once more. The door clicked shut behind her, the sound echoing in the silence that followed.

I stood there for a moment, processing what she had said. I wasn't a prisoner, but I wasn't exactly free, either. I could move around the estate, but I would always have someone watching me, keeping me in line. The idea of it made my skin crawl, the reality of my situation sinking in even deeper.

I walked over to the window, staring out at the vast gardens that surrounded the estate. The sun had dipped below the horizon now, the last rays of light fading into the twilight. The estate was beautiful, there was no denying that. But it wasn't my world. It wasn't my life.

And it wasn't where I belonged.

But for now, it was where I was. I was stuck in this place, with no way out, no idea what the future held. And as much as I wanted to fight against it, to demand my freedom, I knew it would be a losing battle. Not until I figured out what was really going on.

Taking a deep breath, I turned away from the window and made my way back to the chair. I sat down heavily, my mind racing with questions that had no answers. The only thing I knew for sure was that I needed to talk to Alessandra again. I needed to know why she thought this was the only way, and what she expected me to do now. But deep down, I knew—no matter what answers she gave me, no matter how many apologies she whispered—it wouldn't be enough to fix what had been broken. It wouldn't bring back the woman I had once loved, or the man I had been before her world devoured mine.

Chapter 4

Behind Closed Doors

Alessandra

The weight of expectation wrapped around me like a steel vice as I made my way down the long corridor toward the meeting room. My heels clicked against the polished floor, each step deliberate, rehearsed—an echo reminding me of of the woman I needed to be. The cool air brushed against my skin, but it did nothing to quell the heat of anxiety simmering just below the surface. The estate, once a place that offered me security and shelter, now felt like an elaborate stage, its shadows waiting to swallow me whole if I misstepped.

This meeting would be my first major test. And Marco would be there to watch me either pass or burn.

I stopped outside the double doors, inhaling deeply, and pushed them open.

Inside, the air was thick with tension. Conversations stopped mid-sentence as every pair of eyes fixed on me. The room smelled of wood polish and expensive cigars, a familiar scent that had clung to my father like a second skin. Now, it was a reminder that his shadow still lingered here.

I walked to the head of the table, my movements steady, deliberate. The room was large, its walls lined with dark wood paneling, the table a solid expanse of polished mahogany. My father had sat at the head of this table for years, his authority unquestioned. Now, as I took his place, the weight of his legacy bore down on me.

Nico, ever loyal, was already seated to my right, his gaze steady and reassuring. But to my left, Marco sat with his arms crossed, his expression a mix of anger and suspicion. He had been my father's right-hand man for years, and I knew he resented the power shift, resented that I now occupied the seat of authority. The rest of the men—lieutenants who had served under my father, their loyalty forged in blood and fear—watched me with a mix of skepticism and curiosity.

"I called this meeting to address the future of the family," I began, letting my voice carry with confidence, even though my pulse pounded in my ears. "Recent events have shaken our foundation, but our purpose remains unchanged. We move forward together."

The room was silent, but the tension crackled like static in the air.

Marco leaned forward slightly, his eyes narrowing. "Recent events, huh? Is that what we're calling your father's murder now?" His tone was sharp, and his words cut like glass.

The silence heavy with unspoken things. Marco's eyes bore into me, his jaw tight. He was daring me to prove that I was more than just my father's daughter, that I was worthy of the position I had claimed.

"I'm aware that recent events have left some of you... unsettled," I continued, choosing my words carefully. "My father's death has changed many things, but our goals remain the same. We are here to protect and expand this family's legacy. That means making difficult decisions, and it means standing together."

A murmur ran through the room, but it was Marco's voice that cut through the noise. "We all know how you got this position," he said, his tone hard, edged with contempt. "What we don't know is why. What was so important that you had to take the old man out?"

The question hung in the air like a loaded gun. I could feel the eyes of every man at the table on me, waiting for my response. Marco's challenge was clear—he was questioning not just my authority, but my motives. In his mind, I was either power-hungry or weak, and neither option boded well for my leadership.

Nico leaned forward, ready to defend me, but I held up a hand, signaling him to stay silent. This was my battle to fight. I met Marco's gaze head-on, my expression as cold and unyielding as his.

"I did what needed to be done," I said, my voice steady, unflinching. "This family is facing threats on all sides—internal and external. My father's methods served us well for many years, but times have changed. I'm here because I'm willing to do what's necessary to ensure the family is taken care of the way it should be but in the ways that I deem best."

Marco's eyes narrowed, the anger simmering just below the surface. "You think you can just step in and take over? This isn't some game, Alessandra. You may have taken the title, but respect is earned, not inherited."

A murmur of agreement rippled through the room, and I knew Marco was testing the waters, gauging how much support he had among the others. If I didn't assert my authority now, if I didn't prove that I was capable of leading, I risked losing everything.

"I understand that," I replied, my tone sharpening. "I'm not asking for blind loyalty. But I am demanding respect. Not just because of my name, but because I've earned it. You all know what my father was capable of, but I'm not him. I'm prepared to lead this family in my own way, and that means making hard choices. If any of you have a problem with that, speak now."

The room fell into a tense silence. Marco glared at me, his defiance clear, but he said nothing more. The rest of the men exchanged glances, their loyalty divided, their uncertainty palpable.

Finally, one of the older lieutenants spoke up, his voice gruff but measured. "What's the plan, Donna?"

The use of the title wasn't lost on me, and I seized the moment. "There's a business deal on the table, one that's been in the works for months. We'll finalize it, but on our terms. We need to send a message that nothing has changed—that this family is still strong, still united."

"And if the deal falls through?" Marco asked, his tone challenging.

"Then we'll adapt," I replied firmly. "But we won't show weakness. Not now, not ever. Anyone who doubts that can leave, but know this—you leave, you're out for good. There will be no second chances, no protection from the family."

The ultimatum hung in the air, and for a moment, I wondered if anyone would stand. But no one did. They were testing me, pushing me to see if I could handle the pressure. I had passed the first test, but I knew it wouldn't be the last.

As the meeting continued, the tension eased slightly, but the undercurrent of doubt remained. I made my decisions carefully, balancing firmness with fairness, knowing that every move I made was being scrutinized. When the meeting finally ended, I felt a wave of exhaustion wash over me, but I couldn't afford to show it.

Marco was the first to leave, his expression dark as he stalked out of the room. Nico lingered behind, his gaze warm with reassurance.

"You did well," he said softly.

But I wasn't sure if it had been enough.

Once I was alone, I allowed myself a moment of weakness. The weight of the day's events settled heavily on my shoulders, the enormity of what I had taken on crashing down around me. But there was no time for doubt, no time for hesitation. The family was mine to lead, and I would not fail.

As I left the meeting room, a message arrived—one of my father's rivals was testing the waters, making a move that could threaten everything. I felt a surge of anger and determination. They would see that I was not to be underestimated. They would see that the Navarra family was stronger than ever, under my rule—for now.

But even as my anger fueled me, Steven's face flashed in my mind. His words from earlier still echoed in my head, tearing through my resolve: "I don't know who you are anymore."

I forced the thought aside. I couldn't afford to dwell on him—not when the family was at risk. But deep down, I knew the real battle wasn't in the meeting room or against rival families. It was in the space between me and Steven, in the war between love and loyalty.

And I wasn't sure which one I'd already lost.

Chapter 5

Mourning has Broken

Alessandra

The funeral was over, but the weight of it was just beginning.

I leaned my head against the cold glass of the car window, the rain streaking down in thin rivulets, blurring the world outside. My breath fogged the glass, creating small patches of condensation that faded as quickly as they appeared—like memories I couldn't hold onto. The steady drum of rain matched the dull pounding in my skull, a rhythm I couldn't escape.

It was done. My father was buried. His name carved into marble alongside generations of Navarras who had lived and died by power, by fear, by the violence of their legacy. I should've felt something—a sense of finality, maybe relief. But all I felt was the suffocating weight of what I'd done pressing harder against my chest with every mile that brought us closer to the estate.

Nico sat quietly beside me, his presence grounding in the way it had always been. He didn't speak right away, but I could feel him watching me. Nico knew me too well to offer platitudes.

"Are you okay?" His voice was low, careful. The kind of tone you'd use with someone standing too close to the edge.

I closed my eyes, letting the question hang in the air for a moment before answering. "I don't know what I'm supposed to feel." My voice was steadier than I expected, but that wasn't exactly comforting. I'd learned how to bury things deep—grief, guilt, fear. The problem was, they always had a way of clawing their way back to the surface.

"You don't have to figure it out today," he said softly.

But I did. There was no time to grieve. No time to fall apart. Not when half the family was still questioning whether I deserved to sit in the chair my father had left behind. Not when Marco was circling like a vulture, waiting for me to slip up so he could swoop in and claim what he thought should be his. Not when I had bigger plans no one else knew about and no idea if I was strong enough to make them happen.

I opened my eyes and straightened in my seat. "How did it go with the men?" I asked, shifting the conversation away from me and toward what mattered.

"They played their parts," Nico said, his gaze never leaving me. "Respectful. Loyal. But you know how that is—half of them meant it, the other half were performing for the sake of appearances."

I nodded, the answer exactly what I'd expected. The funeral had been less about mourning my father and more about reinforcing the power structure I was now at the head of. The men had gathered like predators, watching, waiting, testing to see if the new Donna was weak.

"And Marco?"

Nico exhaled through his nose, a small shake of his head. "He kept his mouth shut today, but it won't last."

Of course it wouldn't. Marco had been my father's right hand for years, never in line to be heir but powerful enough to make things difficult for me now. I could already feel the cracks forming beneath me, Marco's influence spreading like a slow poison among the men who still saw him as a better fit for leadership.

"He's testing me," I said quietly.

"He's waiting for you to give him an opening," Nico corrected. "You can't give him one."

I met Nico's gaze, and for a second, I saw the flicker of something deeper—something that reminded me he wasn't just a consigliere or a trusted advisor. He was someone who had known my mother before she'd been forced into a life she hadn't chosen, someone who had watched me grow up and had always tried to shield me from the worst of it.

"I won't," I said, more to myself than to him.

We fell into silence after that, the hum of the car engine and the steady patter of rain filling the space between us. I let my thoughts drift, replaying the funeral in my mind—the way Marco had stood at the front, his expression neutral but his eyes sharp, watching everything. Assessing every word, every move I made, as if he were already planning how to take me down.

I hated him. Not just for what he was doing now, but for the way he had stood by my father all those years, enabling the man who had turned me into this—cold, ruthless, capable of pulling a trigger and ending a life.

By the time the estate came into view, the familiar stone walls rising up from the mist, I had already made up my mind. If Marco wanted a fight, I'd give him one. But it wouldn't be on his terms.

As the car came to a stop, Nico opened the door and stepped out first, holding the umbrella over me as I followed. The rain had slowed to a drizzle, but the cold air bit at my skin, a reminder that the world didn't care about my grief. It would keep spinning, and I'd have to keep moving with it.

We entered the estate through the side entrance, avoiding the main hall where I knew the staff would be cleaning up after the reception. As we made our way toward my office, Nico walked in step with me, his presence as steady as ever.

"Have you checked on him today?" I asked, lowering my voice as we passed one of the maids.

Nico didn't have to ask who I meant. "He's fine. Still angry, but he's not causing any trouble."

I nodded, relief and guilt tangling together in my chest. Steven was the one thing I couldn't afford to lose, but he was also the one thing I couldn't figure out how to hold onto without destroying him in the process.

I paused outside my office, my hand resting on the door handle. "Thank you, Nico. For everything."

He gave me a small, understanding smile. "You don't have to thank me. Just be careful. Marco isn't your only enemy."

"I know," I whispered, pushing the door open and stepping inside.

As the door closed behind me, I leaned against it for a moment, my breath coming in slow, measured inhales. The funeral was over, but the fight for control had only just begun.

And if I wanted to survive it, I'd have to be willing to fight like hell—even if it meant becoming everything I swore I'd never be.

Chapter 6

Taking Care of Business

Alessandra

The rain-washed air was refreshing as I stepped out onto the balcony, the sprawling estate stretching out before me like a kingdom. One I had only just begun to rule. It should have felt like power. Instead, it felt like standing at the edge of a precipice.

The sun had barely risen, casting long shadows over the manicured lawns and gardens, but the day's work had already started.

The estate was alive with activity. Men patrolled the grounds, their sharp eyes scanning the perimeter for threats, while others moved between the garage and the main house, likely discussing supply routes and logistics. Inside, the kitchen staff bustled about, preparing for the day ahead. Everything ran like a well-oiled machine, yet I felt the cracks forming beneath the surface.

Respect in this world was not inherited. It had to be taken. Earned.

And I intended to earn it today.

From the moment I'd decided to pull the trigger, I began working to consolidate my position, asserting my authority over the men who had served my father. It wasn't easy—many of them were loyal to his memory, not to me.

Nico had advised me to take a more hands-on approach, to show them that I wasn't just a figurehead. That's why today, I would be handling several matters personally—both on and away from the estate. If I wanted to secure my leadership, I couldn't afford to delegate the difficult tasks.

I descended the stairs, my heels clicking with purpose against the marble floors. A low murmur of voices drifted from the meeting room, and as I reached the doorway, the conversation inside quieted.

Good.

I stepped in, my gaze sweeping over the men seated around the mahogany table. The air was thick with unspoken doubts. Some of these men had known me since I was a child. Others had fought beside my father for years. All of them were now my responsibility.

Nico sat to my right, his presence a quiet pillar of support. Marco, on the other hand, lounged in his chair to my left, his arms crossed over his broad chest. His expression was unreadable, but his silence was its own challenge.

I took my seat at the head of the table.

"There's a situation," I said, cutting straight to the point. "One of our shipments was intercepted by the Valenti family last night."

A ripple of tension passed through the room. The Valentis had been waiting for an opportunity to test us, and now they had one.

Marco leaned forward, his voice edged with skepticism. "And what do you plan to do about it?"

I met his gaze without hesitation. "We take it back."

A smirk twitched at the corner of Marco's mouth. "Bold move."

I ignored the bait. "A team is already en route to handle it. The Valentis will be given one opportunity to return what's ours peacefully." I let my gaze sweep across the room. "If they refuse, we send a message."

One of the older lieutenants, Romano, cleared his throat. "A show of force could escalate tensions. Are you prepared for war?"

The room fell silent, waiting for my response.

I exhaled slowly, keeping my expression cold, unreadable. "We don't start wars, but we don't roll over, either. If we don't respond, they'll see it as weakness. And weakness invites vultures."

Marco leaned back, unimpressed. "And if this backfires?"

I felt a flash of irritation but didn't let it show. Instead, I tilted my head slightly, offering him the faintest of smiles. "Then I suppose we'll find out who's really loyal to this family."

Marco held my gaze for a long moment before a slow, knowing grin spread across his face. "Fair enough."

It wasn't agreement. But it wasn't opposition, either.

For now, that would have to be enough.

By midday, I was in the back of a sleek black car, Nico beside me, as we made our way to meet with Vieri—a business associate my father had worked with for years. The drive through the city was smooth, but my mind was anything but.

"Marco is waiting for you to slip," Nico said, breaking the silence.

"I know."

"He's going to push you, test you. The others are watching."

"I know," I repeated, staring out the tinted window at the passing streets. "And I'll handle it."

Nico nodded but didn't look entirely convinced.

The restaurant Vieri had chosen was discreet—dim lighting, high-end decor, the kind of place where illegal deals were made over expensive wine and overpriced steaks.

I walked in like I belonged there. Because I did.

Vieri was already seated in a private booth, a glass of whiskey in his hand. He rose when he saw me, offering a polite but measured smile. "Alessandra. You look well."

"I'm alive."

He chuckled, motioning for me to sit. "That's a good start."

I took my seat, Nico standing a few feet away, arms crossed. Vieri studied me for a long moment, as if trying to decipher whether I was truly my father's daughter.

"I was sorry to hear about Lorenzo," he said finally. "We had... an understanding."

"So I've heard."

He swirled his drink, watching me over the rim. "Lorenzo knew how to do business. He knew how to keep things in balance. I trust you intend to honor that tradition?"

I rested my hands on the table, keeping my posture relaxed, unthreatened. "Traditions evolve, Mr. Vieri. Balance is necessary, but so is adaptation."

His smile didn't falter, but I saw the flicker of interest in his eyes. "Adaptation comes at a cost."

"Everything does."

Vieri set his glass down with a quiet clink. "Then let's discuss adjustments."

I already knew what he wanted—higher cuts, stronger guarantees. The question was how much I was willing to give without setting a precedent of weakness.

I leaned in slightly, lowering my voice just enough to make him listen carefully. "I respect our arrangement, and I value the partnership my father built with you. But let me be clear—this is not a negotiation where one party walks away with everything."

Vieri studied me, then chuckled, shaking his head. "You do remind me of him."

That wasn't a compliment.

But it meant he saw me as someone worth dealing with.

After another ten minutes of careful back-and-forth, we reached an agreement—one that ensured his continued support without giving him more control than he deserved.

When I stood to leave, Vieri spoke again. "Careful, Miss Navarra. There are people waiting for you to fall."

I met his gaze, my voice steady. "Then I hope they're patient. They'll be waiting a long time."

The meeting ended on a positive note, with Vieri agreeing to the new terms. As Nico and I left the restaurant, I allowed myself a small moment of satisfaction. It wasn't a victory, not yet, but it was a step in the right direction.

Back at the estate, I stood in my father's office, staring at the chair he had once occupied.

I had survived another day. Another test.

But Marco was waiting. The Valentis were waiting. The entire city was waiting to see if I would rise—or fall.

And then there was Steven.

A secret I couldn't afford. A risk I couldn't let go.

I ran a hand over the surface of my father's desk, feeling the weight of his choices, the power he had wielded so effortlessly.

This was my world now.

I just had to make sure I survived it.

Chapter 7

Rumors in the Ranks

Alessandra

The numbers blurred together, twisting and shifting as I stared at the spreadsheets in front of me. The columns of figures should have made sense—profits, shipments, accounts—but the weight of everything else pressed in too heavily, making it impossible to focus.

I exhaled slowly, rubbing my temple. The dim glow from the desk lamp cast flickering shadows across the surface, the low hum of the estate settling into its morning routine outside my office. Beyond these walls, men moved with purpose, alliances shifted with every whispered conversation, and my control over this empire was still fragile, held together by sheer force of will.

And at the center of it all was the secret I was struggling to contain.

Steven.

He was still here, hidden away in the western wing—the part of the estate that hadn't been used in years. Only a handful of staff knew, carefully chosen to avoid suspicion. I had taken every precaution to ensure that no one spoke out of turn. But in a house like this, with eyes and ears in every darkened corner, silence was never guaranteed.

A sharp knock at the door cut through my thoughts.

I straightened, smoothing my expression into something calm and unreadable. "Enter."

The door opened, and Nico stepped inside, his movements measured. He closed the door behind him, locking it. That alone told me this wasn't just a routine check-in.

I leaned back in my chair, forcing a steady breath. "What is it?"

Nico didn't sit. Instead, he crossed the room slowly, his posture carrying a rare stiffness. "We need to talk."

My pulse quickened, but I kept my tone even. "Then talk."

He studied me for a beat before speaking. "There are whispers among the men. About Steven."

Cold crept up my spine, but I didn't move. "Go on."

Nico exhaled, running a hand through his hair. "They know someone's here. Some of them are starting to put it together."

The walls felt like they were pressing in.

I had been careful—really careful—but of course, it wasn't enough. Secrets were currency in this house, and Marco was the kind of man who knew how to make people spend.

I forced my voice to remain steady. "Who's talking?"

"Nothing direct," Nico admitted. "But Marco's stirring the pot. Dropping hints. Saying leadership can't afford liabilities. That emotion has no place in this world."

Marco.

Of course, it was him.

I clenched my jaw, my fingers tightening around the edge of my desk. He wasn't just testing me—he was waiting for me to make a mistake, to prove him right. He wanted the men to doubt me, to see me as weak, as reckless.

And if enough of them believed it, I wouldn't just lose their loyalty.

Nico lowered his voice. "Alessandra... if this gets out of control, someone will handle it for you."

The meaning behind his words was clear. Someone would kill Steven if they saw him as a threat to the family.

I stood abruptly, the chair scraping against the floor.

I had to end this.

I found Marco exactly where I expected him—leaning casually against the wall in the main hall, talking to a group of my father's former lieutenants. The conversation halted the moment they saw me approach.

Marco barely moved, but his smirk deepened. "Donna."

I tilted my head slightly. "A word."

The other men hesitated, exchanging glances, but Marco didn't argue. He gave a casual wave, dismissing them, then followed me down the hall. I led him into one of the smaller meeting rooms, a private space with high-backed chairs and dark wood paneling. The door clicked shut behind us, leaving only silence.

Marco leaned against the table, arms crossed over his broad chest. He looked relaxed. Amused, even.

I was done playing games.

"I know what you've been doing," I said coolly.

His expression didn't change. "You'll have to be more specific."

"Whispers," I said. "About liabilities. About leadership. About what happens when emotions get in the way."

Marco chuckled. "Just making conversation."

I stepped closer, my heels clicking against the hardwood. "Let's get something straight. Steven Porter is under my protection. If anyone moves against him, they move against me."

Marco's smirk faded slightly, but his eyes gleamed with something darker. "You really think the men will accept that?"

"They don't have a choice."

He pushed off the table, stepping into my space, his voice dropping to a near whisper. "You're gambling, Alessandra. With all of our lives. If he talks—"

"He won't."

"Can you be sure?"

I held my ground, my voice ice. "Yes."

Marco studied me for a long moment, searching for cracks. I gave him none.

Finally, he exhaled, shaking his head with a smirk. "You're not Lorenzo."

"No," I said. "I'm worse."

His expression flickered—just for a second—but I saw it.

Good.

I stepped back, adjusting the cuff of my sleeve as if this conversation had been nothing more than an inconvenience. "Tell the men to drop it. This discussion is over."

Marco's lips curved into something resembling amusement. "Of course. If you say so, Donna."

The title sounded like mockery, but I let it slide. For now.

He left the room without another word.

I didn't move until the door had clicked shut behind him. Only then did I allow myself a slow, steady exhale.

This wasn't over.

Marco was waiting for me to slip, to give him the reason he needed to take control. The men were waiting to see if I was strong enough to lead. And Steven—God, Steven—was a secret I couldn't afford, a risk that had the power to destroy everything.

But I had made my choice.

And if anyone thought they could take that from me, they were welcome to try.

Chapter 8

Silence and Solitude

Steven

The days had started to blur together, each one a repetition of the last. I had lost track of time—whether it had been days or weeks since I'd been smuggled into this estate, hidden in the west wing like a dirty secret.

The wing itself felt abandoned, forgotten. The high ceilings and elaborate chandeliers belonged to another time, their grandeur dulled by dust motes caught in slanted beams of afternoon light. Some rooms still bore white cloth draped over furniture, as if the space had been left untouched since a time when its inhabitants mattered. I doubted anyone other than the staff assigned to me ever ventured this far.

And that was exactly the point.

My world had shrunk to a carefully curated existence—gym, walks in a sectioned-off part of the gardens, three meals delivered with quiet efficiency. My phone was dead, my laptop probably discarded or buried in some pile of confiscated contraband. The outside world continued without me, oblivious to the fact that I had vanished.

The only people I saw regularly were Maria, who brought my meals, and Vince, my ever-present watchdog.

Vince was a wall of silence and indifference. The man was built like a bouncer, with arms thick enough to snap a person in half, and a stare that told me he had no intention of making small talk. If I spoke, he rarely acknowledged it. If I joked, he didn't so much as smirk. He followed me to the gym in the mornings, standing off to the side like a gargoyle while I worked out.

I had tried to push him, test his limits. But no matter what I did—whether it was lingering too long in the gym, asking him outright how long they planned on keeping me here, or staring him down in the mirror—Vince never reacted. He was here to watch. Not to engage.

That didn't stop me from trying.

"You ever get bored?" I asked one afternoon, wiping sweat from my forehead as I finished my last set of pull-ups. "Or is standing around glaring at me all day actually entertaining?"

Vince didn't answer. Didn't blink.

I huffed a laugh, shaking my head as I grabbed my towel. "You know, this whole thing is pointless. If I wanted to run, don't you think I'd have tried already?"

Nothing.

"Jesus," I muttered, more to myself than him.

Later, when Maria arrived with lunch, I saw my opportunity.

She set the tray down as usual, adjusting the placement of the silverware with quiet precision. There was something almost maternal about the way she worked—making sure the plate was centered, refolding the napkin if it had shifted. It reminded me of home, of my mother's gentle fussing over the simplest things, and that ache for familiarity nearly undid me.

"Maria," I said carefully, my voice softer than I intended.

She paused, turning to me with raised brows. "Yes, Mr. Porter?"

I hesitated. This was stupid. Reckless. But I had to try.

"I... I need to get a message to my family," I said, keeping my voice low. "They don't know where I am. I just need them to know I'm okay."

Maria's fingers twitched at the edge of the tray. For a moment, I thought she might consider it. Then she darted a glance toward the door—the same way she always did when she sensed Vince was close.

Her voice was barely above a whisper. "I can't."

The two words landed like a punch to the gut.

I nodded, trying to swallow the lump in my throat. "Right. I get it."

Maria's eyes softened. "I'm sorry," she murmured, like that would make it easier. "I have a family too."

Of course she did.

"Don't worry about it," I said, forcing a smile I didn't feel. "Thanks for the food, Maria."

She lingered for half a second longer, as if searching for something to say. But there was nothing, and we both knew it. Without another word, she gathered her things and left, closing the door behind her with the softest click.

I exhaled sharply, running a hand through my hair as I stared at the meal she'd left behind. Suddenly, I wasn't hungry.

That night, I laid in bed, staring at the ceiling, feeling the weight of my circumstances settle over me like a suffocating blanket.

My family must have noticed by now. Mitch would be the first to panic, his voicemails growing more frantic by the day. Nate would be the one taking action, searching for me through his connections, following the breadcrumbs of my last known movements.

And my mother... she would be waiting by the phone, wondering if today would be the day I called.

I clenched my jaw, forcing myself to stay still even as every part of me screamed for action.

Maria wasn't going to help. Vince was untouchable.

But I had learned one thing in all my years as a journalist: every system has cracks.

I just had to find them.

If I couldn't force my way out, I would chip away at my cage, one piece at a time.

Because no matter what Alessandra believed—no matter how much she thought she was protecting me—I wasn't hers to keep.

And sooner or later, I was getting out of here.

Chapter 9

An Impossible Situation

Alessandra

I paced the length of my private quarters, my bare feet brushing softly against the cool hardwood floor. The golden morning light streamed through the tall windows, but it did little to ease the chill creeping through me. The plan had been born out of desperation, a last-ditch effort to protect Steven and silence the murmurs of doubt growing louder within the family. But now that the moment was here, the weight of what I was about to do pressed down like a stone on my chest.

Marriage.

The word settled like a stone in my chest, heavier than I expected. It wasn't just a strategy; it was a declaration, a binding contract that would entangle Steven in this life forever. I had spent my entire existence fighting against my father's world, dreaming of something outside of it. And yet, here I was, about to drag Steven deeper into it with me.

The word settled in my mind, heavy, unshakable. I had spent all night turning it over, trying to convince myself it was just a necessary step—a practical solution to an impossible situation. But I knew that wasn't the whole truth.

I had wanted to marry Steven once.

The memory hit me with startling clarity, as vivid as if it had happened yesterday.

I had found the ring.

It was late one night in our off-campus apartment during our senior year. Steven had been in the shower, and I had been searching for one of his T-shirts to sleep in, rummaging through his dresser when my fingers brushed against a small velvet box tucked away in the back of a drawer. My breath had caught in my throat, my pulse hammering as I lifted it out with trembling hands.

I shouldn't have opened it. But I did.

Inside, nestled in the soft fabric, was a ring. A diamond solitaire—elegant, understated, perfect.

A wave of emotion had crashed over me so suddenly that I had to sit down. I slipped it onto my finger, staring at the way it caught the light, how it looked like it belonged there. Like it was meant to be there.

For one fleeting moment, I let myself imagine it—Steven dropping to one knee, his warm, steady hands reaching for mine, asking me to spend forever with him. I imagined saying yes. I imagined a life that was ours alone, untouched by my family's world.

And then reality had come crashing down, cold and merciless.

It would never happen.

I had known it then, just as I knew it now.

My father had already decided my future. I had bargained with him for four years, fighting for every stolen moment I had with Steven. And when time ran out, when my father had finally demanded my return, I hadn't even been allowed to say goodbye.

Steven never got the chance to propose.

I had left.

He had kept the ring.

I turned abruptly, forcing the memory aside. It didn't matter anymore. The past was dead.

And right now I didn't have the luxury of second-guessing. The whispers were growing louder. Marco was pushing, seeding doubt among the men, testing my grip on the family. I had to act before those whispers turned into something I couldn't control.

I left my room, my heels clicking sharply against the marble floor as I made my way down the hall. The estate felt colder today, its grandeur hollow. Every door I passed, every stretch of empty space, felt like it was closing in around me, suffocating me under the weight of responsibility.

I found Nico in his office, the door slightly ajar. The scent of leather and aged paper lingered in the air, mixing with the faint trace of cologne he always wore. His office was like him—calm, disciplined, untouched by the chaos beyond its doors.

He didn't look up immediately, his focus on the stack of reports in front of him. He was always reading, always analyzing. A man who had survived this world not by brute force, but by knowing how to stay three moves ahead.

As I entered, his expression softened when he saw me. "Alessandra," he greeted, closing the file in front of him. "What's on your mind?"

I hesitated in the doorway for half a second, then stepped inside and closed the door behind me.

"I need your advice," I said, moving to the chair across from him.

His brow lifted slightly, but he didn't look surprised. "I'm listening."

I took a slow breath, steadying myself before I spoke. "The rumors are spreading faster than I anticipated. Marco hasn't said anything outright, but he doesn't have to. He's making sure the men start asking the right questions."

Nico sighed, his gaze sharpening. "About Steven."

I nodded. "They know someone's being kept on the estate. And they're close to figuring out who."

He didn't speak right away. Instead, he studied me in that way he always did—like he was searching for answers I hadn't yet spoken aloud. His silence made my pulse tick faster.

"They won't see him as just a man you care about," Nico said finally. "They'll see him as a liability. A threat to the family."

"I know," I said, my voice barely above a whisper.

The admission felt heavier now, pressing against my ribs. Marco had been circling, testing my authority, waiting for the moment to strike. He wasn't stupid—he knew better than to make an outright move against me. But he could stoke the fire, plant doubt, let someone else act in his stead.

Nico folded his hands on the desk. "What do you want to do?"

I swallowed hard. "I'm going to marry him."

For the first time in a long while, Nico's expression cracked. His lips parted slightly, and for a beat, he simply stared at me. Then, slowly, he leaned back in his chair, considering.

"That's a bold move."

"It's the only move I have left," I admitted. "If he's my husband, he's protected. The men won't question his presence here. He won't be seen as an outsider or a threat."

Nico exhaled through his nose, thoughtful. "And if he refuses?"

The words hit harder than I wanted them to. I flexed my fingers in my lap, forcing my voice to remain steady. "Then I'll have to find another way to keep him safe."

Nico was silent for a long moment. I watched him closely, noting the way his fingers tapped once against the desk—a rare tell, one I had learned meant he was weighing his options.

Finally, he spoke. "This binds him to us forever, Alessandra. To you. To the family. Once he's in, there's no way out."

I knew that. I had spent all night thinking about it, imagining every outcome. Steven might hate me for this, but it was the only way.

Still, Nico's next words made my breath hitch.

"Are you doing this for him?" His voice was quiet. "Or for yourself?"

The room felt impossibly still.

I opened my mouth, but no words came.

"Because once you do this," Nico continued, softer now, "you don't get to undo it. He'll be marked as one of us. And if he ever tries to leave..." He let the words hang, the implication clear.

If Steven left, he wouldn't just be walking away from me. He'd be breaking a vow to the family. And the punishment for that... was death.

Nico sat in silence for a moment, his gaze thoughtful. "Do you think Steven will agree to this?"

I bit my lip. "I don't know. He's angry. Hurt. I've put him through so much already. But I have to try."

His gaze held mine, measuring. Then, finally, he nodded.

"Then you'd better convince him."

I exhaled slowly, nodding in return.

I stood, but before I could turn to leave, I hesitated. There was one more thing I needed to ask.

Nico's chair creaked as he leaned back, giving me time to think. I studied him, wondering if he had ever faced a choice like this. Had there been someone he had loved, someone he had to let go for the sake of duty? I had never asked him about his personal life—he had always kept that part of himself carefully guarded—but now I couldn't help but wonder.

"Nico," I said softly, "have you ever been in love?"

His lips pressed into a thin line, and for a moment, I thought he wouldn't answer.

For the first time since I had known him, Nico looked away first. His jaw tensed, his fingers tightening slightly against the desk.

But then he sighed, a sound filled with years of memories and regrets. "Yes," he admitted. "A long time ago. But love doesn't always fit neatly into the world we live in. Sometimes, it's the thing that saves you. And sometimes, it's the thing that destroys you."

I swallowed hard, his words hitting closer to home than I wanted to admit.

"Alessandra," he said, his tone gentle but firm, "if you do this, make sure it's for the right reasons. Because once you pull Steven into this world, you won't be able to give him back the life he had before."

I nodded, even though doubt still gnawed at the edges of my resolve. "I'll talk to him," I said. "I'll explain everything."

Nico stood, walking around the desk to place a reassuring hand on my shoulder. "Whatever happens, I'm here. But just know, this won't be easy."

I looked up at him, gratitude swelling in my chest. "Thank you, Nico."

He nodded once, and I turned toward the door, my mind already spinning with the next step. Whether it was for the family or for myself, I would ask Steven to marry me.

I had made my decision.

Now, I just had to convince Steven to make his.

And whatever his answer was, I would face it head-on—just as I had faced everything else since the day I pulled the trigger that changed our lives forever.

Chapter 10

A Proposal

Steven

I'd been asking to see her for days.

Every time, Vince gave me the same cold response: "Miss Navarra is busy."

Alessandra was avoiding me, and after everything—after what she'd done—I needed to know why.

I wasn't sure how much longer I could stay locked in this estate without losing my mind. The luxury of my surroundings had long since lost its appeal. The food, the gym, the quiet—it all felt like a distraction, a way to dull my senses.

But I wasn't stupid. I knew what was happening.

They wanted to keep me comfortable. Compliant.

This time, when I demanded to see her, Vince didn't hesitate. He made a call, then nodded. Follow me.

The walk through the estate felt different. The halls were vast and eerily quiet, the kind of quiet that held secrets, the kind that watched you. I should have been used to it by now, but it still sent a prickle up my spine.

By the time we reached her office, something hot and restless twisted in my chest.

Vince barely had time to open the door before I pushed past him, stepping inside without waiting for permission.

Alessandra stood behind her desk, her hand hovering over a stack of papers. The scent of her perfume lingered in the air. The warm, familiar scent was distracting. It softened the space, made it feel less like a prison and more like her.

She turned at the sound of the door, her eyes widening slightly before she masked it quickly, a perfect expression practiced, controlled.

"Steven." Her voice was smooth, but there was something underneath it. Something careful.

I didn't let her say anything else.

"No." The word came out sharp, cutting the air between us. "No more excuses. No more evasions. I'm done waiting for you to decide when I'm worth your time."

Her jaw tightened, but I didn't miss the flicker of emotion in her eyes—guilt, hesitation.

"I'm not avoiding you," she said, stepping around the desk. "But you don't understand what's been going on. My father's death—"

"Your father's death," I cut in, my anger slicing through her words like a blade. "Don't talk about it like it was some unexpected tragedy. We both know it wasn't."

Her breath hitched but she didn't look away.

"You made that choice, Alessandra." My voice was lower now, harder. "You pulled the trigger. You took his place. And now you're keeping me here, like I'm the one who can't be trusted."

Her lips parted slightly, but whatever response she had, she swallowed it back.

"I did what I had to do to keep you safe," she said finally, quieter this time. "My father was dangerous. You know that."

I laughed, but it was hollow, empty. "And now you're in his place.

So what's next? How long do you plan on keeping me locked up here? A week? A month? Forever?"

She exhaled, slow and steady, like she was holding herself together by force. "I'm trying to protect you."

My blood ran hot.

"If you leave, you're dead," she continued, her voice rising slightly. "If they find out who you are and why you were here, you won't last a day."

"Maybe," I admitted. "But at least it would be my decision. Not yours."

Something in her gaze shifted, and for the first time since I walked in, she looked away.

"I'm trying to give you more than that," she said finally. "I'm trying to give you a life. But the only way to do that is for you to stay under my protection."

I ran a hand through my hair, my anger giving way to something heavier.

"How, Alessandra?" My voice was raw, edged with frustration. "How do you expect me to live like this? You think I can just forget who I am, what I believe in, because you say it's the only way to survive?"

"No." She took a breath. Steady. Controlled. "But I can give you something to believe in. I can give you a place here. A reason no one can question."

Her words hung between us, heavy, weighted with something I couldn't name yet.

"What do you mean?" My stomach twisted. "How?"

She took a step closer, her gaze locking onto mine. "We need to get married."

Silence.

The air shifted, thick with something I couldn't process fast enough.

I blinked. "What?"

"It's the only way to keep you safe," she said, her voice measured but filled with something dangerously close to desperation.

I let out a short laugh, but it wasn't amusement. It was disbelief.

"You're joking." My voice sounded far away, foreign. "This is some kind of twisted joke, right?"

"I'm serious."

She didn't waver. Didn't blink.

Marrying her would make me untouchable. It would cement me in the family, make my presence unquestionable.

But it would also make me one of them.

I shook my head, stepping back like I needed the distance to breathe. "You actually expect me to agree to this?"

She stepped forward, closing the space between us, her eyes burning into mine. "I don't expect you to understand. But I'm asking you to trust me. To believe that this is the only way."

I hated her in that moment.

Hated how much she still owned me, even now.

Hated that no matter how much anger burned through me, there was a part of me that still wanted her.

Still loved her.

I exhaled sharply, turning away before she could see just how much that truth destroyed me.

"I need time," I muttered.

Alessandra nodded. "Take it."

I walked out, the door closing behind me with a finality that felt like a death sentence.

Because that's what it was.

No matter what I chose—I'd lose something.

And that might just be the most unforgivable thing of all.

Chapter 11

The Weight of Power

Alessandra

The study smelled of cigar smoke and aged whiskey, remnants of my father's reign that refused to fade. His presence was everywhere—his framed portrait looming over the fireplace, his collection of leather-bound books untouched on the shelves, the heavy oak desk where he had ruled with an iron fist. This room had been his command center. Now, it was mine.

I stood by the window, watching the distant horizon as the sun dipped lower, its golden light stretching long shadows across the estate grounds. The ring I never received still weighed in my pocket, a ghost of a life that had been stolen from me.

I had made my choice, offered Steven something that wasn't just protection—it was a cage lined with silk and promises. A foolish part of me had hoped that maybe, just maybe, he would say yes without hesitation. Not because of strategy. But because he still wanted me.

I had known better.

A sharp knock at the door pulled me from my thoughts. I turned, my pulse steadying as Nico stepped in, his expression unreadable.

"We have a problem," he said.

There was always a problem.

I exhaled, already bracing myself. "What is it?"

Nico closed the door behind him, his presence a quiet force of control. "Matteo's making moves," he said, his voice low. "He's been testing the men, feeling them out. Having quiet conversations with those still loyal to your father. He's making promises he can't keep—because he's expecting to take what isn't his."

A slow, sharp anger curled through my chest. So this was it. The first real challenge to my rule.

"Where is he now?" I asked, my voice cold.

Nico held my gaze. "Waiting in your office. Marco brought him in."

I rolled my shoulders, smoothing out any trace of tension. "And Marco?"

"Watching. Seeing how you handle this."

Of course he was. Marco had always been a problem, but Matteo? He was a threat. And I needed to make an example of him.

I turned to Nico, my voice quiet but firm. "Make sure Marco is there when I deal with him. He needs to see exactly what happens when someone crosses me."

Nico gave a slow nod, the barest flicker of approval in his eyes. "Understood."

I left the study without another word, my heels clicking against the marble as I walked to my office, where a man's fate had already been decided.

The moment I entered the office, the atmosphere shifted.

Matteo stood stiffly in the center of the room, trying to mask his unease, but his fingers twitched at his sides. Marco stood off to the side, arms crossed, watching with cool detachment. He wasn't here to defend Matteo. He was here to see what I was going to do.

I walked to my desk with deliberate slowness, letting the silence stretch, forcing Matteo to stew in his own anticipation. When I finally spoke, my voice was sharp, cutting through the room like a blade.

"I hear you've been making promises, Matteo."

He straightened, feigning confidence. "The men have concerns. They need stability."

I let out a low, humorless laugh. "And you think you're the answer to that?"

Matteo's mask faltered, his Adam's apple bobbing in his throat. "Your father led with strength. He wouldn't have let this family be weakened by—"

I moved fast.

Before he could finish that sentence, I was in front of him, the sharp click of my gun the only sound in the room.

Matteo froze, his breath hitching as he stared down at the weapon now aimed just below his ribs. The air in the room thickened, every muscle in his body locking into place.

"You think I'm weak?" I asked, my voice soft, dangerous.

He swallowed, his throat working hard against his pride.

"I didn't say that."

"But you meant it," I murmured. I leaned in just enough for him to feel the weight of the moment. "So let's be clear, Matteo. I'm not my father. I don't pretend to be. But make no mistake—I will do what he would have done. And if you ever—ever—try to take what's mine again..." I pressed the gun lightly against his stomach, my meaning unmistakable.

His face drained of color, his bravado crumbling under the threat.

I let the silence stretch, let his fear settle deep into his bones. Then, slowly, I lowered the weapon, stepping back with cold, measured control.

"Now get out of my sight."

Matteo hesitated, like a man who wanted to fight but knew he would lose. His gaze flicked to Marco, looking for support.

Marco didn't move.

Smart man.

With a stiff nod, Matteo turned and strode toward the door, but I wasn't done.

"Matteo."

He stopped.

I let the next words come out slow, deliberate. "You're alive because I allow it. Don't make me reconsider."

His jaw tightened, but he nodded once and left, the door closing behind him.

I let out a breath, holstering my weapon.

Marco studied me for a moment before finally speaking. "Your father wouldn't have hesitated."

I met his gaze, unwavering. "And yet, the lesson was learned."

He didn't argue.

Good.

By the time I was back in my study, the adrenaline had faded, replaced by the crushing weight of exhaustion.

Then my phone buzzed.

I glanced at the screen—and everything else ceased to matter.

A rival family was making their move.

A slow breath filled my lungs, my fingers tightening around the phone until my knuckles whitened. The world was closing in, and there was no room for mistakes.

I squared my shoulders, exhaling through my nose.

I had made my choice.

Now, I had to survive it.

Part Two

Treading Dark Waters

Chapter 12

Ghosts of the Past

Steven

The west wing library was silent except for the soft crackling of the fireplace, the scent of aged leather and polished wood thick in the air. Afternoon sunlight filtered through the tall windows, stretching across the floor in golden slashes, but the warmth didn't reach me.

I sat hunched over a book I hadn't touched, my fingers gripping the edges of the pages, turning them absently without reading a single word. The quiet should have been calming. Instead, it pressed down on me like a weight, thick and suffocating.

This was what my life had become—endless days in a beautiful cage.

I ran a hand over my face, rubbing at the scruff on my jaw. A week ago, my life had been my own. I had a purpose, chasing down stories that mattered, exposing corruption in places where no one else dared to look. But now? Now I was just a shadow of myself, trapped in a world I had spent years fighting against.

And Alessandra—she had turned everything on its head with that proposal.

The moment she had said the words, I felt like the air had been knocked from my lungs. *We need to get married.* Five words that had haunted me ever since. Words that hurled me back in time.

Graduation night. A small, velvet box buried in my dresser drawer, the ring tucked inside—simple, elegant, something I knew she'd love. I had rehearsed the proposal a hundred times, imagining the way she would light up when I dropped to one knee, the way she'd laugh, tell me I was an idiot for making such a big deal out of it before saying yes.

But I never got the chance.

Because instead of slipping that ring onto her finger, she had disappeared. No goodbye. No explanation. Just gone.

Now, years later, she was offering me the thing I had once wanted more than anything—but it wasn't the same. This wasn't love. It was control. It was survival.

I pushed back from the desk, the chair scraping against the hardwood, my movements sharp, restless.

I couldn't keep doing this—pacing the same halls, running in circles inside my own mind, trying to reconcile the past with the present.

My past self, the man who had wanted to marry her back then, would have said yes without hesitation. But he didn't know the truth about her world.

The man I was now? The one who had spent years chasing the corruption that ran through families like hers and poisoned entire countries? He should say no.

But then there was the way she had looked at me when she said it. The desperation in her voice. The fear she was too proud to name.

I should have felt nothing but anger. And I did—but it wasn't the only thing.

I scrubbed a hand through my hair and pushed to my feet.

Sitting here wasn't going to give me answers. I needed to see her.

Needed to hear her explain why she thought marriage was the answer to all of this.

With a steadying breath, I turned for the door.

One way or another, I was getting the truth. Even if I hated every word of it.

Chapter 13

A Shadow of the Future

Alessandra

The day had begun like any other—a relentless series of calculated moves—but one message from Nico had set a fire beneath my carefully laid plans.

Vito Valenti wanted a meeting.

Not a casual check-in, not a diplomatic conversation—a meeting.

It meant one thing: he wanted something. And men like Vito didn't ask for things they couldn't take by force.

As the car wove through the city streets, I stared out the window, barely registering the towering skyline. What did Vito really want?

Power? He had it. Influence? He already controlled more than most.

Territory. That was the only thing he didn't have enough of.

The Navarra family held key sectors in Brooklyn and the docks, and my father had always limited how far Vito's reach extended within our domain. He didn't trust him. And now, with my father gone, Vito saw an opening.

A way to either break me or use me.

Nico sat beside me, his silence more telling than words. He was giving me space to think.

"Thoughts?" I finally asked.

Nico exhaled, still watching the road ahead. "He wants something big. Be ready for that."

I nodded, already knowing he was right.

When the car pulled up to a small, unassuming restaurant on the outskirts of the city, I felt my muscles tighten. It was one of Vito's safe houses, the kind of place where deals were struck and debts were collected.

Inside, the air was thick with the scent of garlic, wine, and slow-burning cigars. The lighting was low, the kind of dim glow that made everything feel more intimate—and more dangerous.

Vito Valenti was waiting.

He sat in a private booth, his thick fingers wrapped around the stem of a half-filled wine glass. His dark eyes gleamed as he looked up, flashing a slow, knowing smile.

"Alessandra," he greeted, rising to his feet. "It's been too long."

I met his gaze evenly, offering a polite nod. "Vito."

He gestured toward the seat across from him. "Come. Sit. We have much to discuss."

I slid into the booth, every movement deliberate. Nico stayed close, arms crossed as he positioned himself just out of reach but never out of sight.

Vito's gaze flicked between us before he chuckled, swirling the wine in his glass. "You bring protection now? I'm hurt."

I tilted my head slightly. "You'll get over it."

His laughter was warm, but it didn't reach his eyes.

We both knew this wasn't a social call.

"I wanted to offer my condolences," Vito said smoothly. "Your father was a great man."

I nodded, letting the silence stretch.

Let him wonder how much I agreed.

Finally, he leaned forward, all pretense of small talk fading. "Let's get to it, then. You need my help, and I need your cooperation. Seems simple enough, doesn't it?"

I steeled myself. "What exactly do you need, Vito?"

His smile widened. Like a man who'd been waiting for that question.

"Territory," he said, the single word carrying weight. "Your father was stubborn about keeping me out of certain areas. I think it's time we reassess those boundaries."

I leaned back slightly, feigning nonchalance. "And in exchange?"

Vito took a slow sip of his wine before setting the glass down with precision.

"I ensure your position is untouchable. I bring the weight of my influence behind you. No more questioning whispers. No more Marco stirring discontent." He tilted his head. "I make you untouchable, Alessandra."

I forced my expression to remain impassive, but inside, rage twisted in my stomach like a knife.

"You want Brooklyn."

"And the docks," he confirmed, his voice pleasant, like we were discussing the weather.

He didn't just want power.

He wanted a war.

I pressed my fingers against my thigh beneath the table, a steadying anchor as I kept my voice controlled. "The docks are ours."

"They're a liability in your hands," Vito countered. "The Valentis can make better use of them. And as for Brooklyn—" He spread his hands. "You don't need all of it, do you?"

A slow, deep breath. My nails dug into my palm.

This was a test.

If I agreed too quickly, he'd see weakness. If I fought too hard, he'd push me until I had no choice but to fold.

So I played the game.

"I appreciate the offer, Vito," I said smoothly, meeting his gaze without flinching. "But my father built this empire with intention. I won't dismantle it for convenience."

The smile on Vito's face didn't waver, but his eyes sharpened like a blade.

"I understand. You're trying to prove yourself. I admire that." He leaned in just slightly. "But you should know—I don't make the same offers twice."

Another unspoken threat.

I picked up my water glass and took a measured sip, allowing the silence to stretch.

Then I said, "I'll consider your terms."

Vito's expression flickered—just for a second.

He hadn't expected me to delay.

Good.

"Don't take too long," he said, his voice light, but the warning heavy.

I nodded, rising from my seat. "Enjoy your evening, Vito."

He didn't stop me as I turned to leave.

But as I stepped out into the night air, the weight of the conversation settled over me like a noose.

Vito wasn't just making a request. He was laying the foundation for war.

And whether I accepted his terms or not, he was going to take what he wanted.

Which meant I had one option left.

I had to take him out first.

Chapter 14

Revisiting the Past

Steven

The garden was quiet, but not peaceful. The roses, once carefully tended, were beginning to grow wild, creeping past their neatly trimmed borders, reaching for the stone pathways in tangled defiance. The scent was thick, too sweet, almost suffocating in the warm afternoon air. The longer I stayed in this place, the more it felt like everything Alessandra touched was a contradiction—something beautiful, but dangerous.

And then I saw her.

She stood among the flowers, her back to me, a pale column of a throat exposed as she tilted her head up toward the sky, eyes closed. She looked... tired. Not just physically, but bone-deep, like the weight of her world had finally started to settle into her skin.

Something about the way she stood—rigid yet vulnerable—pulled me forward before I could stop myself. I hated her for what she had done. I hated this place, this cage she called protection. But I hated the unanswered questions more.

I cleared my throat. "Alessandra."

She turned slowly, like she'd already known I was there, but had been hoping I wouldn't speak. The moment her gaze locked onto mine, I felt it again—that pull, sharp and unrelenting.

"Steven." Her voice was quiet, careful.

The garden around us felt suddenly too small, too enclosed. I clenched my fists, resisting the old instinct to close the space between us.

"Is this where you come to justify everything you've done?" My voice came out harsher than I intended, but I didn't take it back.

Her lips parted slightly, a flicker of something—guilt?—crossing her face before she shuttered it away. "I come here to think." She glanced away, toward a deep crimson rose in full bloom. "To remember why I made the choices I did."

I scoffed. "And what choices are those, Alessandra? Keeping me here like a prisoner? Lying to me? Killing your own father?"

She flinched. It was slight—so quick I almost missed it—but it was there.

Good. I wanted her to feel it.

"You don't understand—"

"Then help me understand!" The words snapped out of me, raw and sharp-edged. I stepped closer, forcing her to meet my gaze. "Help me understand how the woman I loved, the woman I was going to spend my life with, became this." I gestured at the estate around us, the garden, her. "Because I don't see that woman anywhere."

She inhaled slowly, like she was steadying herself against the force of my words. But then, finally, she spoke.

"I never wanted to hurt you." Her voice was softer now, almost fragile. "I never wanted any of this."

"Then why?" I demanded, the anger rising up again, twisting with something else—something darker, more painful. "Why did you leave? Why did you push me away?"

Alessandra looked down, the mask slipping for just a second. "Because I didn't have a choice."

I exhaled sharply, shaking my head. "Bullshit. You always had a choice."

Her head snapped up, and this time, there was fire in her eyes. "No, I didn't!" Her voice cracked, and for a moment, the composure she clung to so desperately unraveled. "You didn't know my father, Steven. You didn't know what he was capable of. If he had found out about us, he would have destroyed you."

The conviction in her voice made my stomach tighten.

Had I been wrong?

I had spent years believing she left because she didn't love me enough. Because she hadn't wanted a life with me. But what if... what if she had been protecting me all along?

"You could have told me." My voice was quieter now, but no less intense. "We could have figured it out together."

Her laugh was bitter. "And what would we have done, Steven? Run? Hide? My father had eyes everywhere. There was no escaping him."

I raked a hand through my hair, frustration mounting. "So instead, you just disappeared? Do you have any idea what that did to me?"

She lifted her chin, her eyes glistening. "I know."

The words were barely a whisper, but they sliced through me all the same.

"I was going to propose to you," I said before I could stop myself. The moment the words left my lips, I saw her body tense.

Her breath hitched.

I swallowed hard, pushing through the lump in my throat. "That night. Graduation. I had the ring." I let out a hollow laugh. "You were supposed to be my future."

Alessandra's hands curled into fists at her sides, her lips parting like she wanted to speak, but no words came.

And then, in a voice so quiet I almost missed it, she whispered, "I found it."

I froze. "What?"

She swallowed. "The ring. I found it. Before I left."

The air between us felt impossibly thick. My chest tightened as I pictured it—her, standing in my apartment, finding the small velvet box tucked away in my desk drawer.

"I tried it on." Her voice was barely audible, but I caught every word. "I loved it. And I knew I'd never get to wear it."

Something in my chest cracked open.

"You should have told me," I said hoarsely.

"I couldn't." She exhaled shakily. "Because if I let myself believe, even for a second, that we had a chance... I never would have left."

Silence stretched between us, raw and painful.

She took a step closer, her voice laced with quiet desperation. "I know I hurt you. I know you may never forgive me. But I'm here now, and I am asking you, Steven... to trust me."

I clenched my jaw, torn between the love I had never been able to kill and the reality of everything she had done.

"I don't know if I can," I admitted.

Her face fell, but she nodded. "Then take your time."

As I turned to leave, I felt her eyes on my back, burning into me like a brand.

I had spent years wanting answers. Now that I had them, I wasn't sure what to do with them.

But one thing was certain—no matter how much I wanted to walk away, part of me never would.

Chapter 15

The Rift Grows

Alessandra

The message came at dawn.

I was already awake, sitting at my desk, staring at the half-empty glass of whiskey I hadn't touched in hours. Sleep had been impossible. My mind kept replaying my last conversation with Steven, his words cutting deeper than any blade.

I don't know if I can forgive you.

I had expected as much, but hearing it aloud made it real in a way I wasn't prepared for.

A knock at the door broke the silence. I straightened, my face smoothing into the unreadable mask I had perfected over the years.

"Enter."

Nico stepped in, his expression unreadable, but there was tension in the set of his shoulders. He shut the door behind him, took a breath, and said, "It's Marco. He's gone."

I already knew what was coming next, but I let him say it.

"He defected. He went to Vito."

I leaned back in my chair, exhaling slowly. So, he finally made his move.

I had known Marco was waiting for an opportunity, circling like a vulture ever since my father's death. He had resented me the moment I took over, and now that I had rejected Vito's "offer," Marco saw his chance. Coward. He hadn't even stayed to fight. He'd run.

Nico was watching me carefully, waiting for my reaction. Most people would expect fury, a violent outburst, something dramatic. But I had learned a long time ago that rage was a weapon best wielded coldly.

I tilted my head, considering. "Where is he now?"

"He's not with Vito yet," Nico said. "He's still in the city, trying to negotiate his place."

A slow smile curved my lips. "Then we still have time."

Nico didn't flinch, but I caught the slight shift in his stance. He knew what was coming. He just didn't want to be the one to say it first.

"Bring him to me." My voice was quiet, even. A simple command.

A pause. Then, "Alessandra—"

"Don't," I cut him off, standing. "You know what has to be done. If we let this go, Marco won't be the only one to cause trouble."

Nico's jaw tensed, but he nodded. "I'll take care of it."

I turned to the window, my arms crossing over my chest. The estate was still, the early morning light casting long shadows over the gardens.

"And Nico?" I said without looking at him.

"Yes, Donna?"

"When you bring him to me, make sure there's an empty car waiting."

A beat of silence. Then Nico understood.

They brought him to one of our old warehouses by the docks, a place my father used to use for business deals that required discretion.

Marco was already bloodied when Nico dragged him in. His lip was split, and one eye was swelling shut. But despite the bruises, he still had the audacity to smirk when he saw me.

"Alessandra," he said, spitting blood onto the floor. "I was wondering when you'd call me in for a meeting."

I didn't respond right away. Instead, I paced in a slow, deliberate circle around him, taking my time, letting the weight of the moment settle.

He was tied to a chair, hands bound behind him, his legs spread slightly for balance. But there was no balance in this situation. He was already dead. He just hadn't accepted it yet.

"You went to Vito," I said finally, my voice smooth, almost conversational.

Marco shrugged as best as he could. "I had to look out for myself. You understand, don't you? It's not personal."

I smiled at that. "Not personal?" I echoed. "You betrayed the family. You betrayed me. And you think that's not personal?"

His smirk faltered, but he recovered quickly. "You made a mistake, Alessandra. Turning down Vito. The world is changing. You can't run this family like your father did."

I crouched in front of him, close enough that he could see the amusement in my expression. "You're right," I murmured. "I don't run this family like my father did."

Then I pulled out my gun and shot him in the knee.

Marco screamed, his body jerking violently against the chair as pain ripped through him.

I stood, slipping the gun back under my blazer as he gasped for breath, his face contorted in agony.

"You're lucky," I told him, watching as he struggled to focus through the pain. "If my father were still alive, this would've been slow. But I'm not him."

I nodded once to Nico.

A second gunshot rang out.

Marco slumped forward, blood pooling at his feet.

The car was already waiting, just as I had ordered.

Nico and the others moved efficiently, wrapping Marco's body and loading it into the trunk. No words were spoken. They knew better than to question my decision.

"We'll leave him outside one of Vito's businesses," Nico said, closing the trunk.

I stepped forward, adjusting my gloves. "Not just anywhere. Leave him at the front door."

Nico gave me a look, but he didn't argue. "And the message?"

I considered for a moment before responding.

"You want my men? Fine. You can have this one."

Nico nodded and signaled to the men. The car pulled out of the warehouse, taking Marco's body to its final destination.

As I watched the taillights disappear into the night, I felt nothing. No guilt, no hesitation.

Just resolve.

Marco had made his choice. And now, I had made mine.

I didn't return to the estate right away. Instead, I took a walk along the docks, the salt air sharp against my skin. My plan had always been to dismantle the Navarra empire quietly—piece by piece, from the inside. But Marco's betrayal had forced my hand.

Vito would retaliate. Of course he would. He had been waiting for an excuse.

Which meant I had to move faster.

I pulled out my phone, scrolling through the encrypted messages that contained everything I needed—the accounts I had already begun to drain, the names of people I could trust to disappear when the time came.

It wasn't enough yet.

I needed more time. More leverage.

I thought of Steven—of the anger in his eyes, the way he had accused me of trapping him in this world.

He has no idea how much I want out too.

But before I could burn this empire to the ground, I had to play my part a little longer.

With one final breath of cold air, I turned away from the docks and headed back to the estate.

The war had begun.

And I was going to end it.

Chapter 16

The Thin Line

Alessandra

The space smelled of rust and old oil, the kind of place where deals were made or bodies were buried. The invitation had come this morning, delivered in the form of a handwritten note—an old-fashioned touch meant to remind me that Vito Valenti did things his way.

I wasn't naive. This wasn't an olive branch. It was a test.

I stepped out of the car, my heels clicking against cracked pavement, every movement slow, deliberate. Vito wanted me to feel like I was stepping into his world, but I refused to play into the illusion.

Inside, the warehouse was dimly lit, the walls lined with stacked crates and the faint hum of flickering overhead lights. Vito stood in the center, leaning casually against an old metal workbench. His men flanked him, their expressions unreadable, though I could feel their eyes watching too closely, gauging every breath I took.

I made them wait. If Vito wanted a show of dominance, I would remind him that I was not my father.

"Alessandra," Vito greeted smoothly, his voice thick with something between amusement and condescension. "You look stunning, as always."

"I didn't come here for compliments," I replied evenly. "What do you want, Vito?"

His lips curled in a knowing smile. "So direct. Just like your father—except he knew when to listen."

I didn't bite. I held his gaze, waiting.

He exhaled through his nose, shaking his head like I was a stubborn child. "Marco was a valuable man. It's a shame things ended the way they did."

I tilted my head slightly. There it is.

"He was a problem the second he crossed the line," I said smoothly. "You should be thanking me that you didn't have to waste resources figuring that out."

Vito's expression didn't change, but I caught the subtle twitch of his fingers against the table—the only tell he allowed himself.

For the first time, silence stretched between us. The tension in the air thickened, crackling like an approaching storm.

Vito chuckled, shaking his head. "I have to say, I'm surprised you're making such dangerous choices, Alessandra."

I crossed my arms. "Or maybe I'm just making the right ones."

His eyes darkened, but he kept his easygoing demeanor, shifting the conversation. "Speaking of choices, I hear you've been rejecting several very generous offers lately."

"And yet, here I am. Still standing."

Vito clicked his tongue, pretending to be amused, but I knew him too well. He was looking for a weak spot, waiting for me to flinch.

"I'm just saying," he continued, "expansion is inevitable. If you're not the one growing, someone else is."

I shrugged. "And yet, you came to me. Twice."

A pause. Just for a fraction of a second. But I caught it. He doesn't like being on the defensive.

Vito's smile never wavered, but the warmth in his expression faded. “War is expensive, Alessandra. I’d hate to see your resources stretched too thin.”

There it was. The real reason for this meeting.

I let the words settle, pretending to consider them before tilting my head slightly. “Sounds like a problem you should be worried about.”

One of his men shifted uncomfortably. Even they weren’t sure how this was going to play out.

Vito exhaled, his mask slipping just enough to show his irritation. “I admire your confidence,” he said, stepping closer. “But I hope, for your sake, it’s not misplaced.”

I didn’t move. “And I hope, for your sake, you didn’t call me here just to waste my time.”

His smile widened, but his eyes remained cold. “Of course not. I just wanted to see where we stand.”

“Oh, I think we both know exactly where we stand.”

A slow nod. A mutual understanding. This meeting was over.

I turned first, making my way back toward the exit, my pulse steady even as tension buzzed beneath my skin. Vito had shown his hand—he wasn’t going to let Marco’s death go unanswered. He wasn’t going to let my refusal of his expansion plans be ignored.

The question wasn’t if he would retaliate. It was when.

As I stepped outside, the cold air filling my lungs, I realized something else.

I had to move up my timeline.

I had a plan—but I had expected to have more time. Now, that luxury was gone.

I climbed into the car, closing my eyes for a moment as I let the gravity of the situation settle.

Vito wasn’t going to wait.

Neither could I.

With a slow exhale, I opened my eyes and gave Nico a single sentence.

“We’ve got plans to make.”

The war had already begun. Now it was time to end it on my terms.

Chapter 17

Questions Left Unasked

Steven

The note was waiting for me when I returned from the gym, placed neatly on the small table by the window. At first glance, it seemed unremarkable—just a simple folded piece of thick ivory paper. But the moment I saw the slant of the handwriting, something inside me twisted.

Alessandra's handwriting.

It was the same careful script she used in college when she'd leave notes in my textbooks—playful challenges about who could solve the case studies first, little reminders that she was always two steps ahead. But this note wasn't playful.

I unfolded it slowly, my fingers brushing against the smooth texture of the paper.

Join me for dinner. 8:00 PM.

Nothing more. No explanation. No apology. Just an order, wrapped in elegance.

I read it again. And then a third time.

Vince stood near the door, watching me with his usual unreadable expression. When I finally looked up, his silence told me everything—there was no choice here.

I let out a slow breath. "Tell her I'll be there."

Vince gave a short nod and left, leaving me alone with the weight of the invitation.

Standing in front of the mirror, I adjusted the collar of the shirt I hadn't worn in weeks. The crisp white fabric felt foreign against my skin, a reminder of another life—one where dressing up meant dates nights, fancy dinners, laughter, and stolen kisses.

Now, it felt like putting on armor.

I tugged at the cuffs, glancing at my reflection. The man staring back at me wasn't the same one who had once loved Alessandra Navarra without hesitation. He looked older. Harder.

And yet, his hands still shook when he thought about seeing her.

The dining room was bathed in dim, golden light, the glow from the ornate chandelier casting soft shadows along the long table. The air was thick with the scent of freshly baked bread, rosemary, and something rich and savory. It should have been comforting, familiar.

But it wasn't.

Alessandra sat at the far end of the table, poised as if she'd been waiting for me for hours. Her dark hair was swept to one side, a simple gold necklace resting against her collarbone. She looked... untouchable.

She had always been beautiful, but now, there was something sharpened about her—something that made my chest ache.

"Steven," she greeted, her voice smooth, unreadable.

I hesitated before moving to the chair opposite her, the space between us feeling like an ocean. As I sat, my fingers grazed the edge of the linen napkin, gripping it just to have something to hold onto.

The first few minutes were filled only with the sound of silverware against porcelain.

I should have said something. I should have demanded answers the second I walked in. But instead, I watched her. The way she cut her food with precise, controlled movements. The way she took slow sips of wine, eyes never leaving mine.

Finally, I set down my fork. The metal clinked against the plate, too loud in the quiet room.

"How many people have you killed?"

The question came out before I could stop it, low and rough.

Alessandra didn't flinch. She didn't even blink. She simply placed her knife down, folding her hands neatly in front of her.

"Enough," she said.

The word punched through me.

"Enough?" I echoed, my voice sharper now. "What does that even mean, Alessandra?"

She sighed, tilting her head slightly. "It means I do what I have to."

Her voice was too calm, too controlled.

My hands curled into fists under the table. "To protect your family?" I pushed. "Or to protect yourself?"

Her lips parted slightly, but instead of answering, she picked up her wine glass and took a slow sip. When she set it down, she met my gaze head-on.

"Is there a difference?"

I stared at her, the woman I had loved, the woman I had planned a future with. The woman who was now a stranger.

"Was it all a lie?" I asked, my voice quieter now. "Everything we had—was it just some sick game to you?"

Something flickered in her expression. A crack in the armor.

"No," she whispered.

The single word nearly undid me.

She leaned forward slightly, her voice quieter now, as if she was telling me a secret. "I loved you, Steven. I still do. But love doesn't change reality. And the reality is, I've done things I can't undo. I've made choices that haunt me. That will always haunt me."

I swallowed hard, my throat tight. "And you think that justifies everything?"

She exhaled slowly. "No. But it's the only way I know how to keep you safe."

I pushed back my chair abruptly, the legs scraping against the floor. The sound was jarring in the otherwise silent room.

"I need some air," I muttered, standing.

She stood, too. "Steven—"

Her voice cracked, just barely, but she caught herself.

I turned away, moving toward the door, my heart pounding so hard I could feel it in my fingertips.

I needed distance. I needed to breathe.

As I stepped outside, the cool night air hit me, but it did nothing to quiet the storm inside.

I wanted to hate her. I needed to hate her.

But the worst part?

I still loved her.

And I didn't know if I could survive that.

Chapter 18

On a Precipice

Steven

By day, the grand hallways and manicured gardens could almost convince me I wasn't a prisoner. But at night, when the silence stretched and the shadows deepened, it was impossible to ignore.

I walked aimlessly through the grounds, hands shoved deep into my pockets, trying to outrun the thoughts that chased me. The evening air was crisp, cool against my skin, but I barely felt it.

Alessandra's words from dinner still echoed in my mind. I've done things I can't undo. I've made choices that haunt me.

I had wanted a confession. I had wanted truth.

Instead, she had given me something worse—understanding.

Because despite all my anger, despite everything I had told myself... a part of me did understand.

That realization clawed at my chest, twisting into something I wasn't ready to name.

I found myself at the gardens, the scent of roses thick in the night air. The paths were perfectly maintained, lined with carefully placed lanterns casting a soft golden glow. But the beauty of it all felt wrong, too curated.

Just like her.

I sank onto a stone bench, elbows on my knees, head in my hands.

What was I still doing here?

The sound of footsteps pulled me from my thoughts.

Soft. Unhurried.

I didn't need to look up to know who it was.

She stopped a few feet away, the lantern light catching the edges of her dark hair, casting delicate shadows against her skin. She didn't speak right away. Instead, she just watched me, the way she always did when she was calculating something.

I sighed. "You really don't know how to leave well enough alone, do you?"

"Steven." My name was barely more than a whisper.

I finally looked up. And there it was—that thing in her eyes that I couldn't name, that I couldn't escape.

Regret.

Exhaustion.

Something dangerously close to pleading.

"I'm sorry to disturb you," she said carefully, the words unnatural on her lips. "But I couldn't leave things the way they were."

I let out a short, humorless laugh. "You mean the way you left them?"

Her lips pressed together. "I didn't choose this."

I scoffed, shaking my head. "You keep saying that. That you didn't have a choice. That it was all out of your hands. But every time I look at you, Alessandra, I see someone who's completely in control."

Her jaw tightened. "Control is an illusion, Steven. One I have to maintain every second of every day, or I lose everything."

I stood up, the anger simmering just beneath my skin. "Lose what? More men? More power? Is that really what keeps you up at night?"

Something broke in her expression then, something raw flashing behind her carefully constructed walls.

"No." Her voice was quieter now, but it held more weight than before. "You. I lose you."

I stared at her, my pulse hammering.

She took a hesitant step forward, her arms crossed like she was holding herself together. "I know I've hurt you," she admitted, her voice trembling just slightly. "And I know I've made mistakes that you might never forgive. But everything I've done, I did to protect you. Even if it meant losing you in the process."

God.

The worst part was that I believed her.

I wished I didn't.

I wished I could cling to my anger, let it shield me from everything she was saying. But standing here, looking at her, I saw the same Alessandra I had once worshipped.

And I saw the wreckage of what was left of her.

I exhaled sharply, dragging a hand down my face. "You think that makes it better?"

"No," she admitted. "I think it makes it real."

Her voice cracked slightly at the last word, and I hated that it made my chest ache.

She took another step forward.

This time, I didn't move away.

We were inches apart now, the scent of her perfume wrapping around me, pulling me back into memories I'd spent years trying to bury.

"I never wanted this life," she said, and for the first time, she sounded tired. "And I hate what it's turned me into."

I swallowed hard. "Then stop."

She let out a shaky breath, her hands tightening at her sides. "I can't."

The honesty of it wrecked me.

My hand lifted before I could stop it, brushing against her cheek, my thumb wiping away a tear she hadn't even realized had fallen.

Her breath hitched.

She leaned into the touch, just slightly.

And for the briefest, most dangerous moment, I considered it.

I considered closing the distance. Letting go of all the reasons I should hate her, all the reasons I should walk away.

But reality came crashing back.

We weren't in college anymore. We weren't lying in bed, whispering about forever.

She had blood on her hands.

And I didn't know if I could live with that.

I pulled back.

Her eyes flickered with something—pain, maybe, or understanding.

"I can't either," I said, voice rough. "I can't pretend that any of this is okay."

She nodded, just once. "I know."

The silence stretched, heavy and suffocating.

I took a step back. "I need time."

Alessandra didn't try to stop me this time. She just stood there, arms wrapped around herself, watching as I turned and walked away.

I didn't stop.

I didn't look back.

But as I stepped into the shadows of the estate, my pulse still racing, I knew one thing with absolute certainty.

No matter how far I ran, no matter how much I told myself I hated her...

I would never be free of Alessandra Navarra.

Chapter 19

Stakes and Threats

Alessandra

The drive to Vito Valenti's estate was shorter than I expected, yet each passing mile coiled tighter around my ribs. I sat in the back seat, staring out the tinted window, counting streetlights like they were seconds ticking down to something inevitable.

Vito had sent the invitation through a messenger—an old-fashioned power play meant to remind me of two things: this was his game, and I was playing on his board.

I let my nails dig into my palm, feeling the crescent indentations bite my skin. Not for long.

Beside me, Nico sat stone-faced, his fingers tapping a slow rhythm against his knee. He didn't need to say anything—I knew what he thought of this meeting.

"It's a trap," he had warned earlier. "He wouldn't call you here unless he thought he had something over you."

And I had a feeling that I already knew what that something was.

Steven.

Marco sold him out before he died.

The realization had settled in my stomach like lead, heavier with each moment that passed. I should have known—should have expected it. Marco wasn't the kind of man to go quietly. Even in death, he had made sure to leave a mess behind.

And now, Steven was the leverage.

The car rolled to a stop, the driver stepping out to open my door.

I didn't move at first. Just breathed. Let the weight settle. Let my mind sharpen.

Then, with the kind of slow, measured control my father had taught me to wield like a weapon, I stepped out.

Vito's estate had always been grand, but in a way that felt curated—meant to impress, to intimidate. The marble floors gleamed, the chandelier overhead sparkled just so. Even the air smelled expensive, like cigars and old wealth.

The guards barely acknowledged us as we passed, though I felt their eyes track every step I took.

Good. Let them watch. Let them wonder what I'd do next.

Vito waited in his private study, a glass of wine in hand, his posture too relaxed. His smile—thin, knowing—curled at the edges as I walked in.

"Alessandra," he greeted, as if we were old friends catching up over dinner. "Welcome, welcome."

I didn't smile. "Let's not pretend this is a social visit."

Vito chuckled, setting his glass down. "No, I suppose not." His gaze flicked to Nico, then back to me. "But you can't blame a man for trying to keep things civilized."

I didn't sit. I wasn't going to let him dictate the flow of this conversation.

His smile didn't falter. If anything, he seemed amused by my refusal to play along.

"You've done well since our last meeting," he said, leaning back in his chair. "Handling your father's empire, dealing with traitors—impressive. But we both know there's still work to be done."

I met his gaze. "If this is about the territories again—"

"My dear," he interrupted smoothly, "this is about a much more pressing concern."

A pause.

A shift in the air.

Then—the kill shot.

"Marco came to me before his unfortunate demise." He exhaled as if in mock grief, shaking his head. "And do you know what he told me?"

I didn't move. Didn't breathe.

I knew, but I needed to hear him say it.

"He told me you've been harboring a journalist. A rather... famous journalist." Vito's lips curled. "Steven Porter."

My stomach turned to ice, but my expression didn't so much as flicker.

"That's quite the secret you've been keeping," Vito mused. "And quite the risk."

Nico tensed beside me, but he knew better than to speak. This was my moment.

I tilted my head, schooling my expression into something bored. "And?"

Vito's eyes gleamed. "And it makes me curious, Alessandra. Why go to such lengths to keep him alive?"

Because he was mine. Because I loved him. Because if I let him die, I wouldn't recognize myself anymore.

I let out a slow breath. "He's a liability. I'm controlling the situation."

Vito tsked, his amusement growing. "Control. Such a funny thing. Fleeting, really."

I didn't respond.

Vito leaned forward now, his voice dropping to something calculated. "You've made me an offer before, Alessandra. A partnership.

And I've been generous, patient." He paused. "But it seems to me that trust between us isn't quite... balanced."

I met his gaze head-on. "What do you want?"

A beat of silence. Then—

"I want a real alliance," he said smoothly. "A binding one."

A cold chill slithered up my spine. "Meaning?"

"I want a say in certain operations. A... seat at the table for things your father refused to let me touch."

Nico stiffened. "That's not an alliance, that's a takeover."

Vito merely shrugged. "Semantics."

I exhaled slowly. "And if I refuse?"

His smile widened. "Then I suppose our mutual friend Mr. Porter might become a very public problem."

A noose. Tightening.

I clenched my fists behind my back, nails digging into my palms. My mind spun through scenarios, calculations.

I needed time.

I nodded once, a slow, deliberate motion. "I'll think about it."

Vito's smile didn't waver. "That's all I ask."

The drive back to the estate was silent.

Nico broke it first.

"We can't let him dictate terms," he said, voice tight. "This was a threat. He's testing how far he can push you."

"I know," I murmured, staring out the window. The city blurred past, streaks of light and shadow.

He hesitated. "What are you going to do?"

I thought about Steven. About Vito's warning. About Marco's last act of betrayal.

And I thought about my plan.

The one I hadn't told anyone about yet.

I inhaled slowly, centering myself. I had to move faster.

I turned to Nico, my voice steady.

"We get ahead of him," I said. "We make our move before he can make his."

Nico studied me, then nodded.

No more waiting. No more playing defense.

It was time to end this.

Chapter 20

The Only Way

Steven

The pounding of my feet against the treadmill did little to drown out the war in my mind.

I pushed harder, increasing the speed, the incline—anything to force my body to work harder than my thoughts. The steady rhythm of exertion was usually enough to clear my head, to give me control over the chaos.

Not today.

Not after her.

Sweat dripped from my brow, my breath coming in ragged gasps, but still, I kept going. Kept running.

But I couldn't outrun the truth.

Alessandra's proposal wasn't just an offer. It was a crossroads.

And no matter how fast I ran, it was still there, waiting for me.

Marry her.

The words clawed at my brain, digging deeper with each replay. I'd spent days trying to convince myself that the idea was absurd, that there had to be another way.

But the longer I sat in this house, trapped under the weight of their power, the clearer it became.

This wasn't just about survival anymore.

This was my chance.

I slammed the STOP button, the treadmill slowing beneath me as I doubled over, hands braced on my knees, lungs burning. The gym was empty except for Vince, leaning against the far wall, arms crossed, silent as ever.

He didn't say anything as I stood upright, wiping sweat from my face with the back of my hand. He didn't need to.

I already knew what he was thinking.

This isn't your world. You don't belong here.

But that was the problem, wasn't it? I was here. And whether I belonged or not didn't change the fact that I was standing in the middle of a game I never agreed to play.

But if I was going to be a piece on their board, I'd decide what kind of piece I was for myself.

By the time I was back in my room, freshly showered and changed, my mind had finally settled into something resembling clarity.

Marrying Alessandra had once been my dream. A lifetime ago, when we were nothing more than two college kids in love, I had planned our future down to the smallest details.

Now, it felt like the ultimate betrayal.

Of my integrity. Of everything I stood for.

And yet...

It was also my best shot.

My only shot.

I dropped onto the edge of the bed, rubbing my hands over my face.

If I married Alessandra, I wouldn't just be a prisoner anymore. I'd be part of the inner circle. I'd have access to information I could never get otherwise.

The Navarra empire had been a mystery I'd spent years trying to uncover, a web of secrets and corruption that had ruined lives—including my own. If I became one of them, I could finally see the full picture.

Maybe even use it.

The thought made my stomach twist.

I was a journalist, a truth-seeker. I had built my life around exposing people like the Navarras. And now, I was considering aligning myself with them?

I exhaled sharply, leaning back against the headboard, staring at the ceiling.

But what other choice did I have?

I was tired of being powerless. Tired of waiting for someone else to decide my fate.

This way, I had control.

And if I played it right, maybe—just maybe—I could still finish what I started.

The idea felt reckless. Dangerous. But wasn't that what I did best? Wasn't that the only way to get the truth?

If the Navarras wanted to use me, they'd have to learn—I wasn't a pawn. I was a player.

And I was done waiting for permission.

A knock at the door pulled me from my thoughts.

I sat up, composing myself as Vince stepped inside. He held out a single piece of paper—folded neatly, bearing a familiar, delicate script.

Alessandra's handwriting.

Steven,

We need to talk.

My office. 8 PM.

- Alessandra

No demand. No explanation.

But the meaning was clear.

This wasn't over.

I let out a slow breath, staring at the note.

The decision had already been made.

I was going to say yes.

But not for her.

Not for love.

For me.

For control.

For the endgame.

I stood, tucking the note into my pocket as I grabbed a clean shirt.

Time to play my part.

Chapter 21

Nothing More to Say

Steven

The estate was shrouded in an eerie silence, the kind that made every breath feel too loud, every movement feel weighted. As I walked through its darkened corridors, my footsteps echoed off the marble floors, a stark reminder of how alone I truly was in this place.

My body ached from earlier—muscles sore, skin still warm from the exertion—but the physical strain was nothing compared to the war raging in my mind.

This was it.

The decision I had spent days wrestling with.

I was about to walk into her office and give her my answer.

A decision that should have belonged to us, years ago, made out of love, made under stars and whispered promises. Instead, I was making it in the cold, calculated silence of a house that felt more like a prison with each passing day.

I hesitated outside her office door, my hand hovering over the handle.

This isn't doubt, I told myself. This is just reality hitting you in the face.

With a deep breath, I pushed the door open.

Alessandra sat at her desk, bathed in the golden glow of a single lamp. Shadows stretched across the room, elongating the angles of her face, making her look both powerful and achingly alone.

The first thing I noticed wasn't the exhaustion in her eyes or the way her fingers tensed around the papers in front of her.

It was the gun.

Resting within reach.

And the way her hand instinctively curled around the handle when I entered.

It was a reflex. A split-second calculation.

For a moment, the air between us was razor-thin, stretched tight with unspoken words, unreadable thoughts. Her fingers stayed on the gun just a second too long before she realized it was me. Then, slowly, she released her grip, moving her hand away.

But she had reached for it.

She had considered it.

My stomach twisted. Not in fear, but in realization.

Alessandra had always been guarded, cautious. But never like this.

Once, she would have smiled the moment she saw me, her shoulders relaxing, her guard dropping effortlessly. Now? Now, she lived in a world where even I was a potential threat.

I stepped inside, closing the door behind me. She said nothing at first, just watched me. Waiting.

"Steven," she finally spoke, her voice even, though I caught the hint of something beneath it—relief, tension, something she was trying to hide.

"You said we need to talk," I said, forcing my gaze away from the gun and onto her. "Let's talk."

She leaned back slightly, measuring me. Her exhaustion was

evident—the tightness around her eyes, the stiffness in her posture—but it didn't dull the sharpness in her gaze.

"Have you made your decision?"

I took another step forward. "I have."

Her fingers twitched slightly—like she was bracing for impact.

I didn't look away.

"I'll marry you."

Nothing. No visible reaction at first.

Then, slowly, she leaned back in her chair, her eyes narrowing, like she was picking apart my words, trying to decipher my angle.

"This isn't how I imagined this going," she admitted. Her voice was softer now, thoughtful. "But I have only ever wanted to keep you safe. And I truly believe I can do that."

I laughed, but there was no humor in it. "Safe?" I repeated, shaking my head. "You're asking me to marry into a world I've spent my entire career exposing. This isn't about safety, Alessandra. This is about power. Control."

Her expression hardened, her walls snapping back into place. "Think what you will. But if this is what it takes to keep you and your family safe, then so be it."

My family.

I had been so focused on what this meant for me that I hadn't stopped to think about them.

"My family," I said, my voice low, almost dangerous. "Are they in danger?"

She sighed. Not dismissively, but with the weight of someone carrying a truth she didn't want to say out loud.

"As long as they're connected to you and you're seen as an enemy, they'll always be in danger," she admitted. "But if you become part of the family, they would fall under my protection, too. Your family... they always held a special place in my heart."

The words felt like a punch to the gut.

I thought of my mom, my brothers. How easily their names could become weapons in this world. How quickly their lives could be changed, destroyed.

Alessandra had spent holidays with them. Laughed with them over dinners. She had been loved by them.

And now, their safety was tied to her. To this choice.

I clenched my jaw, looking away for a moment, trying to steady the storm inside me.

"It was never meant to be like this," I murmured, almost to myself.

She didn't respond.

Because we both knew the truth.

It was meant to be like this. Because there was never another path. Not with a father like hers. Not with a past like ours.

Maybe we had been doomed from the start.

I exhaled sharply, grounding myself.

"Let's just get it done," I said, forcing the words out before I could second-guess myself. "No more delays."

She studied me for a moment longer, her eyes lingering on my face like she was searching for something—doubt, hesitation, regret.

Then, she nodded.

"I'll make the arrangements."

No fanfare. No grand declarations.

Just cold, transactional acceptance.

I turned without another word, walking toward the door. My fingers tightened around the handle, but I hesitated for just a second before pulling it open.

Something about that moment, that quiet pause, felt like the last breath before a deep plunge into unknown waters.

And then I walked out.

The door shut softly behind me, and I moved through the darkened halls, each step cementing the reality of my decision.

I wasn't sure what this marriage would bring.

But I knew one thing.

I wasn't stepping into this as a victim.

I wasn't being forced into anything.

If Alessandra wanted me to be part of this world, I would be.
But on my terms.
This wasn't just about survival.
This was about justice.
And if the Navarra family thought they could control me...
They were about to learn otherwise.

Chapter 22

The Wedding

Steven

The garden was bathed in the warm hues of sunset, the golden light filtering through the trees, casting long shadows across the manicured lawn. A soft breeze rustled the leaves, carrying with it the scent of roses—deliberate, no doubt. Everything about this moment had been designed.

It was perfect.

And yet, I couldn't breathe.

I stood there, my hands clasped loosely in front of me, my pulse a steady, deafening drum in my ears. This should have happened at a different time, under different circumstances. It should have been us, choosing this life together. Instead, the reality of the moment pressed down like an iron weight on my chest.

Alessandra stood across from me, poised, calm. The ivory-white of her tailored suit softened her, made her seem almost untouchable. In another life, I would have thought she looked ethereal—otherworldly, even. But in this one, I saw the steel beneath the silk.

And still, it shook me.

Because for a second—just a second—she looked like my Alessandra. The one I had loved. The one I had once dreamed of spending my life with.

But that woman was gone.

The priest's voice broke through my thoughts, steady and unwavering. He was a man who had seen things, who had likely performed ceremonies for men who would have people killed by morning. And yet, here he was, binding us together with vows meant for a love that no longer existed.

I swallowed hard as he spoke the words.

"Do you, Steven, take Alessandra, to be your lawfully wedded wife...?"

The pause felt endless.

I felt Alessandra's gaze on me, waiting, unreadable.

Do I?

It didn't matter. The answer had already been decided.

"I do."

The words felt foreign in my mouth.

Alessandra's voice was softer when it was her turn.

"I, Alessandra, take you, Steven, to be my lawfully wedded husband..."

Her tone was even, almost tender. If I didn't know better, I would have believed she meant it. And maybe, deep down, some part of her did. But the words weren't ours anymore. They belonged to something bigger, something darker.

The final declaration came like the last toll of a funeral bell.

"You may kiss the bride."

For a moment, neither of us moved.

And then, I stepped forward.

Her lips were soft, warm, familiar in a way that made my chest ache. It should have felt wrong, should have felt like another weight on my shoulders, but for those few seconds, the world stopped.

I let myself sink into it.

Let myself feel it.

The way she leaned into me, the way her breath hitched slightly.

For a moment, we weren't in this world.

We were back in another one—one where we were just two people in love.

But then, just as quickly, I pulled back.

And reality came crashing in.

The dining room was intimate, the long table set with pristine china and crystal glasses that reflected the glow of candlelight. A meal fit for royalty sat in front of us, but neither of us had touched it much.

The silence between us was thick, stretching over the table like an invisible wall. Alessandra picked at her plate, her usual sharpness dulled, her movements more hesitant than I had ever seen them.

It wasn't supposed to be like this.

I wasn't supposed to be sitting across from her, wearing a wedding band that felt wrong on my finger, trying to figure out what this meant for both of us.

She finally reached into her jacket, pulling out a small box and sliding it across the table.

"I wanted to give you something," she said softly.

There was something unreadable in her voice—not quite uncertainty, not quite vulnerability, but close.

I hesitated before opening it.

Inside, a sleek key fob and a brand-new cell phone rested against the black velvet lining.

I frowned, looking back at her. "What's this?"

"The key is to a car parked in the garage," she explained. "And the phone is yours to use. It's not your old one, but it's untraceable."

A beat.

"You're not a prisoner here, Steven."

I stared at the key and the phone, my grip tightening slightly.

You're not a prisoner.

It was a nice thought. A tempting illusion.

But a key given by a captor is still a chain.

And a phone they provided was a leash.

I looked up at her, searching for something—a tell, a sign, a reason to believe she meant this.

All I found was exhaustion in her eyes.

"Thank you," I said finally, my voice gruff, edged with something I couldn't quite name.

She nodded, almost relieved. "Vince will show you the garage tomorrow."

I gave a short nod, pushing the box closed, setting it aside. I didn't touch it again.

Later that night, I sat on the edge of the bed in the room that was now ours, staring at the objects she had given me.

The key. The phone.

Freedom in one hand. Control in the other.

It should have made me feel something—relief, maybe. Or maybe even hope.

But it didn't.

Because the truth was, I was never meant to be here like this.

We were never meant to be this.

Strangers bound by circumstance, not by love.

And yet...

I looked down at my ring, twisting it absently between my fingers.

If this is my reality, I have to own it.

I had made my decision.

And I would live with it.

But I wasn't done fighting.

Because now, more than ever, I knew what I had to do.

And I wasn't going to let the Navarra family dictate the rest of my life.

Not when I had my own war to wage.

Not when the person sleeping in the next room—my wife—was both my greatest weakness...

And my greatest weapon.

Chapter 23

Family Ties

Alessandra

The office door clicked shut behind me, the quiet sound swallowed by the vastness of the space. It was nearly two in the morning, and exhaustion pressed against the edges of my mind, but I had no intention of sleeping. Not tonight. Maybe not for a while.

I moved toward my desk, a familiar ritual by now. The wedding ring on my finger felt foreign, an uncomfortable weight I had yet to get used to. I turned it slowly, letting the metal catch the low glow of the lamp as I sank into my chair.

I should have been focused on the documents in front of me—the dismantling plans I had spent months perfecting. But instead, my thoughts drifted back to the evening. To Steven. To the way he had looked at me when he'd said I do.

Not with love. Not with hate.

With resignation.

I let out a slow breath, pushing the thought away as I reached for my pen, tapping it against the edge of my desk. I had a plan. I had a purpose. Getting distracted by emotions wouldn't change that.

Still, as I stared at the pages detailing the steps I had carefully mapped out—the quiet undoing of the Navarra empire—I hesitated.

Should I tell him?

Would he even believe me?

The thought of sharing my plan with Steven sent an unexpected wave of doubt through me. He still saw me as the enemy, as the woman who had betrayed him. Would it make a difference if he knew the truth? If he saw that I wasn't building this empire, I was dismantling it?

I wanted to believe it would. But wanting something didn't make it real.

My fingers tightened around the pen, frustration bubbling under my skin.

This wasn't how my life was supposed to go.

My mind wandered to a memory where Steven sat across from me on the bed in his dorm room where we were studying.

"You hate this," Steven had said, leaning back in the uncomfortable library chair, arms crossed over his chest as he watched me highlight yet another paragraph from my economics textbook.

I barely looked up. "I don't hate it," I muttered.

"Alessandra." His voice was laced with amusement, but when I met his gaze, his expression was serious. "You're miserable."

I wanted to argue, to tell him he was wrong, but we both knew better.

Steven had been the first person to ever really see me—not as a Navarra, not as the heir to a fortune built on blood and power, but as a person. And he had seen right through the carefully curated version of myself I had tried to present.

"You always talk about books like they mean something."

"They do," I had said, closing my textbook. "They're the only things that ever made me feel like there was something beyond all this. Like I could be more than what is expected of me."

Steven had watched me for a long time before shaking his head with a smirk. "You're gonna change everything one day, Alessandra."

"Or," I had said, "I'll become exactly what everyone expects me to be."

He had frowned at that, like the idea of me being anything but free physically pained him. "No. That's not you."

But he had been wrong.

Because in the end, I had become exactly what I was meant to be.

I blinked, forcing the memory back down where it belonged.

Steven had believed in me in a way no one else ever had. But belief had never been enough.

The girl who had dreamed of literature and art history was long gone, buried under the weight of expectation and duty. The woman sitting here now—trapped in an office filled with the ghosts of her father's empire—was proof of that.

I looked at the documents spread before me, the careful dismantling of everything the Navarra family had built.

It wasn't for me anymore.

It was for him.

For the life we had lost.

For the future I was still trying to salvage, even if Steven never knew it.

I leaned back in my chair, rubbing my temple. Steven had been the only person who ever believed I could be more than my name. But that was a long time ago. He wasn't that man anymore. And I... I wasn't that woman.

Still.

Would it be so dangerous to tell him?

Would it be so dangerous to let him see the truth—that I wasn't building this empire, I was tearing it down?

I reached for my glass of whiskey, lifting it to my lips before pausing, my hand hovering midair.

If I tell him, he'll know the risk I'm taking. He'll know what I'm planning.

But if I don't...

I exhaled sharply, setting the glass back down.

No.

I couldn't tell him. Not yet. Not until I was certain.

I leaned forward again, pen finally meeting paper.

If I was going to dismantle this empire, I needed to be smart. And that meant keeping Steven in the dark—for now.

Because the moment he knew the truth, he would have to make a choice.

Stay.

Or betray me.

Twenty minutes later, I sat back, staring at the documents spread before me. My plans were taking shape, but before I could move forward, I needed to secure my position.

I reached for my phone and dialed Nico.

He answered on the first ring. "Donna."

I didn't hesitate. "Send a message to the family. Steven is one of us now. Anyone who lays a hand on him—or his family—will answer to me."

There was a pause. Then Nico's voice, measured. "Understood."

And then... hesitation.

"You know this won't stop them all, Alessandra. Some will test you. Some will wait for the right moment."

"Then we'll make sure they don't get the chance," I said, my voice cold. "Keep a close watch on Steven's family. If anything feels off, I want to know about it immediately."

"I'll handle it," Nico assured me.

I closed my eyes, nodding even though he couldn't see me.

"Thank you, Nico."

"Always," he replied before the line went dead.

The office was quiet again.

I sat there, motionless, my fingers grazing the papers in front of me, my thoughts spiraling back to Steven.

To the way he had looked at me across the dinner table.

To the way he had hesitated before saying I do.

To the moment our lips met, when—for just a second—the rest of the world had ceased to exist.

And to the sharp, aching loss I felt when he pulled away.

I should have expected it. I should have welcomed it.

But I hadn't.

Because for the briefest of moments, I had let myself believe that maybe—just maybe—there was still something left between us.

I exhaled, steeling myself, forcing the foolish thought out of my head.

There was no room for love here. No room for nostalgia.

Only survival.

Only the plan.

I looked down at my hands, flexing my fingers before picking up my pen again.

One step at a time.

That was how I would survive this.

That was how I would save us both.

Even if Steven never knew it.

Part Three

The Power Struggle

Chapter 24

No Place Like Home

Steven

The drive to my mother's house felt longer than it should have, the familiar route now laden with the weight of everything I'd been through. The wedding ring on my finger, a cold reminder of my new reality, glinted in the afternoon sun as I tightened my grip on the steering wheel. A sigh escaped me, heavy with the knowledge that I had to remove it before I saw her. I couldn't explain this—not to her, not to anyone.

I pulled into the driveway, cutting the engine as the house came into view. It looked the same as it always had, the front porch framed by the same white railing my father had painted years ago, the garden beds still meticulously maintained, just as he had left them. But as I sat there, staring at the house that held so many memories, I felt a chasm open up between the life I'd known and the one I now inhabited.

Slowly, I reached for the ring, twisting it off with a feeling of deep reluctance. The metal felt cool and foreign against my palm, and for a moment, I just held it, staring at the circle that bound me to Alessandra. It was more than just a symbol; it was a reminder of everything I'd sacrificed, everything I'd lost. My thumb brushed over the smooth band before I slipped it into my pocket, out of sight but never truly out of mind.

I stepped out of the car, the autumn leaves crunching underfoot as I made my way up the path. The door opened before I could knock, and there she was—my mother, her face lighting up with relief at the sight of me.

"Steven!" she exclaimed, her arms already outstretched as I approached. I stepped into her embrace, letting her warmth seep into me, a small comfort in the chaos of my mind.

"Hey, Mom," I murmured into her hair, the familiar scent of her shampoo tugging at something deep inside me.

She pulled back, her hands still on my arms as she looked me over, her eyes narrowing slightly. "Where have you been? It's been months. You didn't call. I was worried sick."

"I know," I said, forcing a smile that I hoped was reassuring. "I'm sorry. I had to go after a lead—it all happened so fast. I didn't have time to call."

Her eyes searched mine, a mother's intuition digging deeper than I was comfortable with. She was silent for a moment, just watching me, and I could see the worry lines etched into her face, lines that hadn't been there before. I swallowed, the lie I'd spun feeling like a stone in my throat.

"I'm just glad you're home," she finally said, her voice softer now, tinged with that worry she couldn't quite shake. "Come in. I made your favorite."

I followed her inside, the familiar creak of the floorboards beneath my feet bringing a flood of memories. Everything was as it always had been—the photos on the walls, the smell of coffee and something sweet baking in the kitchen, the cozy clutter of a home well-lived in. But there was a tension in the air that hadn't been there before, a subtle shift that made everything feel just a little off-kilter.

"Sit down," she said, gesturing to the kitchen table as she busied herself with the oven. "I'll get us some coffee."

I watched her move about the kitchen, her hands deft and sure as she poured the coffee and pulled a tray of cookies from the oven. She placed a plate in front of me, the cookies still warm and gooey, just like when I was a kid. I managed another smile, this one more genuine, as I reached for one. "These look great, Mom."

She smiled back, but there was something in her eyes—a flicker of concern, of unspoken questions. "You've been gone so much lately," she said, her tone casual but with an undercurrent of worry. "I know your job takes you all over, but I thought you were going to be staying closer to home for a while. After everything..."

"I know," I said, taking a bite of the cookie to buy myself a moment to think. The sweetness of the chocolate melted on my tongue, a brief distraction from the conversation. "It was just one of those things. A lead came up out of nowhere, and I had to follow it. It was...important."

She nodded, but I could see the doubt in her eyes, the questions she wasn't asking. "You're always chasing something, Steven." She reached across the table, placing her hand over mine. "But you know you can't run forever."

The weight of her words settled over me, a reminder of the life I'd left behind, the life that had been simple and full of promise. But that life was gone now, replaced by something darker, something I couldn't escape.

"I'm home now," I said, offering her another smile, though it felt more like a grimace. "At least for a little while."

She searched my face again, and I could see the worry etched deeper into her features, the lines around her eyes more pronounced than before. "You look tired, Steven. Are you sure you're okay?"

"I'm fine," I lied, forcing the words out past the lump in my throat. "Just a little worn out. It was...a tough assignment."

She nodded, her hand slipping from mine as she took a sip of her coffee, her eyes never leaving me. "You're working too hard. You need to take care of yourself."

"I will," I promised, though I wasn't sure how much of it I believed.

We sat in silence for a while, the only sound the ticking of the clock on the wall. I could feel the tension between us, the unspoken words hanging heavy in the air. She didn't push, didn't pry any further, but I could see the questions in her eyes, the worry that she couldn't quite hide.

Eventually, she stood up, clearing the dishes from the table. "I'm just glad you're safe," she said, her back to me as she busied herself at the sink. "That's all that matters."

"Yeah," I said quietly, the weight of the ring in my pocket a constant reminder of the lies I was living. "Me too."

As she washed the dishes, I let my mind drift, the memories of my father surfacing once more. He had always been there for me, always had the answers when I needed them. But now, I was on my own, navigating a world that felt more dangerous and uncertain than ever before.

I could still hear his voice, calm and reassuring, telling me to trust my instincts, to do what was right, no matter the cost. But what was right in a situation like this? How could I reconcile the love I had for Alessandra with the world she was a part of, the world I was now tangled in?

As I sat there, staring at the remnants of my mother's cookies, I felt the weight of my choices pressing down on me. I had made my decision, chosen my path, but it didn't make it any easier. The guilt gnawed at me, the lies I was telling her, the secrets I was keeping.

My mother turned back to me, a soft smile on her face. "You know, your father used to say that no matter where you go, you can always come home. This will always be your home, Steven."

"Thanks, Mom," I said, trying to keep the emotion out of my voice. "That means a lot."

She walked over to me, placing a gentle hand on my shoulder. "Just promise me you'll be careful, okay?"

The ache in my chest deepened, the pain of knowing that I couldn't promise her that, not really. But I nodded anyway, giving her the reassurance she needed, even if it was just another lie.

"I promise," I said, forcing a smile as I stood up. "I'll be careful."

She pulled me into another hug, and I let myself sink into it, savoring the comfort of her embrace, the simplicity of it all. But as much as I wanted to stay in that moment, to hold on to the life I had known, I knew that it was slipping away, just like everything else.

When she finally let go, I stepped back, reaching for my coat. "I should get going," I said, my voice steady even as my heart ached.

She nodded, though I could see the disappointment in her eyes. "Come back soon, okay? Don't be a stranger."

"I won't," I promised, though I knew it was another promise I might not be able to keep.

As I walked out the door, the ring still heavy in my pocket, I felt the familiar pull of the life I had chosen, the life that was now inescapable. And as much as I longed for the simplicity of the past, I knew there was no going back.

There was no place like home, but home was no longer the same. And neither was I.

Chapter 25

Off Balance

Steven

The office smelled the same—coffee, stale printer ink, and the faint metallic tang of too many overworked computers humming at once. But it felt different.

Or maybe I was the one who had changed.

I stood at the entrance, momentarily lost in the whirlwind of voices and keyboard clicks, before the familiar sound of my name snapped me out of it.

"Steven?"

I turned to see Doug striding toward me, his expression a mixture of relief and exasperation. "Man, where have you been?" His voice carried over the newsroom, drawing the attention of a few nearby reporters.

"Hey, Doug." I forced a casual smile, gripping the strap of my laptop bag tighter. "I know. I—" I hesitated, already feeling the lie forming on my tongue. "—had to follow a lead. Came up last minute. No time to check in."

Doug folded his arms, cocking an eyebrow. "Uh-huh. That's

funny. That's exactly what I told the editor when he was demanding to know where you'd vanished to." He let out a low chuckle, shaking his head. "Guess I nailed it."

I smirked, but the weight in my chest didn't lift. "Yeah, well… it wasn't much of a story in the end. Total dead end."

Doug studied me for a beat too long. "You sure about that?"

I exhaled. "Yeah. I wouldn't be standing here if it had been worth something."

Doug nodded, though the skepticism never fully left his face. "Well, I hope you're ready for some heat, because the boss was not happy." He jerked his head toward the editor's office. "Better get in there before he comes looking for you."

I gave a quick nod and made my way across the floor. Every step felt heavier, the distance to that door stretching with the weight of what I was about to do.

I knocked twice before pushing it open.

Alan Wilkes, my editor, was sitting behind his desk, glasses perched low on his nose, red pen in hand. He looked up, eyes narrowing the second he saw me. "Well, well. If it isn't the missing journalist."

I shut the door behind me, bracing myself. "Hey, Alan."

Alan tossed his pen onto the desk, leaning back in his chair. "You better have a really good reason for ghosting us, Porter. I was this close—" He held up two fingers, barely an inch apart. "—to running a missing person's report on you."

I forced a small laugh, though nothing about this was funny. "Yeah… sorry about that. The lead I was chasing took me off the grid."

Alan's gaze sharpened. "Funny thing. The last thing you sent in was that Navarra piece. Then poof. Gone." He drummed his fingers on the desk. "You don't just disappear after submitting a story like that, Steven. You especially don't disappear when that story could get people killed."

I swallowed hard. "You didn't run it."

Alan shook his head. "No, I didn't. And do you want to know

why? Because you weren't here to verify any last-minute changes. Because sources went dark after you vanished. Because I wasn't about to put this paper—and my ass—on the line for a story when the guy who wrote it had literally gone missing."

I exhaled, tension coiling in my shoulders. "I appreciate that."

Alan studied me, his expression shifting. "You're not here to pick up where you left off, are you?"

I hesitated. He was good—too good.

I shook my head. "No."

Alan sighed, rubbing a hand over his face. "A real shame. You were one of the best."

The words hit me harder than I expected. But I pushed through. "I need to step away, Alan. Maybe for good."

He didn't look surprised. If anything, he just looked... resigned. "And this has nothing to do with the Navarras?"

I forced a smile that didn't reach my eyes. "No."

A long silence stretched between us before Alan finally nodded. "Alright. I won't ask questions you don't want to answer." He picked up his pen again, already moving on. "But if you ever decide to come back, you know where to find me."

I gave him a tight nod before turning for the door.

Just as I stepped out, my phone buzzed in my pocket. I pulled it out, glancing at the screen—only to feel my breath hitch.

Nate Porter.

I had barely given my mother my new number, and she had immediately given it to my FBI agent brother.

Fantastic.

I exhaled, bracing myself before answering. "Nate."

"Steven." His voice was even, but there was an edge to it. "Where have you been?"

I walked toward the stairwell, away from the newsroom. "I was following a lead. It turned out to be nothing."

"Bullshit."

I froze mid-step.

Nate never swore.

"You disappeared for months after submitting a story about one of the most dangerous families in the city," he continued. "And now you're suddenly back, with a new phone number? You expect me to believe that's a coincidence?"

My grip on the phone tightened. "I don't know what you want me to say, Nate."

"How about the truth?"

I reached the stairwell, leaning against the wall. "I can't do that."

Silence.

Then, a sigh. "Mom's worried. Mitch's pissed."

Guilt twisted in my stomach.

"I get it," Nate said, his voice softer now. "You're always chasing something, Steven. But this? This feels different. Whatever you're caught up in—" He hesitated. "—be careful. Because if I find out you're in real trouble? I will get involved."

My throat felt tight.

"I hear you," I managed.

"Do you?"

I let out a breath. "Yeah. I do."

Another silence, then, "Call Mitch. You owe him that much."

The line clicked dead.

I stared at my phone, my pulse hammering.

I had walked into this office today thinking I could hold onto pieces of my old life. That maybe, just maybe, I could balance both worlds.

But as I stood there, the weight of my choices pressing down on me, I knew the truth.

That life was gone.

And the more I tried to pretend otherwise, the more the lies would bury me alive.

Chapter 26

No Going Back

Steven

The city lights flickered against the windshield as I drove, the low hum of traffic and the occasional horn filling the silence in the car. I kept my hands tight on the wheel, my knuckles white, my thoughts still heavy from the conversation with Nate. I shouldn't have answered his call. I shouldn't have called Mitch either.

But after months of silence, after lying to my own family about where I'd been, where I was now, I needed to hear their voices—needed to remind myself that part of my life still existed.

I reached for my phone, hesitating for just a moment before dialing Mitch's number and putting the call over the speakers.

It rang twice before he picked up. "Hey, little brother! Finally decided to call your favorite sibling, huh?"

I smirked despite myself. "Yeah, sorry about that. I've been a little busy."

"Busy? Busy like 'almost getting yourself killed' busy? Because

Nate's been acting like you pulled some kind of Jason Bourne stunt. You good?"

His concern was wrapped in humor, but I could hear the genuine worry underneath.

"I'm fine, Mitch. Just... got caught up in something bigger than I expected."

"Caught up, huh?" There was a pause, and I could practically hear the gears turning in his head. "Mom was worried sick. She thought you were finally going to stick around for a while. Then you disappeared, just like that."

I swallowed against the guilt pressing into my chest. "I know. I didn't mean to worry her. It was all last minute, and there wasn't time to explain."

"Explain? Hell, Steve, you've always been the one to rush headlong into danger, but this felt different. Nate said you were working on something really dangerous."

I kept my eyes on the road, gripping the steering wheel tighter. "It was. But I'm back now, or at least trying to be."

"Trying?" His voice lost its teasing edge. "What's really going on with you?"

I exhaled sharply, shaking my head. "It's complicated, man. I wish I could explain, but I need you to trust me right now. Just know that I'm okay."

Silence stretched for a long beat before he sighed. "Alright, Steve. I trust you. Just... don't go disappearing again, okay?"

A small laugh escaped me, the tension easing just a little. "I'll do my best. Thanks, Mitch."

"No problem, man. And hey, when you're ready to talk, I'm here. No judgment, just brotherly advice and maybe a beer or two."

"Sounds good. I'll call you soon."

We said our goodbyes, and I ended the call, setting the phone down beside me. But the conversation lingered, settling over me like a weight.

It was the same thing with Nate, with my mom. They wanted

answers I couldn't give them. Not without putting them at risk. And the longer I stayed in this life, the more tangled everything became.

A flicker in my rearview mirror pulled my attention. A dark sedan, trailing behind me, just far enough to seem casual—but I knew better.

I made a right turn, then another. The car followed.

My pulse quickened, a slow burn of adrenaline working through me.

I changed lanes, weaving through traffic, testing their patience. But they didn't speed up, didn't fall back. They were good. Trained.

I took another turn, this one abrupt. The tires screeched slightly, but when I glanced back, they were still there.

My stomach tightened. Who was following me?

Vito? Someone from his camp? Someone who had caught wind of my presence in this world?

I wasn't naïve enough to think I had slipped back into my old life unnoticed. And if they were tailing me now, it meant I had already made a mistake.

I exhaled sharply and made a final, sharp left into an empty parking lot, slamming the brakes. The car behind me hesitated—too long. Then, slowly, it pulled over a few spaces away, making no attempt to hide.

For a split second, I debated my options. Confront them? Call Alessandra? Walk away?

But before I could move, the driver's side door opened, and Vince stepped out, his large frame blocking the glow of the streetlights.

My jaw clenched.

I threw the car into park and got out, slamming the door behind me. "Are you serious?" I snapped, my voice bouncing off the concrete.

Vince didn't flinch. "Boss's orders," he said simply. "You get freedom, not invisibility."

I stared at him, the anger in my chest shifting into something heavier. Of course. Of course Alessandra wasn't going to just let me walk around the city unchecked. Of course she had me followed.

I let out a humorless laugh, shaking my head. "So what? You babysit me now?"

"Security detail," Vince corrected. "Nothing more."

"Bullshit."

He didn't argue.

I took a step closer, lowering my voice. "Let me guess—she's been tracking my phone too?"

Vince didn't answer, but his silence said everything.

I clenched my jaw, turning away for a moment, trying to shove down the frustration that was threatening to boil over. I knew why she was doing this. I knew she thought she was protecting me. But this wasn't protection. This was control.

And I was so sick of being controlled.

After a long moment, I forced myself to breathe, to push the fury down where it wouldn't get me killed.

"You tell her I don't need a shadow," I said, my voice hard. "And if she doesn't trust me to handle myself, then she never should have given me that car."

Vince sighed. "Steven—"

"No." I cut him off. "You can follow me back to the estate if you want. But after that? Stay out of my rearview."

I didn't wait for a response. I got back in the car, slamming the door shut before peeling out of the lot. Vince's car followed, but I didn't look back again.

I knew he was there. Just like I knew I was never really free.

And that thought—more than anything else—terrified me.

Because if I wasn't free, then what was I?

A prisoner? A husband? A pawn?

Or something worse?

I didn't know anymore.

Chapter 27

Controlled Demolition

Alessandra

The office was quiet, save for the faint ticking of the grandfather clock in the corner. I should have been exhausted—it was late, and the weight of the day hung heavy on my shoulders—but sleep had long since stopped coming easily.

I sat at my desk, papers spread before me, detailing the next steps in a plan that had been years in the making. The dismantling of the Navarra empire would not be swift, nor would it be easy. But it was necessary.

For years, I had told myself that power was the only way to survive. That to keep the family intact, I had to rule with the same ruthlessness as my father. But the deeper I went into this life, the more I realized that holding onto power wasn't the answer. It was the problem.

The Navarra name had been synonymous with dominance, wealth, and bloodshed for generations. But I had no interest in preserving an empire built on corruption and fear. I wanted to undo it—piece by piece, decision by decision, until there was nothing left for men like Vito Valenti to claim.

The first time I voiced this to Nico, I expected resistance. After all, Nico had been by my father's side for years. He had upheld the Navarro legacy, enforced its laws, and ensured its survival. If anyone had reason to stop me, it was him.

But when I told him the truth—when I finally admitted that my goal wasn't to rule but to end—he had let out a long, weary breath, closed his eyes for a moment, and then nodded.

"Good," he had said.

That was all. A single word, but it had carried a weight I hadn't expected.

I had looked at him then, really looked at him. The man who had stood at my side, who had trained me, protected me, ensured that I lived long enough to take my father's place. And for the first time, I saw something in him I hadn't seen before.

Relief.

Not because he didn't believe I could rule—no, he had made his loyalty to me clear the day I took my father's life. But because he had seen what this life did to men like him. And maybe, deep down, he had always hoped I would be the one to break the cycle.

I exhaled, pushing the memory aside as I heard footsteps approaching.

The door opened without a knock, just as it always did when Nico entered. He moved with the quiet confidence of a man who had nothing left to prove. His face, lined with years of loyalty and violence, remained impassive, but his eyes flicked to the documents on my desk before meeting mine.

"You're ready to move forward?" he asked.

"I am," I said, leaning back in my chair. "We start pulling out of Queens first. The businesses there will go quietly—we liquidate assets, cut ties, and make it look like a shift in strategy, not a collapse."

Nico gave a small nod, as if he had expected nothing less. "And the men?"

"They won't suspect a thing at first," I said. "If they think we're restructuring, they'll follow orders. But when the bigger pieces start to fall, that's when we'll need to be careful. Some will stay loyal. Some will see an opportunity."

Nico leaned against the edge of my desk, crossing his arms. "And Vito?"

"He's watching," I admitted. "Waiting for a crack in the foundation. He wants to see how far he can push before I push back."

"You won't give him that chance," Nico said simply. It wasn't a question. It was a fact.

I let out a short, humorless laugh. "No, I won't. When we burn this empire down, I'll make sure there's nothing left for him to take."

Silence stretched between us, but it wasn't uncomfortable. It was the quiet understanding of two people who had seen too much, endured too much, and were ready to see it all end.

"You never questioned me," I said after a moment.

Nico tilted his head slightly, as if considering the statement. "You never gave me a reason to."

I studied him, the man who had been the closest thing to a father I had ever known. "You could have stopped me. When I told you what I planned, you could have said no."

Nico's expression softened just enough that I caught a glimpse of something unspoken. "I was never going to stop you, Alessandra," he said. "Because I know what this life does to people. And I don't want that for you."

I knew he was tired, that he wanted nothing more than to walk away from this life, to find some semblance of peace. But there was no retirement in our world. The only way out was to be without a kingdom—or to be dead.

"I wish I could offer you more, Nico," I said, my voice softer now. "I know how much you've sacrificed. You deserve more than this."

He shook his head, a small, weary smile tugging at the corners of his mouth. "There's nothing more for me, Alessandra. My life has been this family, and it will end with this family. I swore to protect the Navarras, and I will see it through to the end. Whether that end is mine, or the empire's, it makes no difference. But I won't leave you to face this alone."

I felt a pang of gratitude for his loyalty, but also a deep sadness for the life he had lived, the life he had been forced to live. Nico had been more than just a trusted advisor; he had been a father figure in many ways, guiding me through the treacherous world I had inherited. But now, we were both caught in a web of our own making, bound by promises and oaths that neither of us could break.

A silence stretched between us, weighted with things neither of us could change.

"I need you to keep an eye on Vito," I said finally, shifting back to business. "He's been testing the waters, escalating small problems into bigger ones. If he makes a move, I want to know about it first."

"You will," Nico assured me.

I gave a tight nod. "Good. Then we move forward. Piece by piece, the Navarro empire falls."

Nico pushed off the desk and straightened, his expression unreadable once more. But as he turned toward the door, he hesitated.

"You're doing the right thing," he said quietly.

The words caught me off guard. Not because I didn't believe them, but because hearing them from Nico made them feel real in a way they hadn't before.

I swallowed hard, then nodded. "Let's just hope I survive long enough to see it through."

Nico smirked, the closest thing to amusement I'd seen from him in weeks. "You will."

And with that, he was gone.

I sat there for a long moment after he left, staring at the papers in front of me. The blueprint of my father's empire, the empire I was about to dismantle, piece by piece.

For years, I had been trapped under the weight of my last name, forced into a role I never wanted. But now?

Now I was finally making my own choices.

And I would see this through to the end, no matter what it cost me.

Even if it cost me everything.

Chapter 28

A Silent Observer

Steven

The Navarra estate was a place of quiet power, but that power was built on secrets—secrets I needed to uncover. I had spent the past few days acclimating myself to the rhythms of the house, the people, the way everything operated. The staff was efficient and discreet, the guards stationed in strategic but subtle positions, the lieutenants of the Navarra family always hovering nearby. It was an ecosystem, a carefully maintained structure that had been built over generations.

And I was an intruder in it.

I played the part of the observant husband well—asking questions that seemed harmless, appearing curious rather than suspicious. I studied the way the estate functioned, how orders were given, how information flowed. But more than anything, I watched Alessandra.

She moved through this world as if it had always belonged to her, and in a way, it had. But there was something more. The way she spoke to Nico, the way she handled disputes, the quiet determination in her eyes—it was controlled, methodical. And yet, beneath it all, I could sense something shifting.

I wasn't the only one watching.

I had noticed him before—a quiet, looming figure always nearby, never obtrusive but always present. Nico.

He was Alessandra's shadow, her enforcer, her most trusted man. More than that, he was the one who had been in her life the longest. I didn't know how much he knew about me, about us, but I had the distinct feeling that I wasn't just another person under his scrutiny.

Which was why I wasn't surprised when he finally approached me.

I was in one of the smaller hallways off the west wing, heading toward what I had learned was one of the estate's private offices. I had intended to spend some time there, reading through documents I had managed to obtain—trying to piece together more about the Navarra operation.

But before I could turn the handle, I felt the shift in the air.

Nico stepped out from the shadows, blocking my path.

I didn't startle. I had been expecting this.

"Steven," he said, his voice a gravelly warning, as if he had already decided how this conversation would go.

I met his gaze, keeping my expression neutral. "Nico."

"You've been making yourself comfortable," he said, not bothering with pleasantries. "Walking around, asking questions. You looking for something?"

There was an unspoken challenge in his voice, one I couldn't afford to lose.

"I'm trying to understand the world I married into," I said evenly. "If I'm going to be part of it, I need to know how it works."

Nico stared at me for a long moment, his dark eyes sharp, unreadable. "And why is that? Why the sudden interest?"

"Because Alessandra needs someone she can rely on." I kept my voice steady, my posture relaxed, even as my instincts screamed at me to be careful. "I may not have been born into this life, but I'm in it now. And if she trusts me enough to make me her husband, I need to be useful to her."

Nico's expression didn't change, but I could feel the weight of his scrutiny. "Trust," he repeated, almost like he was testing the word.

I didn't react.

"You're not like us, Steven," he continued, taking a slow step forward. "You weren't raised in this world. You didn't grow up with its rules. You don't understand what it takes to survive in it."

I clenched my jaw. "Then teach me."

Something flickered in his gaze. "You think this is something you can just learn?"

I shrugged. "Everything is learned. No one's born into power knowing how to wield it. They have to be taught."

Nico's lips pressed together, and I knew he was assessing me, deciding if I was worth the time—or the threat.

"I've protected Alessandra since she was a child," he said, his voice quieter now, more dangerous. "I was there before you, and I'll be here long after you. So let me be very clear, Steven—if you ever become a problem for her, I'll deal with you myself."

There was no bravado in his words. No empty threats.

I believed him.

I nodded slowly. "I'd expect nothing less."

Nico exhaled, studying me once more. Then, after a long pause, he said, "There are things at play that you don't understand. But you could be an asset if you wanted to be."

I kept my expression neutral. "I'm listening."

"Not here." Nico glanced at the closed office door, then back at me. "When you're ready to know what's really going on, you'll come to me."

Then, without another word, he stepped past me and disappeared down the hall, leaving me standing there, my pulse pounding in my ears.

I had expected resistance, had expected suspicion. But this... this was something else.

Nico hadn't dismissed me outright.
He had invited me in.
And that was more dangerous than anything else.
Because now, I had to decide whether I wanted to play along.
And if I did...
I had to make sure I played the game better than anyone else.

Chapter 29

The Danger of Subtlty

Steven

The tension between me and Alessandra had been shifting, subtly, dangerously.

I had been keeping my distance, trying to remind myself of the mission, of my purpose. But something kept pulling me back.

Maybe it was the way she looked at me sometimes, when she thought I wasn't watching. Or maybe it was the way the past crept into our present when we least expected it.

It had started with small things. Accidental conversations. Late nights where we both ended up in the same room, neither willing to leave first.

Tonight was one of those nights.

I found her in the library, curled in one of the chairs, a book in her hands. The soft glow of the lamp beside her cast warm shadows along her face, making her look softer, younger—like the Alessandra I used to know.

She looked up when I walked in, her expression unreadable.

"You're up late," I said, moving toward the bar cart and pouring myself a drink.

"So are you," she countered, closing the book but keeping her fingers tucked between the pages, marking her spot. "Trouble sleeping?"

I shrugged, taking a slow sip of whiskey. "Something like that."

A beat of silence stretched between us, thick with things neither of us wanted to say.

Then she sighed, setting the book aside completely. "Why are you really here, Steven?"

The question hung between us, heavy with meaning.

I opened my mouth to give her some excuse, some half-truth that wouldn't invite more questions. But instead, what came out was the truth.

"I don't know," I admitted, surprising even myself. "Maybe I just wanted to be near you."

Her breath hitched—just slightly—but I caught it. A flicker of something she tried to hide, something that made my pulse quicken against my better judgment.

"This isn't what I wanted for us," she whispered.

I took a step closer, drawn to her in a way that felt inevitable. "Then what did you want?"

Her lips parted, but no words came.

Before I could stop myself, my hand lifted of its own accord, my fingers brushing a loose strand of hair behind her ear. Her breath caught again, her lashes fluttering for just a second, and it was like stepping into the past—before the lies, before the betrayals, before this life swallowed us whole.

A simple touch.

A moment of familiarity in a world where nothing was familiar anymore.

"I don't know how to do this," she admitted, her voice barely above a whisper.

"Me neither," I murmured.

She didn't move away. Neither did I.

The warmth of her skin lingered beneath my fingertips, and for a second—just a second—I let myself remember. The way she used to fit against me, the way she used to laugh without reservation, the way we used to talk about a future that had never come to be.

And then the moment shattered.

Reality crept back in, cold and unrelenting.

I pulled my hand away, taking a step back before I could let myself fall any further into something I wasn't sure I could crawl back out of.

Alessandra's expression flickered—something unreadable crossing her face before she schooled it into neutrality.

I turned, downing the rest of my drink in one swallow, letting the burn of the whiskey settle deep in my chest.

"Get some rest," I said, my voice rougher than I intended. Then I walked out, leaving her sitting there, alone with the ghosts of what we used to be.

Because I couldn't do this.

I couldn't let myself forget who she was.

And more importantly—who she wasn't anymore.

Chapter 30

Afforded Trust

Alessandra

The estate was never truly silent. Even in the dead of night, there were always distant voices, the murmur of security patrols, the occasional hum of an engine pulling into the garage. But tonight, the quiet felt different. Heavier. Like the walls were holding a secret too dangerous to speak aloud.

I had spent the last few days navigating Vito's encroachments, ensuring that our dismantling efforts remained unseen, and securing my control over my own men. But none of it—none of it—felt as important as the uneasy feeling that had been building inside me. I'd ignored it at first, chalked it up to stress, exhaustion, or even my own paranoia.

But then Vince came to me.

He appeared in my office just after midnight, his presence a shadow against the dim light of my desk lamp. Vince never spoke without purpose, never disrupted my nights unless it was necessary. That alone was enough to make my pulse quicken.

"Ms. Navarra," he said, voice low, controlled. "We need to talk about your husband."

His words sent an immediate chill through me, though I didn't show it. I set my pen down carefully and met his gaze.

"Go on."

Vince hesitated—a rare moment of uncertainty from a man who had spent his life making split-second decisions that determined life or death. That hesitation made it worse.

"He's been asking questions," Vince said. "Subtle, but intentional. Watching. Listening. He's more aware than he lets on."

"What kind of questions?"

"Supply chains, logistics, leadership structure. He's not asking like someone trying to learn. He's asking like someone trying to confirm."

I exhaled slowly, the weight of his words pressing down on me. I had seen Steven lurking on the edges of things, stepping closer, paying more attention. I had wanted to believe that he was trying to understand, trying to find his place in all of this.

"There's more," Vince continued. "I caught him eavesdropping on a conversation between some of the men. It wasn't about anything important—routine work—but the way he froze when he saw me? That wasn't an accident. He's careful, but not careful enough."

I leaned back in my chair, my pulse thrumming at my temple.

"You think he's working against me."

Vince hesitated just long enough to confirm what I already knew. "I think he's a liability. And if he's a liability, Ms. Navarra, we both know what needs to happen next."

The air in the office felt suffocating for the first time in weeks. I clenched my hands together, fingers lacing so tightly that my knuckles ached.

Steven.

Steven, who I had protected. Who I had saved.

Who I had let back in.

I swallowed down the emotion that threatened to surface,

pushing it deep into the cold, hollow space I had carved out for moments like this.

"No one touches him," I said, my voice firm. "Not until I say otherwise."

Vince studied me for a long moment, but he nodded. "Understood."

As he left, I stayed in my chair for a long moment, staring at nothing.

I had given Steven the benefit of the doubt. Given him space. Given him every opportunity to stand beside me.

And he had chosen, instead, to stand against me.

That, I could not forgive.

I stood, my body moving before my mind had fully caught up. I already knew where he would be. He had been spending more and more time in the library, pretending to be lost in books, but I knew better. The library was at the heart of the estate—where men talked freely, where conversations overlapped, where a man pretending to belong could learn more than he should.

I didn't bother knocking when I reached the library doors. I shoved them open hard enough that they crashed against the walls, making Steven jolt to his feet. Papers were scattered across the desk in front of him, notes I couldn't yet make out.

His expression shifted instantly. Surprise. Then recognition. Then something careful—something measured.

"Alessandra?"

"How long?" I demanded, stepping inside, my voice sharp, unwavering.

His brows pulled together. "How long what?"

"How long have you been planning to betray me?"

His jaw tightened, a flicker of something unreadable passing through his eyes. He didn't answer right away, which told me everything I needed to know.

I took another step closer. "Vince told me everything. The listening. The questions. The lies. So tell me, Steven—what exactly was your plan? Infiltrate my world and then burn it to the ground?"

His mouth pressed into a thin line, and for a moment, I thought he wasn't going to answer. But then—

"I was trying to survive," he said, his voice quieter, rougher. "You don't get to play the victim here, Alessandra. You took me. You made me part of this world. What did you think was going to happen? That I would just accept it?"

"I thought you would trust me," I shot back, my heart pounding harder than I wanted to admit. "I thought—"

I cut myself off before I said something I couldn't take back.

Steven's expression flickered. Just for a second. And in that second, I saw the man I had once loved, the man who had once loved me.

"Did you ever mean it?" I asked, the words escaping before I could stop them. "Any of it? The moments between us, the way you looked at me, the way you—"

I swallowed hard.

"Or was it all just part of your game?"

He hesitated—longer than before. And that was what undid me.

"It wasn't a game," he admitted, his voice barely above a whisper.

My breath caught, but I forced myself to hold his gaze, to find the truth in it.

"But it wasn't enough, was it?" I said bitterly.

Steven exhaled, running a hand through his hair. "I don't know what you want me to say, Alessandra. I don't know how to be part of this world."

"Then stop trying to work against me," I snapped.

Silence stretched between us, thick with everything we couldn't say.

Finally, I took a step back. "I don't know if I can trust you," I admitted, my voice quieter now. "And I need to know."

"How?" Steven asked.

I met his gaze. "You'll prove it to me. But right now, I need you to leave."

I turned and walked away before I could change my mind, before I could let the memories of what we used to be cloud the reality of what we were now.

Because trust wasn't given.

It was earned.

And Steven Porter was going to have to earn mine.

Chapter 31

Hidden Intentions

Steven

The estate had never felt so suffocating.

I stood frozen in the library, my mind struggling to process what had just happened. Get out. Alessandra's voice still rang in my ears, cutting through me like a blade.

She didn't trust me.

And why would she?

I had spent weeks watching her, studying her, waiting for the moment I could turn the tables. I had told myself it was survival, that I was just trying to understand the world I'd been forced into. But Alessandra saw it differently. She saw it as betrayal.

And maybe it was.

The realization sat heavy in my chest as I moved toward my room, my thoughts tangled in a web of frustration and guilt. I was packing before I had even fully decided to leave, stuffing a duffel bag with essentials. My hands moved on autopilot—clothes, laptop, the phone she had given me.

I hesitated over the wedding ring.

It wasn't like I had been wearing it much, but I still carried it with me, tucked into a pocket or left on the nightstand. Now, I held it between my fingers, feeling the cool weight of it. This was a symbol of control, obligation, necessity. Not love. Not anymore.

Was it ever?

I exhaled sharply, stuffing the ring into the side pocket of the bag before slinging it over my shoulder. I didn't even know where I was going. Maybe a hotel. Maybe nowhere.

It wasn't until I reached the main hallway that I realized someone was waiting for me.

"Nico."

He was leaning against the wall, arms crossed over his chest, watching me with an expression I couldn't quite place. Not smug. Not angry. Just... knowing.

"Going somewhere?" he asked, his voice as steady as ever.

I shifted the bag higher on my shoulder, meeting his gaze. "I don't know yet."

Nico nodded like he expected that answer. "Let me take you."

Something about his tone made it clear this wasn't a suggestion.

I considered refusing, but what was the point? So, instead, I followed him out the door and into the waiting car.

The ride was quiet at first, the city passing by in a blur of neon lights and late-night traffic. I kept my gaze on the road ahead, trying to figure out why Nico was driving me instead of one of Alessandra's other men.

It wasn't until we turned down a quieter street, pulling up outside an old Italian restaurant, that I realized this wasn't just a ride.

"You hungry?" Nico asked.

I looked over at him, caught off guard by the question. "What?"

"You heard me."

I hesitated, then nodded. Not because I was hungry, but because I wanted to know where this was going.

We stepped inside, the warmth of the place a stark contrast to the cold tension in my chest. The restaurant was nearly empty, just a few scattered patrons sipping espresso at the bar. Nico led me to a booth in the back, and within minutes, a waitress brought over two plates of pasta and a bottle of wine.

I waited for him to speak.

Instead, he took a bite of his food, then nodded at my plate. "Eat."

I didn't touch it. "Are we gonna pretend this is normal?"

Nico smirked slightly. "Normal's a relative thing, Steven. But no, we're not pretending."

I leaned back, arms crossed. "Then let's get to the point."

He studied me for a moment, then set his fork down with deliberate slowness. "I know what you've been doing."

My stomach clenched.

"You think I don't see everything that happens in that house?" he continued, his voice calm, almost conversational. "I saw you watching, listening, testing. Trying to figure out where you could fit in—if you could fit in. And if you couldn't?" He tilted his head. "You'd find another way out."

I didn't deny it.

"Alessandra thinks you're working against her," he said after a pause. "That you were gathering information to take her down."

I swallowed. "And what do you think?"

Nico exhaled, his fingers tapping lightly against the table. "I think you don't know what you're doing."

A humorless chuckle escaped me. "Glad we're on the same page."

Nico's expression didn't change. "I also think you need to hear the truth before you make another mistake."

I frowned. "What truth?"

"Let me tell you a story," he said, leaning back in his chair. His voice was calm, but there was an edge to it.

I said nothing.

"I've been with the Navarra family a long time. Before

Alessandra was born, even. I've seen what loyalty costs, what it gives. And what it takes."

He took a sip of water, eyes locked on me like he was measuring my worth with every word.

"Lorenzo Navarra built an empire," he continued. "Not because he was the smartest. Not because he was the strongest. But because he knew how to control people. He knew how to break them, bend them to his will. He made them believe they had no way out."

My stomach twisted. I wasn't sure where this was going, but I already didn't like it.

"Alessandra was different," Nico said. His voice softened just a little. "She never wanted any of this. She should have been somewhere else. A college professor, maybe. A writer. Anything but this. But she was born into it. And you don't walk away from a life like this without a body count."

Something in his expression shifted, his gaze hardening.

"She killed her father to protect you, Steven."

The words hit me like a fist to the gut.

I had known. Of course, I had known.

But I had never let myself think about it like that.

Not as an act of protection. Not as something she did for me.

The walls of the restaurant suddenly felt too tight, the air too thick. I gripped the edge of the table, forcing myself to breathe.

She had put a bullet in the man who raised her—the man who had built an empire of blood—because he was going to kill me. And then, instead of becoming him, she had spent every second since trying to erase his legacy from existence.

And all this time, I had been planning to bring her down.

I ran a hand over my face, my pulse pounding.

I stared at him, sure I had misheard. "What?"

Nico leaned forward, his voice low, steady. Deadly serious. "She's been working for months to take it apart piece by piece. Cutting ties, closing off operations, moving money where it won't be found. She's not building her father's empire, Steven. She's burning it down."

The words felt like a punch to the gut.

No.

That wasn't possible.

I had spent weeks convincing myself that Alessandra had fully stepped into her father's role, that she had embraced the power, the corruption. I had believed—needed to believe—that she was the enemy.

But now, the enemy was... who?

"You're lying," I said, but the words lacked conviction.

Nico shook his head. "No, Steven. You just haven't been paying attention."

My mind reeled, flipping through every moment, every conversation. The times she hesitated. The way she maneuvered things behind the scenes. The deals she refused to make.

Oh, God.

She hadn't been testing my loyalty to the family. She had been waiting to see if I'd figure it out.

I rubbed a hand over my face, trying to process it all. "Why didn't she just tell me?"

"Because she didn't know if she could trust you," Nico said simply. "And after what she just saw? She's even less sure."

I thought about the way she had looked at me in the library. The hurt behind the anger. The way she had asked me, Did you ever mean it?

My stomach twisted.

I had spent so much time assuming the worst of her. Planning for the worst. And in doing so, I had pushed her further away, reinforcing the very distrust that had gotten me thrown out in the first place.

I looked back at Nico, my voice quieter now. "Why are you telling me this?"

He leaned back, his expression unreadable. "Because I've been where you are, Steven. I know what it's like to be caught between love and duty. Between loyalty and survival. And I know that if you walk away now, you'll regret it for the rest of your life."

His words settled heavily between us.

"You two are more alike than you realize," Nico said, watching me carefully.

I let out a bitter laugh. "That's what you think?"

"That's what I know," Nico corrected. He leaned forward, bracing his arms on the table. "You wanted to take down the Navarra empire. She's already doing it. But she doesn't trust you, Steven. Not yet."

I swallowed hard.

"And you trust me?"

"I trust Alessandra," Nico said simply. "But trust isn't what matters right now. What matters is what you're going to do next."

The waitress dropped off our plates, but I barely looked at the food.

"You think I should go back," I muttered, more to myself than to him.

"I think," Nico said, voice steady, "that you're not done here. And neither is she."

I stared down at the untouched plate of food.

The anger inside me hadn't faded. Neither had the betrayal. But now, layered beneath all of it, was something I hadn't expected.

Understanding.

Alessandra and I had spent all this time pulling in opposite directions, convinced we were enemies. And maybe we still were. But the war we were fighting wasn't against each other.

It was against the past.

I met Nico's gaze again.

"She told me to leave," I said carefully.

Nico smirked slightly. "Then prove to her why she shouldn't have."

The words settled over me, heavier than they should have been.

I had a choice.

I could walk away. Let Alessandra believe I had been working against her. Let her believe that the only person she had ever risked everything for had betrayed her.

Or...

I could prove her wrong.

I swallowed hard, my heart pounding. "How do I fix this?"

Nico gave me a small, knowing smile. "That's up to you."

Chapter 32

Truth in Intentions

Steven

The drive back to the estate was suffocatingly quiet.

Nico didn't say much after our conversation in the restaurant, leaving me alone with my thoughts as the car rolled through the city. The weight of what I had learned pressed against my chest like a vice.

Alessandra had been working to dismantle the empire all along.

I had spent weeks assuming she was the enemy, planning how to take her down, convinced that she had become exactly what I had feared. But all this time, we had been fighting the same war—just from different angles.

And yet... she had thrown me out.

The memory of her voice, cold and sharp, echoed in my head.

"I don't know if I can trust you."

I swallowed hard, staring out the window at the blurred lights of the city. She had every reason not to trust me.

I had worked against her. Spied on her. Assumed the worst.

Why would she let me back in now?

Nico finally spoke, his voice cutting through the quiet. "You know what you need to do."

I let out a slow breath. "Yeah. I do."

But knowing wasn't the same as believing it would work.

By the time we reached the estate, my stomach was in knots.

I stepped out of the car, slinging my bag over my shoulder, and took in the familiar sight of the Navarra estate. The place felt different now, like the walls themselves had shifted under the weight of what I knew.

This wasn't just a prison anymore. It was a battleground.

And I wasn't sure which side I'd end up bleeding for.

I knew where she'd be. Alessandra's office had become her war room, the place where she strategized, controlled, calculated. And if I had any hope of earning her trust back, that's where I needed to go.

I hesitated at the door.

I could almost hear her voice, the sharp accusation from earlier —"How long have you been planning to betray me?"

That moment had been a knife to the gut, not because she was wrong, but because she had every reason to believe it.

I sucked in a breath and pushed the door open.

Alessandra was exactly where I expected her to be—sitting behind her desk, buried in paperwork, her posture tense and unyielding.

She didn't look up right away, but when she did, her eyes narrowed slightly, dark and unreadable.

"Decided not to leave after all?" she said coolly, setting her pen down with deliberate precision.

I closed the door behind me, the click sounding louder than it should have. "I did leave. But I came back. I needed to talk to you."

She exhaled slowly, then leaned back in her chair, crossing her arms. "About what? How you've been watching my every move? Or how you've been planning to take me down from the inside?"

I flinched but held her gaze. "No. About how I was wrong."

A flicker of something—surprise, maybe—crossed her face, but it was gone in an instant.

"Go on," she said, her tone neutral.

I took a step closer, my pulse hammering in my throat. "I thought I was fighting against you," I admitted. "I thought you had become your father. That I had to stop you before you destroyed everything in your path."

Her lips pressed into a thin line, but she didn't interrupt.

"But I was wrong," I continued, my voice lower now. "I didn't see what you were really doing. I didn't realize that while I was planning to take your empire apart, you were already doing it yourself."

She studied me for a long moment, her expression impossible to read.

"And now you want to help?" she asked, voice edged with skepticism.

"I do." I swallowed. "I don't expect you to believe me right away, but I'm done working against you. We want the same thing. And I'm done pretending like we don't."

A silence stretched between us, thick with everything we weren't saying.

Then, softly, Alessandra asked the only question that mattered.

"Can I trust you?"

My throat tightened.

She wasn't just asking about the plan. She was asking about us—about the past, about the future, about whether there was anything left between us that hadn't been completely destroyed.

I stepped closer, resting my hands on the edge of her desk. "I know I haven't given you a reason to trust me," I admitted. "But I'm asking you to let me try. Let me prove it to you."

Her gaze searched mine, looking for something—reassurance, truth, maybe even hope.

But hope was dangerous.

"Why now?" she asked, exhaustion bleeding into her voice. "Why change your mind now?"

I hesitated.

I could have given her a dozen reasons—because I knew the truth now, because I understood what she was trying to do, because Nico had opened my eyes.

But the real reason was simpler.

"Because I still care about you, Alessandra."

Her breath hitched just slightly, but she didn't look away.

"Despite everything, I still care."

Something in her expression flickered—not softness, not yet, but something close. Vulnerability.

I wanted to reach for her, close the distance, but I knew better. This wasn't the time for that.

Instead, I gave her an out.

"I'll be around if you want to talk," I said quietly. "No pressure. No expectations."

Alessandra exhaled, and for the first time since I walked in, her shoulders sagged just a fraction, like she was allowing herself to be tired.

Finally, she nodded. Just once. A small step. But a step nonetheless.

"Okay," she murmured.

It wasn't much.

But it was a start.

Chapter 33

The Burden to Bear

Alessandra

The door clicked softly shut behind Steven, leaving me alone in the suffocating quiet of my office.

I stared at the space where he had stood, my hands clenched into fists, my breath unsteady. I had thought I wanted him gone—that if I forced him to leave, I could push away the doubt, the confusion, the ache of his presence. But I had barely made it through a single minute of silence before I regretted it.

Because now, I was left with the truth.

He had left. And he had come back.

Not because he had no other choice.

Not because he had nowhere else to go.

Because he had wanted to.

I sat heavily in my chair, staring at the papers scattered across my desk. Documents outlining financial closures, supply chain disruptions, carefully orchestrated sell-offs. Each one was another brick removed from the empire my father had built—a slow, deliberate dismantling of a dynasty built on blood and control. It was my life's work. And I was still doing it alone.

I had wanted Steven to stand beside me. That had always been the hope, hadn't it? That when the time came, when I was ready to tear it all down, he would understand.

But he hadn't.

He had watched me like I was the enemy, like I was still the same woman who had let him go all those years ago. Like I was the villain in a story where he was the hero.

And yet, when I looked at him in the library tonight, when I heard his words—I'm sorry. I want to help.—for the first time, I believed him.

A sharp knock pulled me from my thoughts. I knew it was Nico before he even stepped inside.

Of course it was Nico.

He had been watching me since I was a child, standing in the shadows of my father's empire, ensuring that the only thing sharper than my ambition was my ability to survive.

"Are you all right?" Nico's voice was low, steady. Protective.

I let out a slow breath. "I don't know."

He studied me, his dark eyes searching. Then, instead of standing over me like a soldier awaiting orders, he sat across from me, his forearms resting against his knees. Not as a consigliere. As family.

"It's about him, isn't it?"

I should have expected that. Nico had seen everything—the tension, the way Steven and I orbited around each other, neither willing to fully collide.

"He left," I murmured, staring at the surface of my desk. "And then he came back."

Nico tilted his head slightly. "That surprised you."

I exhaled sharply. "Yes."

"And now you don't know if you should trust him."

I finally met his gaze. "I don't know if I can."

A long silence stretched between us. Finally, Nico leaned back, his eyes narrowing slightly. "You want my opinion?"

I hesitated, then nodded.

"He's in love with you," Nico said simply.

The words hit like a punch to the stomach.

I opened my mouth, then closed it again, gripping the arms of my chair. "That's not—"

"Yes, it is," Nico interrupted, his voice patient but firm. "I've been watching him, Alessandra. Not just since he got here. Before that, too. Back when you left him the first time. You want to know what I saw? A man trying to outrun his own heart."

I looked away.

"That doesn't mean you should trust him," Nico continued. "Love doesn't erase mistakes. It doesn't guarantee loyalty. But it does mean one thing—his fight isn't just against you. It's against himself. And that makes him unpredictable."

I pressed my lips together, the weight of his words settling deep inside me.

"You've always been one to follow your instincts," Nico said after a moment. "And they've kept you alive. Trust them now."

I shook my head. "My instincts are the problem. I want to believe him, Nico. But if I'm wrong..."

"If you're wrong, you deal with it," Nico said simply. "Like you always do."

I looked at him sharply. "You think I should let him in?"

Nico was silent for a moment, then sighed. "I think that for the first time in a long time, you have a chance at something real. Something that isn't just about power plays and survival." He shrugged. "If it were me? I'd give him a chance to prove himself. But that's not my call."

It was mine.

It had always been mine.

I sat there for a long time after Nico left, staring at the papers on my desk, my fingers brushing over the ink-stained pages.

This had always been a war. A war against my father's legacy. A war against the men who wanted to control me. A war against a fate I never asked for.

But now, it was something else.

A war against my own heart.

I stood slowly, walking to the window, watching as the estate lights flickered against the dark. Somewhere, out there, Steven was waiting.

For my answer.

For my decision.

For me.

I took a deep breath.

And made my choice.

I also knew he would prove himself. One way or another.

Chapter 34

Crossing the Line

Alessandra

My thoughts were a tangled web of conflicting emotions, each one pulling me in a different direction. Last night's conversation with Nico had helped me clear my mind, but the tension that had been building between Steven and me was far from resolved.

I reached the library, hesitating for a moment before pushing the door open. Steven was there, sitting in one of the leather armchairs with a book in his lap, though his eyes weren't on the pages. He looked up as I entered, his expression unreadable.

"Do you have a minute?" I asked, trying to keep my tone steady.

He nodded, closing the book and setting it aside. "Of course."

I crossed the room and took a seat across from him, the large oak desk between us feeling like a barrier I wasn't sure I was ready to cross. For a moment, neither of us spoke, the silence thick with unspoken words.

"I've been thinking," I began, choosing my words carefully, "about what you said last night. About working together."

Steven leaned forward slightly, his eyes locking onto mine. "And?"

"I want to try," I said, feeling the weight of the decision settle over me. "But I need you to understand that this isn't going to be easy. There are no guarantees, and once we start, there's no going back."

He nodded, his expression serious. "I understand."

"We'll have to be careful," I continued, my voice dropping to a whisper as if speaking too loudly would break the fragile agreement we were forming. "The family, the other families—they're all watching. If they suspect anything..."

"They won't," Steven interrupted, his tone confident. "I'm in, Alessandra. Whatever it takes."

For a moment, I just stared at him, searching his eyes for any hint of doubt, of hesitation. But all I saw was determination, a resolve that matched my own. It was both reassuring and terrifying, knowing that we were about to embark on something that could change everything.

"Okay," I said finally, leaning back in my chair. "We'll start tomorrow. I'll take you with me to a few meetings, let you see how things work from the inside. But you'll need to keep your distance, stay quiet, and observe. We can't afford any mistakes."

"I can do that," he replied, his gaze unwavering.

We spent the next hour discussing the logistics, the steps we would take to ensure that Steven's presence by my side didn't raise any suspicions. It was all business, all strategy, and for a moment, it felt like we were back in the early days of our relationship, when everything had been new and exciting, when we had faced the world together as a team.

But those days were long gone, replaced by a reality that was much darker, much more dangerous. And as much as I wanted to believe that we could work together, that we could trust each other again, there was a part of me that knew better. We were walking a tightrope, and one wrong move could send us both crashing down.

Over the next few weeks, Steven became a constant presence at my side. He attended meetings, sat in on discussions, and observed the inner workings of the family with a careful, calculated eye. To the others, he was just another part of the operation, another cog in the machine. But to me, he was something much more.

I watched as he navigated the world I had grown up in, slipping into the role of silent observer with ease. He was careful, always aware of the eyes on him, always conscious of the danger that lurked just beneath the surface. But there were moments—brief, fleeting moments—when our eyes would meet across the room, and I would see a flash of the man he used to be. The man I had fallen in love with.

And it terrified me.

One night, after a particularly long day of meetings and negotiations, we found ourselves alone in my office, the rest of the estate quiet and still. The room was dimly lit, the only light coming from the lamp on my desk, casting a soft glow over the papers spread out in front of us.

"We need to talk about the next steps," I said, breaking the silence that had settled between us. "The pressure is building. Vito is getting bolder, and we need to be ready for whatever he throws at us."

Steven nodded, his focus entirely on the documents in front of him. "I've been thinking about that," he said, his voice low. "There's a way we can turn the tables, make him think he's got the upper hand when really, we're the ones in control."

I looked at him, curious. "Go on."

He leaned in closer, pointing to a spot on the map spread out between us. "If we can get him to move his operations here, we can cut him off at the source. It'll take some careful planning, but if we pull it off, we can weaken his position without exposing ourselves."

I stood next to him and studied the map, considering his proposal.

It was risky, but it could work. "It's a good plan," I admitted, looking up at him. "But it's going to take perfect execution."

"We'll make it work," he replied, his voice filled with a quiet confidence that sent a shiver down my spine.

For a moment, we just stood there, the tension between us palpable. There was something in the air, something electric, and I could feel it pulling us closer together, even as I tried to resist.

"Steven," I began, my voice faltering as I searched for the right words.

Before I could muster another syllable, his hand brushed against mine. It was a feather-light touch, but it might as well have been a lightning bolt for how it jolted through me. My breath hitched, my skin prickled, and I swear I could feel every callous, every scar on his hands. His touch lingered for a heartbeat too long, and I was a done.

Our eyes locked, and the rest of the world evaporated. The family, the plan, the danger—none of it mattered. It was just him and me, and the electric current that had been humming between us for weeks. He stepped closer, his familiar scent wrapping around me. My body betrayed me, leaning into him like a magnet.

"Alessandra," he growled, his voice low and rough enough to make my knees weak. There it was—that longing, that raw need that mirrored my own. I could've drowned in the sound of my name on his lips.

I didn't move, didn't breathe, as his hand cupped my cheek. His thumb traced my jawline, sending shivers down my spine. His touch was gentle but demanding, like he already owned me. And then his lips were on mine, hot and insistent.

The kiss was an explosion. It wasn't sweet or tender—it was raw, desperate, like we'd both been holding our breath for too long. His hands tightened on me, pulling me so close it was hard to tell where he ended and I began.

"Steven," I whispered, my voice shaking as his lips trailed down my neck. Every touch unraveled me further, every moment dragging me closer to the edge of a line I knew I shouldn't cross.

I should've stopped him. I should've reminded myself of the plan, of the danger. But all I could think about was him—his touch, his voice, the way he looked at me like I was the only thing that mattered.

My resolve crumbled.

The world outside disappeared as the tension between us finally snapped. It was reckless, it was inevitable, and it felt like falling into something we both knew could burn us alive.

I pulled away, the silence pressed in, heavy and suffocating. His eyes held mine, filled with guilt, longing, and something that cut me deeper than any wound ever could.

"This can't happen again," I said, my voice firmer than I felt, the sadness in it unmistakable.

For a moment, he didn't answer. His jaw tensed, and he exhaled sharply, like he was physically holding himself back from saying something more. His Adam's apple bobbed as he swallowed, his hands clenching and unclenching at his sides.

And then, finally—softly, brokenly—he said, "Okay."

But he didn't move.

Didn't step away.

Didn't break eye contact.

And for one excruciating second, I knew—we both knew—he didn't mean it.

After helping me right my clothes and my hair, he stood there for a moment longer, his gaze lingering on mine, before turning and walking out of the office, leaving me alone in the darkness.

The door clicked shut behind Steven, leaving me alone in my office, my breath still uneven, my pulse still racing.

I squeezed my eyes shut and forced a deep inhale, but it did nothing to calm the storm inside me. My body still burned from his touch, my skin still tingled where his hands had lingered, and worst of all—my heart still ached.

I had known better.

I had **known** better.

And yet, when he touched me, when his lips met mine, when his hands gripped me like he was claiming me—I let it happen. I wanted it to happen. And that was the problem.

I let out a frustrated breath, pressing my fingertips into my temples.

This can't happen again.

Not because I didn't want him. Not because I didn't love him.

But because I wanted something real or I wanted nothing at all.

Because if I let myself fall into this, if I let our relationship exist only in the quiet, stolen moments between battles, between strategies, between missions—then it would never be more than that. It would never be more than a distraction.

And I couldn't let myself settle for that. Not with Steven. Not when there was too much at stake.

I pushed back from my desk, pacing the length of the office, arms crossed tightly over my chest. The room still smelled like him—like cedarwood and something deeper, something warm, something safe.

Safe.

My stomach twisted at the word.

Steven was safe now.

That had been my goal from the beginning, the reason I had done everything—killed my father, taken over this empire, worked day and night to tear it down from the inside. I had put my heart, my soul, everything into making sure Steven survived this world.

Now that he was no longer a pawn in my father's game, now that I had ensured he wouldn't be used against me, there was only one priority left.

The Navarra empire had to fall.

And I couldn't let him distract me.

Even if everything inside me screamed that he was the only thing that ever made me feel alive.

I closed my eyes and let myself slip, just for a moment, into the past.

A different space. A different night. A different life.

Our apartment senior year had been perfect—just enough space for both of us, but it had been ours. A warm little corner of the world where we could just be us, where I wasn't Alessandra Navarra, heir to an empire of crime and bloodshed, and he wasn't Steven Porter, the boy who didn't yet know that our love had an expiration date.

I could still picture the soft lamplight, the faint hum of a record player in the background—Fleetwood Mac, maybe? I could never quite remember the song.

I had been curled up against his chest on the worn couch, my legs draped over his as he absently ran his fingers through my hair. It was a small thing, a mindless thing. But even then, I had known I would remember it for the rest of my life.

"Alessandra," he murmured, his voice half-asleep, warm and lazy.

I had hummed in response, pressing my cheek against his heartbeat.

"I think I could stay like this forever."

I had smiled, not letting the sadness creep in. "Yeah?"

"Yeah," he had murmured, shifting just enough to tilt my chin up so our eyes met. His gaze was so open, so trusting. So full of a love I didn't deserve.

I had kissed him then—slow, deep, real.

And I had let myself pretend, just for that moment, that there was no end date.

That I could stay with him forever.

I hadn't known, then, just how much it would hurt to leave him.

And now, standing here in my office, the ghost of that memory wrapped around me like a vice, I knew one thing with certainty:

I wouldn't hurt him again.

I wouldn't let us fall back into something that wasn't real.

Not until it could be.

Not until everything else was finished.

I swallowed hard, pressing a hand to my chest as if that would somehow steady the rapid thrum of my heart.

The past couldn't be changed.

But I could ensure I didn't repeat it.

I forced myself to push the memory aside, inhaling deeply before straightening my spine. I had a job to do.

And so did Steven.

By the time I left my office, the estate was already stirring with morning activity—staff moving through the halls, business as usual. I walked with purpose, letting the familiar rhythm of power and control ground me.

I wasn't going to avoid Steven. That would be weakness. Instead, I would do what I had always done—I would be strategic.

By the time I stepped into the conference room, the men were already gathered, their low murmurs filling the space. Steven was there, too, standing near Nico, his hands tucked into his pockets.

He looked up when I entered, and for just a second, our eyes locked.

A flicker of something passed between us—a memory, a question, an ache.

But then it was gone, buried beneath the weight of everything else.

I forced my expression to remain unreadable as I took my seat at the head of the table. "Let's get started."

The meeting went as it always did—business, logistics, plans in motion. Steven sat beside Nico, listening, observing, absorbing everything. He didn't speak much, but I could feel his presence like a live wire, crackling at the edge of my awareness.

Once or twice, I caught him looking at me.

And once or twice, he caught me doing the same.

But neither of us said a word.

By the time the meeting adjourned, everyone filed out, leaving only Nico, Steven, and me. I busied myself with gathering my notes, pretending I didn't feel the weight of Steven's gaze still on me.

He didn't speak until the door clicked shut behind Nico.

"So," he said, his voice casual but too careful. "That's business as usual, huh?"

I glanced up, arching a brow. "Something wrong with it?"

He hesitated. "No. Just... different from what I expected."

I exhaled slowly, closing my folder. "You're learning."

A beat of silence.

Then, softer—more careful:

"Alessandra."

I looked up.

And there it was.

The weight of everything that had happened between us. The past. The present. The pull that hadn't faded, even now.

My fingers curled into my palm beneath the table.

"We can't," I said quietly.

I saw the flicker of something in his expression—agreement? Disappointment?—before he nodded. "I know."

I swallowed. "We have too much to lose."

"I know," he said again.

For a moment, it felt like he might say something else. Like he might push.

But instead, he just held my gaze a moment longer before pushing off from the table, heading for the door.

I watched him go, forcing my hands to steady as I gathered my things.

This was how it had to be.

For now.

Because I couldn't afford to get lost in Steven Porter again.

Not until the war was over.

And I wasn't sure either of us would survive it.

Chapter 35

The Wreckage of the Past

Steven

I hadn't slept much—if at all.

Every time I closed my eyes, I was right back in that moment with Alessandra, the memory of her melting under my touch replaying over and over like a song I couldn't turn off. Every detail was burned into me—the way her breath caught when I pulled her close, the way her fingers dug into my shoulders like she was anchoring herself to me, the way she had trembled as though the weight of the world was pressing in around us.

But now, in the harsh light of morning, none of it felt real.

I sat on the edge of the bed, staring down at my hands, flexing my fingers like I could still feel her skin beneath them. I exhaled sharply, raking my hands through my hair as I tried to steady the chaos in my mind.

It wasn't supposed to happen.

I had told myself I wouldn't let it. That whatever existed between us was too fractured, too laced with anger and history and unfinished business to be anything other than volatile. And yet, last night, I had caved. She had too. And now, I didn't know where that left us.

I pushed off the bed and walked to the window, shoving my hands into my pockets. Outside, the estate grounds were bathed in early-morning light, the garden paths quiet, untouched. It was peaceful—a stark contrast to the storm raging inside me.

For a few brief moments last night, I had let myself forget. Forget the plan. Forget the revenge. Forget why I was here in the first place.

And that was dangerous.

I grabbed a jacket off the chair and left my room, needing space, needing air. My footsteps echoed in the empty corridors as I made my way through the estate. The place was awake but quiet, the early morning hum of staff moving through their routines, security positioned at their usual posts. No one paid me much attention anymore. I had blended in, just as I had intended.

But now, I wasn't sure I wanted to blend in anymore.

I pushed open the doors to the garden, the crisp morning air a shock to my system. The scent of fresh earth and dew lingered in the breeze, grounding me for a second before my thoughts came rushing back in.

I needed to pull myself together.

Last night was a mistake.

But deep down, I knew that was a lie. It hadn't been a mistake.

It had felt inevitable, like something that had been building between us since the day Alessandra walked back into my life. It had been heat and desperation and something darker, something neither of us could name.

But I also knew this: it couldn't happen again.

I ran a hand down my face, exhaling hard as I sat down on a stone bench.

Because if it did? I wouldn't be able to keep lying to myself about what I really wanted.

I had told myself I was here for justice. That marrying her, staying by her side, was a means to an end. I had let my anger and my past grievances cloud every interaction between us. But last night had cut through all of it.

She wasn't the Alessandra I had known in college.

But she also wasn't the villain I had convinced myself she had become.

And that truth scared me more than anything.

I let my head drop forward, resting my elbows on my knees.

I needed to focus.

The mission hadn't changed. Alessandra and I were supposed to be on opposite sides, even if now we had a common enemy.

But was that really true anymore?

Because if I was being honest, I didn't want to just watch from the sidelines anymore. I didn't want to play some cold, calculated role in her war.

I wanted to fight beside her.

And that? That was even more dangerous than touching her.

I squeezed my eyes shut, the weight of it pressing down on me like a vice.

I couldn't let this distract me. Couldn't let her distract me.

But as I sat there, the echoes of last night still burning in my veins, I knew one thing for certain:

I was already lost.

Chapter 36

A Show of Strength

Alessandra

The map in front of me felt like a battlefield. Every mark, every line, every shaded territory represented more than just land—it represented power, control, and survival. And tonight, I was fighting for all three.

Vito Valenti had made his move.

I stared at the section of the map where he had struck, my pulse thrumming with barely restrained fury. Little Odessa. It was a key port for our operations, a lifeline to distribution channels that had been in Navarra control for decades. And now, it was under siege.

He didn't just test me—he crossed a line.

Nico stood beside me, his usual composed expression tinged with something sharper. Concern. Frustration. Readiness. "He's baiting you," he said, his voice measured but heavy with meaning. "Vito wants to see how much you'll tolerate before you strike back."

I let out a slow breath, my fingers tightening around the edge of the desk. "He thinks I won't retaliate," I said, more to myself than to Nico. "He thinks I'll hesitate."

And maybe, for a second, I had.

Because I knew what came next. A response meant war.

"If we let this stand, it won't just be Vito," Nico warned. "The other families will start circling like vultures, waiting for you to make a misstep."

He was right. Power in this world wasn't just about strategy—it was about perception. If I let Vito get away with this, it would be seen as weakness, and weakness invited death.

I forced myself to exhale, my mind racing through the possibilities. "What did he do exactly?" I finally asked, my voice cold.

Nico's jaw tightened. "He sent men into our docks. They hijacked three shipments, burned another, and left two of our guys beaten so badly they're in the hospital. He made sure the attack was public—sent a message loud and clear that he doesn't see you as the rightful heir to this empire."

I felt my stomach tighten, a slow and burning anger settling deep inside me. This wasn't just a power play. This was personal.

Vito wanted to make me look incompetent. He wanted my men to doubt me. He wanted me to lose control before I could dismantle this empire on my own terms.

I turned to Nico, my voice dangerously even. "How did we respond?"

"We locked down the remaining ports. Increased security. We've sent word that any move against us will be met with force." He paused, then added, "But that won't be enough, Alessandra. They need to see what happens when someone comes for you."

I met his gaze, and for the first time in a long time, I saw something that felt like hesitation in his eyes. He had watched me grow up in this world, had seen me evolve into the woman standing before him now. But he also knew what this meant.

Once I retaliated, there was no turning back.

I clenched my jaw, forcing down the weight pressing against my ribs. This was what it took to lead.

I had spent years trying to distance myself from my father's legacy, but now? I was beginning to understand why he had ruled with an iron grip. Because in this world, mercy wasn't respected—it was exploited.

"What's the best move?" I asked, keeping my voice steady.

Nico studied me for a moment, then stepped forward, placing his hands on the edge of the desk. "We hit back. Not just a message—we take something from him, something that costs."

I nodded slowly. "His men?"

He shook his head. "That's expected. He'll be ready for that. We take what fuels him. His business. His money. We make it impossible for him to function."

I exhaled through my nose, my mind already spinning through the logistics. Vito had spread himself thin in recent months, expanding too quickly, making enemies in the process. If we hit him in the right place, he wouldn't just suffer a loss—he'd start crumbling from the inside.

I made my decision.

"Shut down his supply routes. Cut off his distribution. I want his men scrambling, not knowing where their next paycheck is coming from." My voice was steel now, unwavering. "And Nico?"

His eyes sharpened. "Yes, Donna?"

"Make sure he knows it was me."

Nico's lips curled slightly, a shadow of something close to approval flashing across his face. He nodded once. "Consider it done."

And then—

The door swung open.

Steven stood in the doorway.

His expression was unreadable at first, but the moment stretched too long, his silence too charged, and then I knew—he had heard everything. And apparently, he wasn't happy about it.

Chapter 37

Unforeseen Consequences

Steven

I stood just outside the slightly ajar door, my pulse hammering in my ears. I hadn't meant to eavesdrop. I had come here to talk, to make sure she was alright after last night. To figure out where we stood—not just in the war we were fighting, but with each other.

But then I heard it.

"We hit back. Not just a message—we take something from him, something that costs."

Nico's voice was steady, calculated.

"His men?" Alessandra asked.

"That's expected. He'll be ready for that. We take what fuels him. His business. His money. We make it impossible for him to function."

I sucked in a breath, my hands curling into fists at my sides.

"Shut down his supply routes. Cut off his distribution. I want his men scrambling, not knowing where their next paycheck is coming from. And Nico?"

"Yes, Donna?"

"Make sure he knows it was me."

Her voice was calm. Resolute. Unshaken.

And it hit me like a punch to the gut.

I had spent weeks by her side, watching, learning, understanding the weight of her decisions. But this? This was a declaration of war. And she hadn't said a word to me about it.

The anger came fast, burning hot in my chest. We were supposed to be doing this together. We had agreed—no more secrets, no more lies. But here she was, making decisions that could change everything without me.

I shoved the door open without thinking.

Both Alessandra and Nico turned to face me.

Nico didn't even blink, his expression unreadable as ever. But Alessandra? There was something there—surprise, irritation, maybe even guilt.

"We need to talk," I said, barely keeping my voice even.

Nico gave Alessandra a look, one she clearly understood, because she gave him a small nod. He stepped back, moving toward the door. "I'll give you two a moment."

The door clicked shut behind him, leaving us alone in the dimly lit office.

Alessandra leaned back in her chair, exhaling through her nose as she studied me. "What do you need?"

"Cut the shit," I snapped.

I paced toward the desk, planting both hands on its surface. "You're planning a counterattack?" My voice was sharp, harsher than I intended, but I didn't care. "You made that decision without me?"

Her gaze hardened. "I didn't realize I needed your permission."

"That's not what this is about, Alessandra," I shot back. "We're supposed to be in this together. You told me that. You made me believe that we were working toward the same goal. But now I find out you're escalating things without even telling me?"

She stood slowly, pushing her chair back as she placed her hands on the desk, mirroring my stance. "I don't need to tell you, Steven. I need to lead. I'm still the Donna of this family, and that means I make the decisions I think are best. I don't ask permission first."

Her words struck deep, sharp and cutting, and for a moment, I had nothing to say.

Because the truth was, she was right.

She wasn't my partner in this—not in the way I had wanted. She was the Donna. The one who had been forced to bear the weight of this empire. The one making the hard choices while I played at understanding the world she had been raised in.

But that didn't mean she could just shut me out.

"You keep saying we're in this together," I said, quieter now but no less intense. "But when it comes down to it, you still make the choices alone."

She let out a slow, measured breath, but I saw the flicker of something behind her eyes. Frustration. Exhaustion. A battle she had already fought too many times.

"You don't get it," she said finally, shaking her head. "I can't afford to hesitate. I can't afford to wait for a consensus. If I do, people die. If I misstep, this entire house crumbles. And if you think for one second that I have the luxury of debating every decision with you, then you're still thinking like an outsider."

I flinched at that.

"Alessandra—"

She held up a hand. "No, listen to me. You think you deserve a say in this, but I haven't told you we're equals, Steven. Because we're not."

Her words should have stung more than they did.

But the truth was, she wasn't wrong.

She had grown up in this world, learned to navigate it before she was even old enough to fully understand what it meant. I had only just begun to scratch the surface, still finding my place while she carried the weight of an empire on her shoulders.

She walked around the desk slowly, stopping in front of me. "I know you want to help. I know you want to be part of this. But you have to understand that I'm not running every decision past you because I can't afford to. Because this isn't some political campaign where we weigh our options and choose the best path forward." She exhaled, shaking her head. "This is war. And war doesn't wait for approval."

I swallowed hard, staring at her.

She was right.

And yet—

"If this is war," I said, my voice low, "then you shouldn't be fighting it alone."

Something shifted in her expression. Just for a second. But it was gone before I could name it.

"I'm not," she said simply.

The words hung between us, heavy and unspoken.

I let out a slow breath, stepping back, raking a hand through my hair. "I just—" I paused, trying to find the right words. "I just need to know where I stand with you."

She hesitated. Longer this time.

I couldn't tell if she was weighing her options or weighing the cost of letting me in.

Then, softly—carefully—she said, "By my side."

I exhaled. "Then let me."

She studied me, searching my face for something—maybe doubt, maybe hesitation. Whatever she saw must have satisfied her because she gave a single nod.

"Alright," she said, voice quieter now. "But you need to understand something, Steven. The decisions I make? They're not easy. And if you're going to stand beside me, you need to be ready for what that really means."

I met her gaze. "I am."

She let out a slow breath, nodding. "Then we move forward."

It wasn't an apology.

It wasn't a reassurance.

But it was enough.

For now.

Because even if she wasn't ready to call me her equal, I would make sure I earned my place beside her.

And I wasn't going anywhere.

Chapter 38

A Web of Lies

Alessandra

The weight of leadership had never felt so heavy. Every decision I made now carried the potential to shatter the fragile balance of power that I had fought so hard to maintain. And tonight, that balance had been tested—and broken.

The counterattack should have crippled Vito. We had planned it carefully, calculated every move, ensured every weak spot would be exploited. His supply routes should have been severed. His money should have dried up. His men should have been scrambling, desperate, choking on the weight of my retaliation.

But none of that had happened.

Vito had been waiting for us.

Our men had barely set foot on his territory before they were ambushed. Half of our forces were pinned down before they even knew what hit them. A key shipment we intended to intercept had been rerouted at the last second. And instead of crippling Vito's operations, we had barely scratched him.

Which meant one thing—he knew we were coming.

Someone had warned him.

And that meant someone inside my own walls—one of my men, one of my trusted few—had betrayed me.

I sat in my office, the weight of it all pressing down on me like a suffocating blanket. Who?

The question gnawed at me, sharper than any blade. The walls of my own estate suddenly felt foreign, filled with shadows I couldn't trust. I had built this family on control, on power, on precision. And now, for the first time, I felt something dangerously close to vulnerability.

There is a snake among us.

And I would find them.

I inhaled sharply through my nose, forcing the rising anger to settle into something colder, something I could use. I needed to think. I needed to move.

If there was one thing I knew with absolute certainty—

Whoever betrayed me would not live to regret it.

I should have involved Steven. He was my husband now, my partner in this life of ours, whether it felt like one or not. But I couldn't bring myself to do it. Not yet. The idea of exposing him to more of this world, to the dirty underbelly of what kept this empire alive, twisted my gut in knots. He was already wrestling with the violence and the power plays—how would he handle knowing there was a snake in our midst? How would he react when he found out I kept this from him?

But there was no time to worry about that. I had a job to do.

The truth had to be uncovered, and it had to be done quickly. I couldn't afford to let this betrayal fester, to allow the rot to spread any further within the family. If we didn't root it out now, the consequences would be catastrophic.

I stood and made my way to the door, a sense of resolve hardening within me. Nico would know how to proceed. He had been with the family long enough to understand the stakes, and he would have no qualms about doing what needed to be done. But even as I prepared myself for the confrontation, a part of me hesitated. I had never been one to shy away from the harsh realities of our world, but this... this felt different. It felt personal.

The corridor outside my office was quiet, the usual hustle of the estate subdued, as if the very walls knew something was wrong. I made my way to Nico's office, my footsteps echoing softly against the polished floors. When I reached the door, I paused for a moment, gathering my thoughts before knocking.

"Come in," Nico's voice called from within.

I pushed the door open and found him seated at his desk, papers spread out in front of him. His eyes met mine, and I saw the weariness etched into his features. He looked older now, more tired than I had ever seen him. But there was a sharpness in his gaze that told me he was still very much in control.

"Nico," I began, closing the door behind me. "We have a problem."

He nodded slowly, his expression unreadable. "I'm aware."

"There's a traitor," I said, my voice steady. "I need to find out who it is before they can do any more damage."

Nico leaned back in his chair, his gaze thoughtful. "I'm already on it. Do you suspect anyone in particular?"

"I have my suspicions, but I need proof. I need to be sure before I take action."

He nodded again, his eyes narrowing slightly. "This isn't going to be easy, Alessandra. The men are loyal, but fear can make even the most loyal man do desperate things."

"I know," I replied, the weight of the situation pressing down on me. "That's why I need your help. We need to root this out quickly and quietly. No one can know what we're doing until we have the traitor in hand."

Nico studied me for a long moment, his gaze searching. "And Steven? What does he know?"

I hesitated, the guilt flaring in my chest. "Nothing. I haven't told him. I don't want to involve him unless I have to."

Nico's expression softened slightly, but there was a hint of disapproval in his eyes. "You're still trying to protect him."

"Yes," I admitted. "But I'm also trying to protect us. If he knew... I don't know how he'd react."

Nico sighed, rubbing a hand over his face. "You're playing a dangerous game, Alessandra. But I understand. We'll do this together, quietly. We'll find the traitor and make an example of them."

I nodded, feeling a mixture of relief and dread. "Thank you, Nico."

"Always," he replied, his voice firm. "We'll start with those closest to you. The ones who have the most to gain from your downfall. I'll set up the meetings, one by one. We'll find our man."

The first to be summoned was Rocco, a man who had served under my father for years. He had always been loyal, but loyalty was a fickle thing, easily swayed by fear or greed. As I waited in the small, windowless room where the interrogation would take place, I tried to push away the memory of my father sitting across from Rocco in a similar setting, years ago, grilling him about a failed shipment. Rocco had been steadfast then, unflinching under my father's cold gaze. Would he be the same now, under mine?

The door creaked open, and Nico entered, Rocco following behind him. Rocco's face was as impassive as ever, but I saw the flicker of unease in his eyes as he took in the room. Nico gestured for him to sit, and he did so without protest, his gaze shifting between us.

"Rocco," I began, keeping my voice calm, almost casual. "I need to ask you a few questions."

He nodded, his posture rigid. "Of course, Donna. Whatever you need."

I studied him for a moment, searching for any sign of deception. "There's been a breach in our security. Someone close to the family has been leaking information. I need to know if you've heard anything. If anyone has approached you, tried to buy your loyalty."

Rocco's eyes widened slightly, but he quickly masked his surprise. "No, Donna. I would never betray the family. You know that."

"Do I?" I asked, leaning forward slightly. "I know you were loyal to my father, Rocco. But things have changed. Loyalties can shift. I need to be sure of you."

His gaze flickered, a flash of something—fear, perhaps?—crossing his face. "I haven't spoken to anyone, Donna. I swear it."

Nico remained silent beside me, his presence a silent reminder of the consequences of lying. I watched Rocco closely, noting the slight tremor in his hands, the way his gaze darted to the door as if calculating the distance.

"Do you know who might be responsible, then?" I pressed. "Anyone who has been acting suspiciously?"

He hesitated, his brow furrowing in thought. "There's been some talk, Donna. Some of the men... they're uneasy. They miss your father's way of doing things."

"And you?" I asked, my voice hardening. "Do you miss my father's way?"

Rocco swallowed, his throat bobbing with the effort. "No, Donna. I follow you. Always."

"Good," I said, standing up, signaling that the conversation was over. "You're dismissed, Rocco. But remember—if I find out you've been lying to me, you won't get a second chance."

He nodded quickly, relief washing over his features as he stood and left the room, his footsteps hurried.

As the door closed behind him, I turned to Nico. "What do you think?"

"He's hiding something," Nico said without hesitation. "But I don't think he's the one we're looking for."

"Agreed," I replied, a knot of tension tightening in my chest. "But he knows more than he's saying. Keep an eye on him. If he so much as twitches wrong, I want to know."

Nico nodded, his expression grim. "Who's next?"

"Vince," I said after a moment's thought. "I want to know what he knows."

That evening, Nico returned with a file in hand. He placed it on my desk without a word, his expression grim. I opened it, my eyes scanning the contents quickly. Vince's movements had been monitored closely over the past few days, and the evidence was damning.

He had been in regular contact with one of Vito Valenti's men. The meetings were too frequent to be a coincidence, and they were always held in places where Vince was unlikely to be recognized. He had covered his tracks well, but not well enough. There were records of text messages and phone calls.

"He was hoping to lay the blame on Steven," Nico said quietly. "If something went wrong, he could point the finger at him and walk away clean."

My anger flared, a hot, searing rage that threatened to consume me. Vince had always been resentful of Steven, but to betray the family, to betray me like this—it was unforgivable.

I pushed the file away, leaning back in my chair as I tried to contain the fury that roiled within me. "He'll be made an example," I said coldly, the decision already made. "We can't afford to let this slide. The others need to see what happens to those who betray the Navarra family."

Nico nodded in agreement, but there was a sadness in his eyes that hadn't been there before. "Are you sure about this, Alessandra?"

I met his gaze, my resolve hardening. "Yes. It has to be done."

The next day, Vince was brought to me. He looked as confident as ever, his usual cocky smirk in place. But when he saw the look in my eyes, the smirk faded.

"Vince," I began, my voice steady. "Do you know why you're here?"

He shifted uncomfortably, his eyes darting around the room. "I don't know what you mean, Donna."

I stood, moving around my desk until I was standing directly in front of him. "You betrayed this family. You've been meeting with Valenti's men behind my back, conspiring to lay the blame on Steven if things went wrong. Did you really think I wouldn't find out?"

The blood drained from Vince's face, his eyes wide with shock and fear. He stammered, trying to find the words to defend himself, but I didn't give him the chance.

Vince blinked, his usual smirk faltering for the first time, but then he scoffed.

"I don't know what you're talking about, Donna. Someone's been feeding you bullshit, and if I had to guess? It's probably him." He tilted his head slightly. "Porter's been sniffing around places he doesn't belong, asking questions—"

I held up a hand. "Enough."

Vince froze.

"You really thought you could sell me another lie?" My voice was steady, unimpressed. "That I'd believe my own husband was the one leaking information to the man trying to destroy us?"

I saw the moment real fear crept into his expression.

"This is the last time anyone will question where your loyalties lie," I said, my voice cold and final. "You've made your choice, and now you'll pay the price."

Vince's protests were cut short as Nico signaled to the men standing behind him. They moved swiftly, dragging him out of the room despite his desperate pleas. I watched them go, the cold satisfaction of justice tinged with a bitter aftertaste.

When the door closed behind them, I turned to Nico. "Make sure the others know what happened. Let them see what becomes of those who betray us."

Nico nodded, his expression solemn. "It'll be done."

As I sat back down, the weight of my decisions pressed down on me. Vince's betrayal had been dealt with, but it was just the beginning. There were still threats to my leadership, still men who would challenge my authority.

But as long as I was Donna, I would do whatever it took to protect this family—even if it meant becoming the very thing I once feared.

Chapter 39

The Last to Know

Steven

There was an undercurrent—a shift in the air. Conversations stopped when I walked by. Men who usually stood firm under Alessandra's command kept their heads lower than usual.

Something had happened.

I didn't know what.

But I could feel it in my bones.

I had spent the morning in the library, pretending to focus on financial reports and logistics, but my mind was elsewhere. My instincts were screaming at me, and I wasn't the kind of man who ignored them.

The first real clue came when I noticed Nico moving through the halls, quieter than usual, speaking in hushed tones to Alessandra's men. Normally, he carried an air of silent command, but today, he looked... wary.

Like a man tying up loose ends.

Like a man dealing with something unpleasant.

I caught sight of Rocco in the hallway and waved him over. "Something happen?" I asked, keeping my tone casual.

Rocco hesitated. "Nothing for you to worry about."

Wrong answer.

"Try again," I said, keeping my voice even. "And don't insult me this time."

Rocco exhaled sharply, shifting uncomfortably. "It's not my place, Mr. Porter." He glanced toward Alessandra's office, then back at me. "If she hasn't told you, there's a reason."

And there it was.

Something had happened.

And Alessandra hadn't told me.

A slow burn of frustration curled through my chest, but I forced it down. I wasn't going to lose my head—not yet. I needed facts.

I left the library and started moving through the estate, watching, listening. It didn't take long before I overheard whispers. A name. Vince.

Dead.

That stopped me in my tracks.

I barely noticed the hall I was standing in, the muted conversations of Alessandra's men fading into the background as the pieces snapped together.

Vince had been close—closer than most of the men here. And now, he was gone.

And Alessandra hadn't told me.

I didn't storm into her office this time.

That's what I would've done before—before I started understanding what it meant to live in this world, before I realized that reacting on impulse made you predictable.

No, this time, I knocked.

A pause. Then, "Come in."

I opened the door and stepped inside, shutting it behind me with careful precision. Alessandra sat behind her desk, her expression unreadable. She didn't look surprised to see me. If anything, it felt like she had been waiting.

I walked toward her, slow and deliberate, keeping my anger in check. "Vince is dead."

She didn't flinch. "Yes."

That was it. No excuse. No justifications. Just confirmation.

I studied her, searching for any sign of hesitation, guilt—anything that would make this make sense. "You didn't tell me."

She met my gaze, unwavering. "No, I didn't."

I let out a slow breath, keeping my voice even. "Why?"

Her fingers tapped lightly against the desk before she sat back in her chair. "Because I knew you'd ask me to reconsider."

That stopped me cold.

She wasn't denying it. She wasn't giving me an excuse. She had made this choice fully aware that I wouldn't approve.

My chest tightened, frustration curling under my skin like a slow burn. "We're supposed to be doing this together," I said, my voice lower now.

She exhaled, shaking her head. "You keep saying that, Steven, but you still don't understand what it means to be me."

Something sharp flickered in her expression—something close to exhaustion, but not quite.

"I made a call," she continued. "I made it quickly, decisively, because that's what leadership demands. There was no debate, no second-guessing, because I don't have the luxury of doubt. Vince betrayed me. He was feeding information to Vito. If I had hesitated, if I had waited for your approval, it could have cost us more than just pride—it could have cost us everything."

I swallowed hard.

Because despite everything... I understood.

I hated that I understood.

"You still should have told me," I said, quieter now.

Her lips pressed together, as if considering that. "Maybe," she admitted. "But I needed to see something first."

I frowned. "See what?"

She stood slowly, rounding the desk until she was in front of me. "If you could accept it."

Silence stretched between us, heavy and unspoken.

I wasn't sure what answer she wanted.

But I knew the answer I had.

"I don't like it," I said, my voice rough. "I don't like any of this."

Her gaze softened, just for a fraction of a second. "Neither do I."

The weight of her words settled between us.

And suddenly, I saw it.

Not just the Donna of the Navarra family.

Not just the woman who had orchestrated Vince's death without hesitation.

But the girl I had once known—the one who had fought so hard against this life.

The one who had once wanted out.

Something in my chest twisted.

I took a slow breath. "Next time," I said carefully, "tell me. Even if you think I won't agree. Even if you think I'll fight you on it."

She studied me, weighing my words, and after a long moment, she nodded. "Alright."

It wasn't an apology.

It wasn't even a promise.

But it was all I got.

Chapter 40

Things Left Unsaid

Steven

The library had become my refuge.

It was the one place in this house where I could think, where I could breathe. It had the best view of the garden, where neatly trimmed hedges stood like silent sentries, and where bursts of color from Alessandra's childhood flowers still bloomed despite everything that had changed.

I liked the illusion of it. The idea that something could remain untouched, uncorrupted.

But peace was a fragile thing here. And tonight, I wasn't here for peace.

I was searching.

I had been combing through the shelves for weeks under the guise of reading or research, but my real goal had always been the same—leverage. A way to dismantle this empire from the inside. A weakness. A secret. Something that would change everything.

But the Navarra family didn't exactly keep a "How to Destroy Us" guide lying around.

I sighed, running a hand through my hair. The scent of old books filled the air, heavy with time, but so far, I had nothing.

I moved to the far wall, eyeing the rows of books carefully.

Something felt... off.

The shelving here was unremarkable at first glance, but there was a subtle gap between the edges, as if the wood wasn't quite flush with the others. My fingers skimmed the spines, and one book caught my attention—not for its title, but because the top edge was worn from use.

I pulled.

A soft click.

I stilled.

Slowly, beneath the shelf, a small compartment slid open, revealing a single flash drive.

I stared at it.

Lorenzo Navarra had hidden this. Which meant it was important. Which meant it was dangerous.

I exhaled, steadying myself, before slipping the drive into my pocket. I could look at it later, when I knew I wouldn't be interrupted.

For now, I had something else to focus on.

I went looking for her, my steps carrying me through the estate like I belonged here. Like I wasn't a man walking through enemy lines, playing house in a war I still wasn't sure I could win.

When I reached her office, the door was ajar, but the room was empty.

I frowned, moving on.

I found her in one of the smaller living spaces, tucked away in a quiet corner of the estate.

She wasn't behind her desk, wasn't in her usual crisp, commanding posture. Instead, she was curled up on the couch, staring into space.

And she looked exhausted.

She wasn't in business attire, no sharp blazer or perfectly pressed slacks. Instead, she was in a simple sweatsuit, her hair piled up in a messy bun. She looked younger like this. More vulnerable.

More like the girl I used to know.

I hesitated in the doorway. I had never seen her like this before.

She didn't notice me at first, lost in whatever thoughts were keeping her here, trapped in her own mind. When she finally did look up, her eyes met mine.

And I saw something that made my chest ache.

She wasn't just exhausted. She was carrying a weight she couldn't put down.

I walked over, quiet, careful.

She didn't say anything.

Neither did I.

Instead, I sat down behind her, shifting until I could pull her against me, my chest against her back. My arms wrapped around her, slow and deliberate, giving her time to resist.

But she didn't.

If anything, she leaned into me, her head resting against my shoulder, her body melting into the warmth of mine.

I closed my eyes for a second, inhaling the faint scent of her hair. Lavender and something deeper, something uniquely her.

I wasn't sure how long we sat like that.

Minutes. Hours. A lifetime.

Neither of us spoke.

There was no strategy here, no power plays, no past or future. Just breathing. Just being.

Somewhere along the way, exhaustion finally caught up to us both.

The first light of morning crept in through the curtains, soft and golden, stirring me from sleep.

Alessandra was still in my arms.

Her body was warm and relaxed, the steady rhythm of her breathing brushing against my neck.

It was the first time we had woken up together since college. Since the morning of graduation, when I had thought we had forever.

I felt her shift slightly, her breathing changing as she woke.

Her eyes fluttered open, blinking sleepily up at me.

For a moment, there was no tension. No war. No empire.

Just us.

"Good morning," she murmured, her voice soft, still hazy with sleep.

"Morning," I said, my voice just as quiet.

We stayed like that for a second too long, caught in the space between what was real and what we wished could be.

"I didn't mean to fall asleep," she admitted, pulling back slightly, though she didn't move far.

"Me neither," I said. A small, wry smile tugged at the corner of my mouth. "Guess we both needed it."

"Yeah." She nodded, her gaze flickering down to where our hands had brushed.

She hesitated. Just for a second.

Then she pulled away completely, sitting up.

She smoothed down the fabric of her sweats, a faint, awkward smile playing at her lips. "I should... probably get ready."

"Right," I said, shifting back to give her space.

She stood, stretching slightly before moving toward the door. But then—just as she reached it—she paused.

"Thank you," she said softly, still not looking at me.

"For what?"

A beat of silence.

"For staying."

Then she slipped out, leaving me alone with my thoughts.

I sat there for a long time, staring at the empty space where she had been.

Something between us had shifted. Not fixed, not resolved. But something was different.

I reached into my pocket, fingers brushing against the flash drive.

I had come here to tell her about it.

But I hadn't.

And now, I wasn't sure if I should.

Because whatever was on this drive, it had the power to change everything.

And for the first time in a long time...

I wasn't sure I wanted to.

Chapter 41

Longing for Something More

Alessandra

The small living space was one of the few places in the estate where I could breathe. It was tucked away, forgotten by most, which made it the perfect refuge. I had come here after a long night of battles I couldn't afford to lose, not with the old guard watching my every move, waiting for me to slip up. But this wasn't just exhaustion. It was something heavier, something colder.

I wasn't just tired.

I was losing pieces of myself.

I sank into the couch, staring blankly at the wall, my thoughts circling the same, unrelenting truths. Every move I made was calculated, every decision a thread in the tangled web I had woven to survive. But how many more threads could I pull before the whole thing collapsed? How many more nights like this—nights spent chasing ghosts, ensuring my father's empire didn't devour me whole—could I endure before I became just another version of him?

That thought made my stomach turn.

I told myself I was different. That I wasn't ruling out of greed or power, but necessity. That every order, every calculated act of violence, was another step toward breaking free.

But if that were true... why did it feel so natural?

I let out a breath, pressing my fingers against my temples. It would be easier if I didn't remember what it felt like to be anything else. If I didn't remember what it was like to laugh without caution, to love without consequence.

If I didn't remember him.

I squeezed my eyes shut, but it didn't stop the memory from rising, unbidden.

Steven, grinning at me from across our tiny college apartment, the overhead light flickering as we sat on the floor eating takeout straight from the cartons. His knee bumped mine, casual, familiar, like we were just two people in love, like the world outside that apartment didn't exist.

"You're doing it again," he had teased, pointing at me with his chopsticks.

"Doing what?" I had asked, feigning innocence.

"Overthinking," he had said simply. "You get that look when your brain is going a million miles an hour."

I had rolled my eyes, but he wasn't wrong. He knew me better than anyone, better than I had ever let anyone know me.

And now? Now I was a stranger to myself.

I let my head fall back against the couch, exhaling slowly. I was trapped. Caged by this empire, by my father's legacy, by the choices I had made to keep Steven alive.

Maybe I had been fooling myself all along.

Maybe there was no way out.

I didn't hear him enter. I was too lost in my own head, drowning in my thoughts. But then, suddenly, he was there.

Steven.

I didn't move, didn't acknowledge him at first. Part of me expected him to demand answers, to push me, to remind me—again—that I had shut him out. But he didn't.

He just sat down beside me.

And then, after a long pause, he wrapped his arms around me.

I should have pulled away. I should have reminded him, reminded myself, that this wasn't real. That what we had once been had died a long time ago, buried under lies and regret.

But I didn't move.

Instead, I melted into him, letting my body fold into his warmth, my head resting against his shoulder. I let myself be weak. Just for a little while.

He didn't say anything, and I was grateful for that. I wasn't ready to talk. Not about Vince. Not about the war outside these walls. Not about what this meant—this fragile, stolen moment where I let myself remember what it felt like to be safe.

His hand traced small, absentminded circles against my back, and I hated how much I needed it.

How much I needed him.

Because if I let myself need him, it would destroy me.

I wasn't sure when exhaustion finally dragged me under, but I let it. And for the first time in what felt like forever, I slept.

The first light of morning filtered through the curtains, waking me gently. I felt it before I opened my eyes—the unfamiliar warmth of Steven's body still pressed against mine, his arm draped over me like a shield.

For a split second, I forgot.

Forgot that we weren't the same people we had been in college. Forgot that the world outside this room was still waiting to tear us apart.

I could almost pretend that nothing had changed.

Then reality crashed back in.

I stirred slightly, and Steven woke with me, blinking the sleep from his eyes. He looked at me like he wasn't sure what to say. And I felt that, too.

Because what could we say?

"Good morning," I whispered.

"Morning," he replied his voice thick with sleep.

Silence stretched between us, not unpleasant but heavy. There were too many things we weren't saying.

Steven was the first to shift back, putting distance between us, but he didn't go far. His fingers brushed mine—just barely—as if debating whether to hold on or let go.

I forced myself to move first.

If I let this continue, it would ruin me.

"I should... probably get ready," I said, my voice steady, but my hands betrayed me—fidgeting, slow to leave his warmth.

"Right," he said, nodding slightly. "Of course."

I stood, smoothing down my sweatsuit, suddenly feeling exposed. He had seen too much.

I swallowed hard. "Thank you," I said softly. "For last night."

His lips parted slightly, like he wanted to say something else, something more, but instead, he just nodded.

"Anytime."

I turned, hesitating at the door for half a second before I forced myself to leave. Before I could second-guess myself.

As I walked away, I tried to remind myself that this didn't change anything.

That I was still *donna.*

That I still had a war to win.

But the memory of his arms around me, the quiet way he had held me without asking for anything in return, stayed with me.

Lingering.

Like a ghost.

Like hope.

Like something I couldn't afford to want.

But, God... I wanted to.

Chapter 42

Contingencies

Steven

I had spent the last few hours trying to convince myself that what I found on that flash drive wouldn't change anything. That it was just old files, relics of a dead man's empire.

But deep down, I knew better.

The weight of it burned in my pocket as I made my way toward Alessandra's office, my pulse pounding in my ears. I had considered looking at the files alone, bracing myself for whatever truth was hidden inside before dragging her into it. But the moment my fingers had hovered over the keyboard, something stopped me.

This wasn't just my fight anymore.

Alessandra needed to see it too.

When I reached her office, the door was slightly ajar, and I saw her standing by the window, arms crossed, lost in thought. The softness from this morning—the warmth of waking up beside her—was gone, replaced by the woman who had spent her entire life fighting to survive in a world built for men like her father.

For a brief second, I hesitated.

She turned before I could decide whether to knock. "Steven?"

I stepped inside, closing the door behind me. "I found something."

Her eyes sharpened. "What?"

I pulled the flash drive from my pocket and held it up. "In the library. Hidden compartment in a shelf."

Alessandra's brows furrowed slightly. "I didn't know there was a compartment in there."

My stomach twisted. If she didn't know, that meant her father had hidden it for himself—or worse, for someone else to find after he was gone.

She exhaled, nodding toward her desk. "Let's see what's on it."

I handed it over, watching as she plugged it into her computer. The screen flickered, loading rows of meticulously labeled folders. Operations. Financials. Contingencies. My gut clenched as my eyes landed on one near the bottom.

Active Targets.

Alessandra clicked the folder, and a document opened. A list of names filled the screen.

I scanned the first few, the words blurring together. Names I recognized, names I didn't. But then—

My vision tunneled.

The air felt too thick, the letters on the screen stretching and distorting.

H. Tucker.

The senator. The one I had written about, investigated, tried to expose. The one Lorenzo Navarra had likely had under his thumb.

And then, further down—

I couldn't breathe.

My hands went cold, my pulse hammering so hard it felt like my ribs would crack under the pressure.

I couldn't look away.

Porter, ~~Carl &~~ Julia

Porter, Nathan & Deena

Porter, Mitchell & Tara

My family.

My mother. My brothers. Their wives.

Every single one of them.

The word ACTIVE sat next to each name, clinical and damning.

Alessandra stiffened beside me, sucking in a sharp breath as she read the list. I barely registered the way her fingers trembled against the desk.

I was going to be sick.

"What does this mean?" I forced out, my voice barely recognizable.

Alessandra's lips parted, but no words came out. Then, she swallowed hard and grabbed her phone. "Nico. Now."

Less than a minute later, Nico stepped into the office. His gaze flicked between us, taking in my clenched fists, Alessandra's stiff posture. "What happened?"

Alessandra didn't look at him. She just turned the screen toward him.

The moment his eyes landed on the list, something changed in him. His whole body tensed, his lips pressing into a thin line. A muscle jumped in his jaw, his usual unreadable expression cracking just enough for me to see what lay beneath.

Recognition.

Dread.

Resignation.

Alessandra's voice was tight. "Did you know about this?"

Nico exhaled slowly, dragging a hand down his face. "Not this."

"Then what did you know?" I demanded, barely containing the panic clawing up my throat.

Nico was silent for a beat, then—

"I knew your father had procedures for things like this." His voice was low, grim. "I knew he didn't handle enemies impulsively. He set plans in motion, gave orders that weren't meant to be executed immediately."

I stared at him, unblinking. "So you're telling me these orders were just... waiting?"

Nico met my eyes. "Yes."

Alessandra inhaled sharply.

I gripped the edge of the desk, trying to steady myself, but my legs felt weak. "So what—you're saying someone could be watching them right now?"

Nico didn't answer.

And that silence told me everything.

Alessandra moved first. She grabbed my wrist, her grip firm. "We're shutting this down."

I turned to her, still reeling. "How?" My voice was hoarse. "If they've been waiting for years—if they still think this is an active order—how do we know they haven't already moved?"

Nico answered this time, his tone clipped. "Because they wouldn't move unless someone told them to."

Alessandra's eyes flashed. "Then we find out who's still left, who's still following my father's orders." She turned to Nico. "Start making calls. Pull in every contact we still have."

Nico nodded and left without another word.

The second he was gone, I let out a shuddering breath and ran a hand through my hair. My skin was cold, but my body burned with something I couldn't contain. Fear. Rage. The sheer helplessness of knowing my family had been in danger this whole time.

Alessandra took a step closer, her voice softer now. "Steven."

I squeezed my eyes shut, trying to steady myself.

She was standing right in front of me when I opened them. And what I saw in her face—guilt, regret, something deeper I couldn't name—only made the knot in my chest tighten.

"You met them," I murmured. "You met my parents."

Alessandra's breath hitched.

She had. Once. Back in college, when we were just kids who thought we could outrun the world.

"They treated me like family," she whispered. "Like I belonged."

I swallowed hard. "And now, because of your father—"

Her voice broke slightly, "Steven, I swear to you, I didn't know."

I exhaled sharply, nodding once. I believed her.

But believing her didn't change the reality.

We had to stop this.

I turned toward the computer, my hands steady now. "We shut it down. We protect them."

Alessandra nodded. "And then we finish this."

She wasn't just talking about the list.

She was talking about everything.

We were done playing defense.

It was time to end the Navarra empire once and for all.

Part Four

Changing Tides

Chapter 43

This Fragile Thing

Steven

The garden was quiet, almost too quiet—like the breath before an explosion. The sky was beginning to darken, the last remnants of sunlight casting a golden glow over the estate. It had been a long time since I felt anything close to peace, and even now, I wasn't sure if that was what this was.

I walked beside Alessandra, our steps slow and unhurried, gravel crunching underfoot. The scent of jasmine and roses drifted through the air, a reminder that no matter how much blood had been spilled on this land, there were still things here that could grow. That could survive.

We reached a secluded bench, half-hidden by wisteria. Alessandra sat first, and after a beat, I followed, the silence stretching between us—not uncomfortable, but heavy with everything we hadn't said.

I didn't know how to start, but I knew I had to. The last few weeks had been hell. The weight of what we'd discovered about my family still sat in my chest, tight and suffocating. But with Vito backing off and the immediate threats handled, for the first time in a long time, we had space to talk about something other than survival.

She was the one to break the silence. She always was.

"I didn't think we'd ever get this far," she said, her voice quiet as she stared out at the garden. "There were moments I thought we wouldn't make it."

I exhaled, rubbing the back of my neck. "Me too. But somehow, we're still here."

Her gaze shifted to me, something softer in her expression. "Do you ever think about what happens after all of this?"

"All the time," I admitted.

That seemed to surprise her. She studied me for a moment, like she was trying to figure out whether or not I was lying.

"We've both changed," she murmured, almost to herself.

"Yeah," I said. "We have." I hesitated, feeling the weight of what I was about to say. "But that doesn't mean we can't try again."

Her brows drew together. "Try?"

"A fresh start," I said, turning toward her fully. "Not as the people we used to be. As who we are now."

She let out a quiet breath, her gaze dropping to where our hands rested between us. The space was small—so small—but neither of us had crossed it yet.

"Steven... it's not that simple."

"I know," I said, shaking my head. "I'm not saying we forget everything that's happened. I just—" I sighed. "Back in college, when everything almost fell apart, you asked me if we could start over. I said yes. And we found our way back to each other then."

Her lips parted slightly, the ghost of something—maybe a memory, maybe regret—passing over her face.

"We were different then," she said.

"We were," I agreed. "But I still think we can try. We've faced worse odds."

She let out a small, disbelieving laugh, shaking her head. "That's true."

I hesitated for only a second before reaching for her hand. She didn't pull away. Instead, she let me lace my fingers through hers, her grip hesitant at first before tightening.

"A fresh start," she repeated, like she was testing the words, seeing if they could hold.

I squeezed her hand. "Yeah. If we want it."

She looked at me then—really looked at me. And I saw it, the moment she let herself want it too.

"Okay," she whispered.

And just like that, something shifted between us.

I didn't think about it—I just moved. She did too.

The kiss was slow, careful, almost cautious, like we were afraid that if we went too fast, we'd shatter whatever fragile thing we were trying to build. Her fingers curled into my jacket, pulling me just a little closer, and I felt the tension ease from her, felt her give in to the moment just as I did.

When we pulled back, we stayed close, our foreheads nearly touching, breathing the same air.

Alessandra swallowed hard, her voice barely above a whisper. "We take it one step at a time."

"One step at a time," I echoed.

She nodded, but I saw the flicker of uncertainty in her expression. She was still afraid. Still holding part of herself back. But for the first time, she wasn't pushing me away.

She was choosing to stay.

I could work with that.

Chapter 44

Second First Date

Steven

We stayed there, close and quiet, letting the world slip away for just a little longer. But the silence wasn't heavy anymore—it felt like something new. Not the fragile, uneasy truce we'd clung to before, but something steadier.

Something like hope.

I pulled back just enough to see her face, to study the way her lashes cast soft shadows against her cheeks, the way her lips parted slightly as if she was on the verge of speaking but hadn't quite found the words. I wasn't about to let this moment pass us by.

"Alessandra," I started, my voice low but sure. "What if we did this right?"

She blinked, tilting her head slightly. "What do you mean?"

I let out a breath, the idea taking shape as I spoke. "What if we tried something new? No secrets, no shadows hanging over us—just you and me, starting fresh. Like it's our first date all over again."

A surprised laugh escaped her, soft and disbelieving. "You want to take me on a date?"

I smiled, feeling something loosen in my chest at the sound. "Yeah. A real one. No logistics, no strategy, no looking over our shoulders. Just us."

Alessandra looked at me like she was waiting for the catch, like she wasn't sure whether to believe this was possible.

"Steven," she murmured, shaking her head slightly. "After everything, do you really think we can just... start over?"

I reached for her hand, threading my fingers through hers. She didn't pull away.

"I think we can try," I said. "Not as the people we used to be, but as who we are now."

She was quiet for a long moment, her gaze locked onto mine. And then, so softly I almost missed it, she whispered, "Okay."

I exhaled a quiet breath of relief, squeezing her hand. "Tonight?"

That earned me another laugh, this one warmer, real. "You really don't waste time, do you?"

I shrugged, grinning. "Life's too short."

She sobered at that, nodding slightly. She knew what I meant. How close we had both come to losing everything.

"Alright," she said finally. "Tonight."

And just like that, the world shifted again.

I had spent way too much time picking out the restaurant. It had to be the right balance—somewhere outside the city, far enough that we wouldn't have to worry about prying eyes, but not so remote that it felt like a strategic retreat. I wanted this to feel like something normal, something good.

When I arrived at the estate to pick her up, she was already waiting in the foyer.

And for a moment, I forgot how to breathe.

She wasn't wearing anything overly extravagant—just a sleek black dress, simple jewelry—but it was the effort that made my chest tighten. She had let her hair down, soft waves framing her face, and for the first time in what felt like forever, she wasn't dressed for war.

Alessandra Navarra, the Donna, was nowhere to be seen.

Just Alessandra.

She caught me staring and raised an eyebrow. "Are we leaving, or are you just going to keep looking at me?"

I let out a breathless laugh, offering my arm. "Both, probably."

She rolled her eyes, but her lips twitched into the ghost of a smile as she slipped her hand into mine.

Progress.

The drive was quiet, but not in the way it had been before. This silence wasn't heavy with unspoken words or tension—it was comfortable. The kind of silence that comes when two people don't feel the need to fill every second with noise.

At the restaurant, we were seated in a private corner near the back, the dim lighting casting a warm glow over everything. The conversation started slow, careful, as if neither of us wanted to say the wrong thing. But eventually, it unraveled into something easy.

We talked.

Really talked.

About our lives before all of this, about the things we missed, the dreams we used to have. She told me how she used to sneak out of her father's estate when she was a teenager, just to sit by the water and pretend the rest of the world didn't exist. I told her about the time my brothers dared me to climb the old water tower in our hometown, and how I nearly broke my arm trying to get back down.

For the first time in a long time, there was laughter.

Not the bitter, sharp kind that came after trading barbs or surviving yet another impossible situation.

But real laughter.

And God, I had missed that sound.

After dinner, we walked. There was a small park near the restaurant, and we ended up by the water, the reflection of the moon rippling across the surface.

She sighed, wrapping her arms around herself. "I don't remember the last time I did something like this."

"Like what?"

She glanced at me. "Just... be."

I nodded, shoving my hands into my pockets. "Yeah. Me neither."

A breeze rolled in, tugging loose strands of her hair. I reached out without thinking, tucking them behind her ear. Her breath hitched slightly at the touch, and I felt her still under my fingertips.

I didn't pull away.

Neither did she.

"I'm glad we did this," she said after a moment, her voice quieter now. "I didn't realize how much I missed just... being with you like this."

"Me too." I swallowed, forcing myself to be honest. "I didn't know if we could ever get back here. But now that we are, I don't want to lose it again."

She turned fully toward me then, searching my face.

"Then let's not," she said simply. "Let's keep trying, no matter what happens."

The words hit me like a weight I hadn't realized I'd been carrying was suddenly lifted.

She wanted this. Us.

Even after everything.

"We will," I said, meaning it.

For the first time, I reached for her not out of impulse, not because we were on the verge of losing each other, but because I wanted to.

When I kissed her, it wasn't desperate or claiming—it was slow, careful, like we were both afraid of moving too fast and shattering whatever fragile thing we were building.

She sighed into it, her fingers curling into my jacket, pulling me closer.

When we pulled apart, we didn't step back. We stayed close, our foreheads nearly touching, our breaths mingling in the cool night air.

"One step at a time," I murmured.

She smiled. "One step at a time."

And for the first time in a long time, I let myself believe.

Chapter 45

Follow Her Lead

Steven

The last few weeks had been a strange kind of paradise—dangerous, fleeting, and fragile. Alessandra and I had found a rhythm, something close to normal, and I'd let myself believe we could keep it.

Now, standing in a coffee shop with a newspaper clenched in my hands, I felt that illusion crack wide open.

SENATOR TIED TO NAVARRA FAMILY CRIME EMPIRE.

My name wasn't on the byline. *Doug Stapleton.*

My stomach twisted as I scanned the article. The story wasn't just familiar—it was mine. The one I had started months ago before everything changed. The one I had buried.

I barely noticed as the barista slid my coffee across the counter. My pulse hammered, the words blurring together as I read:

Howard Tucker, a sitting U.S. Senator, had deep-rooted financial connections to the Navarra family, stretching back decades. Contributions masked as legitimate investments. Backroom meetings with Lorenzo Navarra himself.

The article wasn't just damning—it was designed to destabilize.

I knew who was behind it.

Vito Valenti.

I grabbed the coffees and bagels, shoved the paper under my arm, and left.

By the time I reached the house, my thoughts were racing, but I had one priority—Alessandra needed to know.

I found her in the kitchen of all places, sleeves pushed up, knife in hand, slicing into a bell pepper with practiced precision. It was such a normal sight, so unlike the woman who commanded a room with a single glance, that for a second, I almost let myself believe she wasn't about to be blindsided.

Then she looked up, and that softness vanished.

"What's wrong?"

I didn't answer. I just handed her the newspaper.

She wiped her hands on a dish towel before taking it, her expression unreadable as she scanned the headline. But I saw it—the moment she realized what it meant.

The slight tightening of her grip. The way her lips pressed together, jaw clenching just enough to tell me she was already thinking five steps ahead.

"Doug Stapleton," she murmured, her tone calm. But I knew better. This was the kind of calm that came before a gun was drawn. "He wrote this?"

"Not exactly," I said. "I did."

Her head snapped up. "What?"

"Months ago. I never finished it—never could finish it because everything changed. But Doug got his hands on it."

Her eyes darkened. "He didn't just get his hands on it. Someone gave it to him."

I exhaled sharply. "Vito."

Alessandra nodded once, slowly, absorbing the implications.

"Doug didn't have the connections to verify this on his own. That means someone handed it to him, ready to publish. And since Vito's been trying to cause chaos for weeks..."

She didn't finish. She didn't have to.

I ran a hand through my hair. "This was a power play. He wants us scrambling, trying to put out fires while he moves unchecked."

"We need to cut this off before it spreads," she said, already shifting into strategy mode. "If we don't control this narrative, we'll have more than law enforcement breathing down our necks—we'll have people questioning me. And that is not an option."

Her voice was sharp now, commanding. But I wasn't about to just listen and nod.

"I can talk to Doug," I said. "We worked together for years. I can—"

"No."

The answer was immediate.

My stomach tightened. "Alessandra—"

"You can't get involved," she said, cutting me off before I could argue. "Doug's already compromised. You going after him makes us look desperate—and it puts a target on your back."

"Doug is my problem," I shot back. "He stole my work. He used my words, my research, and twisted it to serve Vito. If I don't do something, this could blow up in our faces."

She set the knife down with a sharp click against the cutting board. "Steven, trust me. This isn't just about a stolen story. This is about optics. If you go after Doug, the press will rip you apart. And if Vito gets wind of you sniffing around, he'll make sure you regret it."

I gritted my teeth. "So what? I just stand back and let someone else handle it?"

She exhaled, pinching the bridge of her nose like she was trying to keep her patience in check. "We'll figure out why Doug ran the story, but we'll do it quietly. Nico can dig around, see what he finds. In the meantime, we do not let anyone know we're onto them."

My hands clenched into fists. "I'm not some outsider in this, Alessandra."

Her gaze snapped back to mine, sharp and unwavering. "No, you're not. But you also don't get to play by the same rules as me. If Doug sees you coming, if Vito sees you coming, they'll twist it to their advantage. You think Vito wants to see me squirm? No—he wants you to snap. Because if you do, he wins."

I hated that she was right.

But even more than that, I hated that she had to be the one making this call.

I took a slow breath, forcing down the frustration boiling under my skin. "So what's the plan?"

Alessandra studied me for a long moment before answering. "We do what Vito doesn't expect. We don't panic. We don't chase after Doug like we're desperate. We make sure he knows we see him—but we don't make a move until we're ready."

I nodded, though the tension in my chest didn't ease.

She softened, just a little. "Steven, I know this is personal. But if we let emotions dictate our response, we lose. We do this my way."

I let out a sharp exhale, looking away. "For now."

She didn't argue.

Instead, she picked up the newspaper, folded it carefully, and placed it aside. A silent declaration that she would deal with it—but on her terms.

And as much as I hated feeling like I was being sidelined, I had to remind myself—we were in this together.

Even if it didn't always feel like it.

Chapter 46

Can't Afford Mistakes

Alessandra

Later that evening, I met with Nico in the study. The tension in the room was suffocating.

Steven sat across from me, arms folded, his jaw clenched so tight I thought he might crack a molar.

I hated this.

I hated the distance between us, the doubt in his eyes, the way his fingers tapped against the desk like he was barely containing the urge to lash out.

But what I hated most?

He wasn't wrong.

"We need to assume Vito is behind this," Nico said, cutting through the silence. "He wouldn't risk this kind of exposure unless he had a way to control the fallout."

Steven let out a sharp breath. "Then why did Doug run with it?" His voice was edged with frustration, but I could hear something else beneath it. Something closer to fear.

I didn't answer right away.

Because I didn't know.

Steven turned to me, his hands tightening into fists. "Doug didn't publish this story because he suddenly developed a conscience. Someone gave it to him. Someone made him think this was worth the risk."

Nico nodded. "Either a payoff or a threat."

Steven let out a bitter laugh, shaking his head. "Or the chance to make his career." He exhaled sharply, rubbing a hand over his face. "The thing is... Doug's not stupid. He wouldn't have run this unless he thought he was safe."

I met his gaze. "And that's what scares you."

His eyes darkened. "Yeah."

Because if Doug thought he was safe, that meant someone promised him protection.

Someone powerful enough to keep the wolves at bay.

And right now? There were only two people in this world who had that kind of influence: Vito Valenti... and me.

Steven was still pacing, the newspaper clenched in his fist, his thoughts spilling out faster than he could control them.

He looked away, running a hand through his hair. "This isn't just about Vito. If Doug had my notes, that means someone gave them to him. It could've been my editor." His voice dropped slightly, as if saying it out loud made it more real. "The story made it to submission, but I disappeared before I could follow up. Maybe my editor handed it over. Maybe Doug took it. Maybe he bargained with Vito for the credit." His thoughts came fast and jagged. "I don't know. But I need to find out."

I could see it in his eyes—the same relentless focus I'd seen back in college when he'd spent nights chasing a story, getting too caught up to eat, to sleep. This was the Steven Porter I had fallen in love with. The one who never let go of a thread until he unraveled the whole thing.

And I had a choice.

I could tell him to let it go, to stay out of it, to let me and Nico handle it the way we always did—through quiet negotiations and quiet threats.

But that wasn't who he was.

And if I wanted this—us—to work, I couldn't keep treating him like a liability.

I exhaled slowly, forcing myself to loosen my grip on control, just a little. "Then go talk to Doug."

Steven's head snapped up, his eyes narrowing like he was expecting a fight.

I gave him a small shrug. "You're right. This is your world. You know how it works better than I do."

A beat of silence.

Then Nico scoffed.

I turned, meeting his sharp gaze. "Problem?"

"Yeah," he said flatly. "This is a bad idea."

Steven folded his arms. "You don't trust me."

"I don't trust anyone to walk into a situation blind," Nico shot back. "Doug Stapleton published a story designed to destabilize this family. You think you can just walk in there and ask a few questions?"

Steven's jaw tightened. "I've spent years investigating dangerous men in dangerous places. You think this is my first time dealing with a source who's in over his head?"

"That was different," Nico said. "You weren't a Navarra then."

I felt the shift in the room immediately.

Steven went quiet—not because he didn't have a response, but because he did.

I saw it in his posture, the way his shoulders squared, the way his expression hardened.

And when he spoke, his voice was calm. Controlled. Sharp.

"I wasn't a Navarra when I was standing outside a police station in Mexico City, waiting for a guy who'd been smuggling arms across the border to decide if he was going to give me an interview or have me killed," he said, his voice measured. "I wasn't a Navarra when I was chased out of a hotel in Jakarta because I got too close to a human trafficking ring. I wasn't a Navarra when I was sitting across from a Russian oligarch who didn't know if he wanted to have dinner with me or have me disappeared." He paused. "But I made it out of every single one of those situations. Because I knew when to push, when to back off, and when to run. So, yeah, I think I can handle a meeting with a journalist."

Nico didn't look convinced, but he didn't argue.

Instead, he turned to me. "This is your call, Donna."

I met his gaze evenly. I knew what he was really asking.

Are you sure about this?

I turned back to Steven. He didn't look at me like he was asking for permission. He looked at me like he was asking for trust.

I made my decision.

"He goes."

Nico exhaled through his nose, clearly displeased, but nodded. "Fine. But I'm keeping a man on him."

Steven smirked. "Looking forward to the babysitter."

Nico ignored him, turning on his heel and leaving the room, the door clicking shut behind him.

I barely had a second to breathe before Steven closed the distance between us.

He didn't say anything.

Just looked at me.

And the way he looked at me—like I had just handed him something rare, something he never thought I'd give—sent heat curling through my stomach.

"Thank you," he murmured, his voice lower now, quieter. Rougher.

His fingers brushed over my wrist, slow, deliberate. Not demanding, not insistent—just there.

I swallowed. "For what?"

"For trusting me."

His hand slid up, over my forearm, slow enough that my breath caught. "I know how hard that was for you."

I should have pulled away. Should have told him I didn't need to be handled like this.

But I didn't move.

I let him step in closer, his chest nearly brushing mine.

"Steven—"

Then he kissed me.

Slow and deep, like he was savoring it. Like he wasn't just taking but giving—showing me what it meant to be believed in, to be seen.

I let myself melt into it, into the way he held me—not to claim, not to control, but to anchor.

And when we finally pulled apart, breathless and wanting, he pressed his forehead to mine, his hands firm at my waist.

"Thank you," he whispered, again.

Chapter 47

Name That Lead

Steven

The next morning, I called Doug.

I'd spent half the night staring at the ceiling, playing out different versions of this conversation in my head—ways to approach it, ways to corner him, ways to make him slip up. But when I finally dialed his number, I went with something simple.

"Doug. It's Steven."

A brief pause. Then, his voice, smooth and practiced. "Well, well. Porter. Didn't think I'd hear from you."

I ignored the bait. "We should talk. Lunch?"

Another pause. Then, "Yeah. Sure. Frankie's, noon."

He hung up before I could say anything else.

That wasn't surprising. Doug and I had worked together for years, but we were never really friends. Journalism wasn't the kind of industry that bred friendship. You respected people, you admired their work, but at the end of the day, everyone was looking for the next big story, and loyalty only stretched as far as the next byline.

Still, Doug wasn't an idiot. He knew exactly why I was calling.

Which meant this meeting was going to be a game.

Doug was already there when I arrived, sitting at a booth near the back with a sandwich half-unwrapped in front of him. He looked up as I slid into the seat across from him, his expression unreadable.

"Porter," he said, nodding. "Long time."

"Yeah," I said, setting my drink down. "Quite a story you ran."

His lips quirked up in something that wasn't quite a smile. "That's what they tell me."

I leaned back, folding my arms. "Read like something I'd write."

For just a second, a flicker of something crossed his face. Guilt? Annoyance? I couldn't tell. Then he shrugged. "Not my fault you disappeared. Someone had to run with it."

I clenched my jaw but kept my voice even. "Did Alan give it to you?"

Doug picked up a fry, studied it, then popped it into his mouth. "Don't know what you're talking about."

"Bullshit."

His eyes flicked up to mine, sharper now. "Careful, Porter."

I exhaled, forcing myself to stay calm. "Just trying to understand. That story sat in limbo for months, and suddenly it lands on the front page under your name? Why now?"

Doug didn't answer right away. He took a sip of his drink, his gaze flicking toward the street outside. Then, finally—

"You should be thanking me."

I scoffed. "For what?"

"For keeping your name out of it."

That threw me for a second. "Excuse me?"

Doug sighed, leaning forward. "You ever stop to think about why I ran it and not you? Why Vito—" he stopped himself, but it was too late—"Why whoever gave me that story didn't just slap your name on it?"

My stomach twisted.

"Half the shit I was told about you? If even a fraction of it was true, Porter, you're lucky your name wasn't attached."

His voice was low, his words careful.

I stared at him. "What did they tell you?"

Doug shook his head. "Doesn't matter. The point is, you walked away clean. You should keep it that way."

I clenched my hands under the table to keep them steady.

Doug knew something. Something big.

But he wasn't going to give it up easily.

So I forced a laugh, shaking my head. "Right. Because I should trust that you suddenly grew a conscience?"

Doug smirked. "Call it professional courtesy."

I narrowed my eyes. "More like self-preservation."

He didn't deny it.

The server came by and dropped off my sandwich, but I barely noticed.

Doug pushed his basket of fries toward me like this was just another conversation between colleagues, like he hadn't just hinted that my name had been actively buried.

I wasn't sure what was worse—the fact that Doug knew more than he was letting on, or the fact that Vito, or someone in his orbit, had chosen to keep me out of the story.

Because that meant someone had plans for me.

And I didn't like that one bit.

Doug exhaled and sat back, wiping his hands on a napkin. "Look, man. I don't know what you're trying to do here. But whatever it is, let it go."

I stared at him. "You don't believe that."

For the first time, I saw a flicker of doubt in his expression.

No—he didn't.

Doug knew he'd been played.

He just wasn't sure how much it would cost him yet.

I could work with that.

But not here.

I forced a casual shrug, reaching for a fry. "Sure, Doug. I'll let it go."

Doug watched me for a second longer, then nodded once, like he was satisfied with that answer.

Idiot.

This was far from over.

By the time I pulled up to the house, my mind was spinning.

Doug hadn't given me much, but he'd confirmed what I suspected—someone had given him my work. And someone had made sure I wasn't the one who published it.

I had to tell Alessandra.

I found her in the study, reviewing some documents with Nico. The second she saw my face, she set her pen down.

"What happened?"

Nico leaned back in his chair, watching me closely.

I tossed the newspaper onto the desk. "Doug wasn't surprised to see me."

Alessandra arched an eyebrow. "No?"

"No." I exhaled, running a hand through my hair. "He all but told me I should be grateful my name wasn't on that story."

Nico's expression darkened. "That's quite a thing to say."

"Yeah," I muttered. "Which means whoever gave him that story knew exactly what they were doing."

Alessandra's jaw tightened. "Vito."

"Maybe," I said. "Or maybe my editor. Or maybe someone we haven't even considered yet." I looked at her. "But Doug knows more than he's saying."

She studied me for a long moment, then nodded. "We push him."

Nico frowned. "You really want to make a journalist sweat? That's a good way to get more headlines."

I shook my head. "Not like that. If I go back too soon, he'll shut down. But I can get him to talk."

Alessandra leaned back in her chair, considering.

Then—

"Do it."

Nico's head snapped toward her. "Alessandra—"

"He's right," she said firmly. "Doug won't talk to me. He won't talk to you. But he will talk to Steven."

Nico's expression was unreadable, but I saw the tension in his jaw.

Still, he didn't argue.

Instead, he turned to me. "Then don't screw it up."

I smirked. "I wouldn't dream of it."

Nico rolled his eyes, pushing out of his chair and leaving the room.

The second he was gone, I turned back to Alessandra.

She was watching me, something unreadable in her gaze.

I stepped closer. "You didn't hesitate."

"No," she admitted.

I studied her for a beat. Then, quieter—

"Alessandra."

She exhaled slowly, her fingers brushing the edge of the desk.

Then I closed the space between us.

Slow. Deliberate.

She didn't pull away.

I lifted a hand, brushing my fingers along her jaw.

Her breath hitched.

"Kiss me," she whispered.

So I did.

Not claiming. Not demanding. Just trusting.

And when she kissed me back, I knew—

We weren't just in this together.

We were in this for real.

Chapter 48

Whistleblower

Alessandra

The morning started like any other—until it didn't.

I was at my desk, sifting through financial reports, when Nico burst into the room. He didn't knock. He didn't announce himself. He just strode in, shutting the door behind him with a force that sent a chill through me.

Nico was always composed, even in chaos. But right now? His eyes were sharp, his movements quick and clipped.

Something was very, very wrong.

I straightened in my chair, pushing the reports aside. "Talk."

He tossed a folded newspaper onto my desk. "Tucker just made his move."

I unfolded the paper, my stomach tightening the second I saw the headline:

SENATOR HAROLD TUCKER BLOWS THE WHISTLE ON ORGANIZED CRIME: FBI LAUNCHES MAJOR INVESTIGATION

My breath caught in my throat.

I scanned the article, my pulse pounding with each line.

Tucker had gone public, claiming he was being framed for corruption by undisclosed criminal entities. He painted himself as a victim—an innocent man who had unwittingly been pulled into the depths of organized crime. And in his desperate bid to save his career, he had taken a scorched-earth approach.

He had given the FBI everything.

Or at least, everything he had.

According to the article, Tucker had turned over damaging intelligence on major players within the criminal underworld. The specifics were vague, but it was enough for the FBI to act. Raids were being planned. Arrests were already underway.

And worst of all?

The Navarra name was all over the report.

I forced my voice to remain even. "What exactly did he give them?"

Nico's jaw tightened. "We don't know yet. But it's enough for the FBI to justify immediate action. They're targeting key properties—our businesses, safe houses, financial accounts. They're going to hit hard, and they're going to hit soon."

I swallowed the sharp stab of panic rising in my chest. "And our people?"

Nico exhaled, his expression grim. "Some have already been picked up. Others are going underground."

My grip on the newspaper tightened. This wasn't just a problem. It was a full-blown disaster.

We had been so close to dismantling the Navarra empire from the inside, controlling the fallout before anyone could use it against us. But now? The whole operation was compromised.

And worse—Steven was in the direct line of fire.

I closed my eyes for a brief second, just long enough to pull myself together. "The capos," I said, my voice sharper now. "We need to call them in. Lock down whatever we still control. Anything that isn't compromised, we secure immediately."

Nico nodded but didn't move.

I looked up. "What?"

His gaze darkened. "Steven."

The single word was enough to send ice down my spine.

I pushed back from my desk, already reaching for my phone.

"He's in a dangerous spot," Nico continued. "He might not be tied to us officially, but if the FBI starts pulling at threads, they'll find him. His old investigation. His resignation. His connection to you."

I didn't need Nico to spell it out.

If the Feds came after Steven, they wouldn't just be looking at his time as a journalist. They would dig deeper. They would see his marriage to me. And once they started connecting dots, they wouldn't stop until they had enough to drag him down with the rest of us.

Tucker had set the fire.

Now we had to stop it from spreading.

I pressed the call button, my phone ringing against my ear as I braced myself for the conversation that was about to come.

Steven answered on the second ring.

"Alessandra?" His voice was alert, on edge.

He already knew.

"Tucker just declared war," I said. "And we need to talk. Now."

Steven arrived within the hour, his expression unreadable as he stepped into my office.

The room was thick with tension, the kind that settled in your bones and refused to let go.

Steven sat across from me, his hands resting on his knees, fingers twitching like he was trying to keep himself from bolting out the door. His mind was already moving, working through the angles, looking for a way forward.

"We need to assume Tucker gave them something solid," Nico said. "The FBI wouldn't be moving this aggressively unless they believed it would hold up."

Steven let out a sharp breath. "Then why did he go public with it?" His frustration bled into his voice, but there was something else beneath it—something closer to fear.

I didn't answer right away. Because I didn't know.

Steven turned to me, his jaw tightening. "Tucker's not stupid. He wouldn't do this unless he thought he had protection. Either from the Bureau, or from someone else."

Nico nodded. "He's either got the Feds fully on his side, or he's made a deal with someone who can shield him from whatever fallout is coming."

"Like Vito," I said, the realization settling like a stone in my stomach.

Silence.

Then Steven ran a hand through his hair, his mind clearly working through every possibility, every angle. His voice was quieter when he finally spoke.

"I need to call my brother."

I blinked. "What?"

"Nate," he clarified. "If the FBI is moving on this, he'll know something. Or at the very least, he'll know who to talk to."

Nico scoffed. "Absolutely not."

Steven ignored him, his eyes locked onto mine. "He's my best shot at finding out what's happening on the inside. He might not give me everything, but he'll give me enough."

"No," Nico said, stepping forward. "That's insane. You call him now, and suddenly you're on the Bureau's radar. You think Tucker won't have people watching for leaks? You think Nate won't be pulled in for questioning the second someone realizes he has a direct line to you?"

Steven's jaw tightened. "You think I don't know that?"

"Then why—"

"Because he's my brother, Nico." Steven's voice was sharp now, cutting through the room. "And if I don't call him, he's going to find out the hard way that his name is sitting on a federal watchlist just because he's related to me."

That hit like a bullet.

Nico exhaled sharply, running a hand over his face, but he didn't argue. Because Steven was right.

Tucker had just put a target on every single person connected to Steven, and that meant Nate—FBI agent or not—was at risk.

I stayed quiet, feeling the weight of the decision pressing down on me.

Steven turned to me, his voice steady. "You trust me?"

A loaded question.

I had already trusted him with so much—with my plans, my survival, my heart.

This was a different kind of trust.

But if I told him no, if I shut him out now, I knew exactly what that would do to us.

I inhaled slowly.

Then—

"Call him."

Steven's eyes flickered with surprise before settling into something more resolute. He nodded.

Nico clenched his jaw. "Alessandra—"

"He's right," I said. "If Nate's name is in this mess, we need to know before it's too late."

Nico exhaled through his nose but didn't argue. "Fine. But I don't like it."

Steven smirked. "I'm not sure what chanced but suddenly, you don't like anything I do."

Nico ignored him, already pulling out his phone, likely setting up countermeasures in case this went sideways.

The second we were alone, Steven turned to me, stepping in close. "Thank you."

I swallowed. "For what?"

"For trusting me," he murmured, brushing his fingers along my wrist.

I shivered.

Then he leaned in, his lips brushing against my cheek, slow and deliberate.

Not a demand. Not an apology.

Just trust.

And when he pulled back, I let him go.

Because no matter how much I wanted to protect him—

I needed to let him fight this battle his way.

Chapter 49

In Too Deep

Steven

The message I'd sent had been short.

Call me as soon as you can.

My phone buzzed almost instantly. The pit in my stomach deepened as I picked up the call.

"Hey, Nate." I kept my voice steady, neutral.

"Steven," he replied, his tone clipped. "We need to meet. How soon can you be available?"

I gripped the steering wheel a little tighter. He knows something.

"Where?"

"The old diner off Route 7," Nate suggested. A neutral ground. The place we always went when we needed to talk without anyone listening.

"Two hours," I said before ending the call.

The drive felt longer than it was, the roads stretching endlessly in front of me. My fingers drummed against the steering wheel, the same beat echoing in my chest.

By the time I pulled into the parking lot, Nate's car was already there. He was sitting at a booth in the back, his posture rigid, his face hard as granite.

I slid into the seat across from him, my movements slow, careful. "Nate."

"Steven." His eyes locked onto mine, sharp and unreadable. "What is going on? And don't give me the abridged version."

I nodded, inhaling deeply. "Alright."

Then I told him.

Everything.

I didn't hold back—not about the marriage, not about the flash drive, not about the hit list with our family's names on it.

By the time I finished, Nate was leaning forward, his elbows braced against the table, his expression a careful mask of control. "So let me get this straight," he said, his voice dangerously calm. "You married Alessandra Navarra. And you thought that was the best way to keep us safe?"

I kept my expression neutral, but my pulse was hammering. "It's not what it looks like," I said evenly. "It was the only move I had. The only way to make sure you, Mom, and Mitch weren't put in the crosshairs."

His laugh was humorless. "That's what you're telling yourself? That you had no choice?"

"You think I wanted this?" I shot back, my voice lower now, barely contained. "You think I planned on falling in love with her again?"

Nate's expression darkened, and something flickered in his eyes—something dangerously close to disappointment. "You love her?"

"Yes." No hesitation. No regret. Just the truth.

He exhaled sharply, shaking his head. "Steven, do you even hear yourself? You are married to the heir of the Navarra family. You are inside one of the most dangerous organizations in the country. And now, the FBI is coming down on all of it. On her. On you."

My stomach twisted. "I know."

"Then get out."

My breath stalled.

"Cooperate with the FBI," he continued. "Give them what they need to bring down the Navarras. It's the only way you're going to survive this."

I forced myself to breathe. "You don't understand."

"I understand perfectly." His voice was hard, unwavering. "You're in too deep, and you're making decisions based on emotion instead of logic. That is a mistake, Steven."

I clenched my fists beneath the table. "She's not Lorenzo."

"Doesn't matter."

My jaw tightened. "It matters to me."

Nate sat back, exhaling through his nose, trying to keep his own temper in check. "This isn't about Alessandra," he said, his tone quieter now, more measured. "It's about you. And Mom. And Mitch. And Deena and Tara. You don't think your name is in every file the FBI is pulling right now? You don't think they're looking at your past stories, your connections, wondering why you left your job, why you suddenly disappeared from the journalism world?"

I stayed silent.

Because he wasn't wrong.

"This is a federal investigation," Nate continued. "And once you're in their sights, you don't just walk away."

My stomach twisted. "What are you saying?"

He hesitated. Then—"I might be able to help you. If you cooperate."

I swallowed hard. "You want me to betray her."

Nate's face hardened. "I want you to save yourself."

Silence.

The kind that stretched and frayed and dug in deep.

Then I stood, sliding out of the booth, my hands braced against the table. "I can't do that."

Nate exhaled, shaking his head. "Then I don't know how much longer I can protect you."

Chapter 50

A Future to Believe In

Steven

The drive home blurred past me in a haze of streetlights and distant city sounds.

Nate's words echoed in my head, looping like a song I couldn't turn off.

"Cooperate with the FBI."

"It's the only way you're going to survive this."

"I want you to save yourself."

My fingers tightened around the steering wheel, the leather creaking under the pressure. Save myself?

As if I could just walk away.

As if my survival meant anything if I had to betray Alessandra to do it.

The estate came into view, its gates opening smoothly as I approached. I pulled into the driveway, cut the engine, but didn't move right away. The weight of the conversation I was about to have pressed down on me.

I had to tell her.

The house was quiet, the kind of quiet that settled late at night when the staff had long since retired. I moved through the halls, the familiar paths feeling heavier tonight, like the walls were pressing in.

Alessandra's office door was open, light spilling into the dim hallway.

She was at her desk, her head bent slightly as she studied the documents in front of her. The glow from her desk lamp cast long shadows, illuminating the sharp angles of her face, the slight crease in her brow.

Focused. Determined.

But she looked... tired.

Still, the moment she sensed me, her eyes flicked up, and for a second, something softened in her expression.

"Hey." I leaned against the doorframe. "You look good sitting there."

A small smile tugged at her lips. "Flattery will get you anywhere, but only if you stop looking like someone just ran over your dog."

I huffed a quiet laugh, stepping inside. "Worth a shot."

She stood as I reached her, her gaze searching mine now, reading me like a book she knew by heart. "Steven. What happened?"

I didn't answer right away.

Instead, I reached for her, pulling her into me, pressing my lips to hers—slow, grounding.

She let me.

Let me steal this moment before reality crashed back in.

And God, I needed it.

Because for the first time in a long time, I wasn't just fighting to protect her. I wasn't just fighting for survival.

I was fighting for us.

When I finally pulled back, I lingered, my forehead resting against hers. My hands cupped her face, my thumbs brushing over the curve of her cheekbones.

She looked up at me, searching, waiting.

I exhaled, the words sitting heavy in my chest—words I hadn't said in years. Words that I thought I had buried, convinced they didn't belong to me anymore.

But they did.

They always had.

"I love you, Alessandra."

Her breath caught.

I felt it—felt the way her fingers tightened against my shirt, the way her pulse jumped beneath my fingertips.

For a second, she just stared at me, like she wasn't sure if she had heard me right. Like she wasn't sure if she could believe it.

And then—

"I love you too."

The words came quiet but steady, carrying years of weight, of loss, of everything we had built and destroyed and built again.

And suddenly, none of it—the FBI, Nate, the war waiting for us outside this room—none of it mattered as much as this.

As her.

Her hands slid up my chest, over my shoulders, pulling me back in, kissing me like she needed to memorize it. Like she needed to feel it, to make sure this moment was real.

I let her.

I let myself have this—just for a second.

Because no matter what came next, no matter how many battles we still had to fight, I had just won the most important one.

And I wasn't going to lose her again.

"Tell me what's wrong," she whispered against my lips, her voice softer now, but laced with the steel that made her her.

I swallowed hard.

Reality came rushing back.

And I had to tell her.

I exhaled, letting my hands drop to my sides. "I saw Nate today."

That got her attention. Her expression sharpened, the warmth in her eyes flickering into something more guarded.

"And?"

I hesitated. "He knows everything."

The words hung between us, heavy and irreversible.

Alessandra didn't flinch, but her posture shifted, tension creeping into her frame. "How much is everything?"

"Enough. More than I'd like." I ran a hand through my hair. "He pulled records after the story broke. Connected the dots. And now he's giving me an ultimatum."

Her jaw tightened. "Which is?"

"Help the FBI take down the Navarras or go down with them."

A beat of silence.

Then—her eyes darkened, a slow inhale expanding her ribs. "And what did you tell him?"

"No."

Her gaze flickered, just for a second.

Like maybe she hadn't expected me to say it so easily.

"I told him no," I repeated, stepping closer. "I told him I was with you."

She tilted her chin up slightly, studying me. "Even knowing what that means?"

"Especially knowing what that means."

A muscle feathered in her jaw, her throat working as she swallowed.

Then, slowly, she turned, taking a few steps away. I watched the rise and fall of her shoulders, the way she planted her hands on the desk, fingers pressing into the wood like she needed something to hold onto.

"Steven... this isn't going away." Her voice was quieter now, careful.

"I know."

"He's not going to stop just because you told him no. He's your brother. That means he's going to keep pushing. He's going to find another angle."

"I know."

"And you're still choosing this?"

I crossed the room, moving until I was behind her. Slowly, I wrapped my arms around her waist, pulling her back against my chest.

"Yes."

Her breath hitched, but she didn't resist. Didn't pull away.

I pressed a kiss to the side of her head, my lips lingering at her temple. "We'll figure this out. But we do it together."

She exhaled, her hands resting over mine now, gripping tightly.

"Together," she repeated, softer now.

We stood there like that for a while, the weight of the world pressing down on us, but neither of us willing to let go.

Then, finally, she pulled back, turning to face me.

"We have to be careful, Steven. No mistakes. No missteps."

"I know."

She nodded, more to herself than to me. Then, after a moment —"I need to think."

"Okay."

She hesitated. Then, softer, "Stay?"

I brushed a strand of hair behind her ear, nodding. "Yeah. I'll stay."

We didn't have all the answers.

We didn't know what was coming next.

But for tonight, we had this.

And for now, that was enough.

Chapter 51

The Smoking Gun

Alessandra

The last few days had been a blur of whispered conversations and calculated moves. Every step we took was a gamble, but for the first time, it felt like we were playing offense instead of scrambling for defense.

But we still didn't have a way out.

Not yet.

That thought was pounding at the back of my skull when it hit me.

I sat up abruptly from the couch in Alessandra's office, my heart kicking against my ribs. "The flash drive."

She looked up from her laptop, her sharp eyes narrowing. "What about it?"

I was already on my feet, searching my bag. "We never went through all of it. We got distracted by the hit list and Tucker's name, but there were other files—things we didn't take the time to read."

Alessandra stood immediately, already following my train of thought. "You think there's something else on it?"

I pulled the drive from my bag and turned it over in my fingers. "I know there is. Lorenzo hid this for a reason. If there's even a chance that something in here can shift the heat off us and onto someone else, we have to look."

She nodded, taking the flash drive and plugging it into her laptop. The room was completely silent except for the hum of the computer as the files loaded.

A long list of folders appeared on the screen.

Most of them were labeled in Lorenzo's usual cold, calculated way—single words that gave nothing away until you opened them.

OPERATIONS

CONTINGENCIES

FINANCIALS

ASSETS

ACTIVE TARGETS

We already knew what was inside that last one, and neither of us wanted to reopen it.

But then—

LEVERAGE

Alessandra and I exchanged a glance.

She clicked the folder.

Inside, a series of documents, spreadsheets, and encrypted files filled the screen. Dozens of names. Dates. Account numbers. Offshore holdings.

And then—

"TUCKER - PRIMARY"

Alessandra clicked it, and a series of scanned documents filled the screen.

Bank transfers. Large sums moving between shell companies, tracing back to accounts under Tucker's influence.

Photos. Tucker at private meetings with men who weren't just businessmen, but criminals—Navarra-affiliated associates, including some who were dead now.

Bribery agreements. Proof that Tucker hadn't just been turning a blind eye to organized crime—he had been an active participant.

Alessandra let out a slow breath. "This is enough to bury him."

I scrolled further.

And then—

FBI INTERNAL CORRUPTION - VERIFIED LIST

A knot tightened in my stomach as I clicked it open.

More names.

Agents. Federal prosecutors. A few judges.

But it wasn't just a list of dirty names.

There were payment records. Case files that had been deliberately buried. Internal memos about investigations that were never meant to see the light of day.

My chest tightened as I scrolled, my pulse hammering. "Jesus Christ."

Alessandra's voice was steady, but I could hear the weight behind it. "It's worse than we thought."

I clenched my jaw. "And Nate—he's been working with these people."

Her gaze snapped to mine.

"I don't mean he's compromised," I added quickly. "But if we have this list, that means someone else does too. And if Tucker leaked anything to the FBI, we don't know how much of the bureau is actually clean."

Alessandra's expression darkened. "You think he's in danger?"

I exhaled slowly, my fingers gripping the desk. "I don't know. But if Tucker's pulling strings, I can guarantee he's not doing it alone. And if Nate trusts the wrong people..."

I didn't finish the thought.

I didn't need to.

Alessandra shut the laptop. "We need to go to him."

I nodded.

Because this wasn't just about saving ourselves anymore.

This was about saving my brother, too.

Chapter 52

Taking a Risk

Steven

I sat in my car outside the meeting spot, my fingers tapping against the steering wheel in an uneven rhythm. The street was quiet, but it felt like it was holding its breath, like even the buildings around me knew that something was about to shift.

I hadn't spoken to Nate since our last conversation, and I wasn't sure how this was going to go.

Would he believe me?

Would he even listen?

Would he turn me in?

I exhaled, rolling my shoulders, trying to shake off the nerves crawling under my skin. It wasn't just my future riding on this. If Nate didn't listen, if he dismissed what I had to say, we wouldn't just be back to square one—we'd be out of moves entirely.

And if that happened?

I wasn't sure I could protect Alessandra.

A pair of headlights cut through the darkness, and my pulse

kicked up. I watched as Nate's car rolled into the lot and pulled up beside mine.

He got out a second later, looking exactly how I expected—exhausted, tense, but unreadable. His eyes swept over the lot before landing on me, his expression carefully neutral.

I climbed out of my car, the flash drive heavy in my pocket.

"Nate," I greeted, keeping my voice even.

"Steven," he said, his tone clipped, controlled. "This better be good."

I didn't waste time.

I pulled the flash drive from my pocket and held it out between us.

Nate's gaze flicked to it but made no move to take it. "What is it?"

"Proof," I said. "Tucker. Corruption inside the FBI. Bribery, offshore accounts, buried case files. It's all here."

For a second, he didn't react. He just stared at the drive like it might detonate in my hand. Then, slowly, he met my eyes again.

"And you just happened to find this?"

"In a hidden compartment in the Navarra estate," I admitted. "Lorenzo buried it. Maybe for leverage, maybe as insurance—but it's real. I had no idea how deep it went until we went through it."

Nate inhaled through his nose, finally reaching for the drive. He turned it over in his palm, inspecting it like he could see the weight of its contents just from holding it.

"How do I know this isn't Navarro manipulation?" he asked. "How do I know this isn't something you doctored to throw me off?"

"I didn't doctor anything," I said firmly. "I found it. I read it. And when I saw what was on it, I knew I had to bring it to you."

Nate exhaled, shaking his head slightly. "Steven, do you even realize what you're asking me to do?"

"I'm asking you to look at the truth," I said, stepping closer. "I know you, Nate. You swore an oath to protect people. If you open this, if you see what's in here, you'll realize that the people you think you're working alongside aren't all good guys. Some of them are just as bad as the criminals you're chasing."

His jaw clenched.

That had hit something.

He knew it, even if he didn't want to admit it yet.

"This doesn't clear you," he said after a pause. "Or the Navarras. If anything, it makes you look worse."

"I know that," I said, my voice low. "But you want to know why I brought it to you?"

His brows furrowed.

I took a step closer.

"Because I trust you," I said, the words thick in my throat. "Because I need someone who isn't on the take. I need someone who can do something with this. And because if Tucker gets away with this, if he keeps pulling the strings the way he has been, you and I both know that more innocent people are going to get hurt."

Something flickered in Nate's expression.

A crack in the solid wall of his resolve.

He was listening.

He just didn't want to be.

"You think this stops Tucker?" he asked, testing me.

"No," I admitted. "But it'll throw a spotlight on him. He can't operate in the dark if the whole world is watching."

Nate exhaled heavily, looking at the flash drive again.

"And what about you, Steven?" His voice dropped slightly. "Where does this leave you?"

I swallowed.

He wasn't just asking about the investigation.

He was asking about Alessandra.

About us.

I held his gaze, knowing I couldn't lie to him.

"You already know the answer to that," I said quietly.

Nate's jaw tightened. "Yeah. I do."

Silence stretched between us.

Finally, he slid the flash drive into his pocket and took a step back toward his car. "I'll look at it," he said. "But I can't promise you anything."

"That's all I'm asking," I said.

But before he could turn away completely, I forced myself to say one last thing.

"Nate."

He paused.

"If you do this," I continued, "you're protecting more than just yourself. You're protecting Deena. Mom. Mitch. Everyone. But you're also giving me time to do what I need to do. And not all of that is going to line up with your badge."

His fingers twitched at his side, his whole body tense.

"You'll have to decide if you're willing to accept that," I finished.

Nate turned back to me, and for the first time, I saw it—the hesitation.

Not because he thought I was lying.

But because he already knew what his answer would be.

After a long moment, he said, "Just promise me one thing, Steven."

"Anything."

"If I do this—if I help you—don't make me regret it."

I met his eyes, steady and sure.

"I won't."

And I meant it.

He nodded once, then turned and got into his car.

As he pulled away, I watched his taillights disappear down the road, the weight of what we'd just set in motion settling deep in my bones.

Because this wasn't just about Tucker anymore.

This wasn't just about keeping ourselves out of prison.

It was time to fight.

Chapter 53

A Rising Tide

Steven

I tried to focus in the meeting Alessandra was leading, but my mind was a thousand miles away.

The voices around me—Nico's low, methodical breakdown of Vito's movements, Alessandra's razor-sharp strategy—blurred into background noise. I should have been engaged. This was our fight. Our war. But all I could think about was Nate.

He had the flash drive.

He was probably going through it right now, sifting through secrets that could ruin men and expose the corruption woven deep into this city. He had the power to end this—or to end me.

Would he see it the way I did? Or would he see my name tangled in the mess and decide I was too far gone to save?

My stomach twisted.

I forced myself to sit through the rest of the meeting, nodding at the right moments, adding a comment where I was expected to. But my mind was fractured, spiraling down paths I couldn't control.

When it finally ended, I didn't wait around.

I disappeared into the gym, pushing my body harder than I had in weeks. It wasn't enough. The restless energy didn't leave me, so I spent an hour walking the property, watching the sunset stretch long shadows across the courtyard. Still, the weight didn't lift.

I ended up in the library, pacing the same stretch of floor over and over, my fingers brushing against the spines of books I wasn't reading. Every time my phone vibrated, I snatched it up, only to feel my stomach drop when it wasn't Nate.

By the time hunger finally hit me, the estate was dark. I had no idea how much time had passed.

Had Alessandra eaten?

That thought pulled me out of my head long enough to push me toward her office.

When I found her, she was exactly where I expected—behind her desk, her laptop casting a glow against the sharp angles of her face. She was scanning a document, her fingers idly twisting the ring on her left hand, a habit I'd picked up on when she was deep in thought.

She looked up as I entered, her gaze sweeping over me, instantly reading the tension in my shoulders.

"There you are," she said, voice even but tinged with concern.

I leaned against the doorframe, rubbing the back of my neck. "Yeah. I kind of lost myself today."

Alessandra studied me for a moment before nodding toward the chair across from her. "Come in."

I stepped inside, closing the door behind me. "How's it going?"

"Busy," she said, leaning back in her chair. "Vito's been quiet. Too quiet. Nico's been gathering intel, but we're still in the dark. And Tucker—" Her expression darkened. "We can't ignore him. He's more dangerous now than when this started."

I moved closer, bracing my hands on the edge of her desk. "Nate has the flash drive."

Her fingers stilled against the keyboard.

I exhaled. "He's going through it now."

Something flickered across her face—relief, apprehension, something in between. "Do you trust him?"

"I do," I said immediately. Then, after a beat: "But it's not just about trust. If he sees what's on that drive, I think he'll do the right thing. I just don't know what he'll consider the right thing."

Alessandra nodded slowly, her gaze distant, calculating.

"We need to move quickly," she said, her voice harder now. "Tucker's going to panic once he realizes what we have. And Vito..." She sighed, rubbing her temple. "We need to figure out what he's planning before he makes his move."

I folded my arms, jaw tightening. "He's waiting. Biding his time. But we can't afford to wait. We need to go after Tucker first—expose everything before he can retaliate."

"Agreed," she said, meeting my eyes. "But we have to be smart. Vito will seize any opportunity to undermine us, and we can't give him one."

I let out a slow breath, nodding. "So we make Tucker the priority. Take the heat off us, put it on him."

She stood, moving around the desk until she was right in front of me. When she placed her hands on my arms, I finally exhaled, tension bleeding from my shoulders.

"We'll take them down," she murmured. "Tucker, Vito, all of them. We'll protect what's ours."

I reached up, cupping her face in my hands. "We will."

She nodded, eyes searching mine. But I saw it—the exhaustion creeping into the edges of her expression, the weight of everything pressing down on her.

I hesitated, then asked, "Have you eaten?"

She barely shook her head.

I held out my hand. "Come on. Let me feed you. We can figure out our next steps later."

A small, tired smile ghosted across her lips as she placed her hand in mine.

As we left the office, her fingers still tangled with mine, I glanced at her out of the corner of my eye. If this was all we ever had—this fragile peace between storms—I'd make sure it was enough.

For both of us.

Part Five

Wins and Losses

Chapter 54

A Great Sacrifice

Steven

The diner was a relic of another time. The kind of place where the coffee was strong, the jukebox never worked, and the smell of fried food clung to the walls. It had always been a quiet spot, the kind of place where you could have a conversation without worrying about who was listening.

Tonight, though, it felt like a trap.

The neon sign outside flickered weakly, casting a dull red glow across the parking lot. Inside, the only sounds were the faint hum of the refrigerator and the occasional clatter of dishes from the kitchen. There were no other customers—just us.

That wasn't an accident.

Nate was already there when we arrived, sitting in the back booth, a cup of coffee untouched in front of him. He barely glanced up as we approached, but when his gaze finally landed on Alessandra, there was no mistaking the tension behind it.

"Alessandra," he said, voice carefully controlled. "It's been a while."

His words were polite. His tone was not.

Alessandra didn't flinch. "It has."

That was all she gave him before sliding into the booth across from him. I sat beside her, tension knotting in my spine. I wasn't expecting a warm reunion, but I needed Nate to set his feelings aside —just for tonight.

Nate exhaled through his nose, eyes flicking toward Nico, who stood a few feet away near the entrance. "And him?"

I followed his gaze. Nico was scanning the room, his posture relaxed but his eyes sharp. He didn't like being in a place he couldn't control, and right now, neither did I.

"He's with us," I said. "We trust him."

Nate's jaw ticked. "That makes one of us."

Alessandra didn't let the comment slide. "Nico has done more to protect Steven than anyone else in this room."

"Right. And now he's here, playing bodyguard while we discuss taking down an entire branch of corruption in the FBI," Nate muttered, shaking his head. "Great company you keep, Steven."

I gritted my teeth. "Are we really gonna do this, or are you just here to lecture me?"

Nate leaned forward, resting his arms on the table. "That depends. Are you here to be smart, or are you about to do something that gets us all killed?"

Before he could press, the waitress appeared, setting down the drinks we had ordered earlier—a black coffee for Nate, a tea for Alessandra, and water for me.

"You boys need anything else?" she asked, popping her gum.

"We're good, thanks," I said.

She nodded and wiped her hands on her apron. "Alright, I'm taking my break. Holler if you need me."

With that, she disappeared into the back, leaving the place entirely to us.

Alessandra and I exchanged a glance. I could feel the tension rolling off her, but she kept herself composed.

"You have the evidence," I said, cutting through the hostility. "You have everything we need to take Tucker down. Did you open the flash drive? What did you think?"

Nate hesitated, his fingers tightening slightly around the coffee cup. Then he leaned back, exhaling slowly.

"It's solid," he admitted. "But it's dangerous. If even half of what's on that drive is true, we're not just looking at Tucker—we're looking at a systemic cleanup that goes way deeper than one corrupt senator."

"Which means?" Alessandra pressed.

Nate hesitated, then his voice dropped. "It means this doesn't just go away, Steven. It means the FBI won't just be looking at Tucker—they'll be looking at the Navarras. At you. At her."

Alessandra's expression stayed neutral, but I saw the way her fingers curled slightly against the table. "Then we make sure they have bigger targets," she said simply.

Nate studied her for a long moment. "You really think you can walk away from this clean?"

She didn't answer right away. Then, "I think we can walk away alive. That's the priority right now, isn't it?"

Nate sighed, rubbing a hand over his face. "I don't like this. But I don't see another way."

"You don't have to like it," I said. "You just have to help us finish it."

Nate exhaled sharply. "Fine. But we need to move carefully. If Tucker catches wind of this before we're ready, he'll come down on you with everything he has."

"Then we don't give him the chance," Alessandra said.

We spent the next hour going over the details, refining the plan, and discussing contingencies. Nico stayed nearby, keeping an eye on the parking lot through the diner's front windows, but never intruding on our conversation. His presence was a reminder that, despite the relative calm, we were still in the crosshairs. As the meeting wrapped up, Nate stood, his demeanor still tense but slightly more relaxed.

"I'll contact you when I've set things in motion," he said, slipping the flash drive into his pocket. "But remember—if this goes sideways, I'm out."

"We understand," I said, standing as well. "We'll be ready."

Nate gave us a curt nod before heading toward the door.

And then, in a single breath, it all went to hell.

The first gunshot shattered the quiet.

"Down!" Nico's voice was sharp, cutting through the sudden explosion of sound.

Instinct took over. I grabbed Alessandra and yanked her down, shielding her with my body as another round of bullets tore through the diner windows. Glass shattered, raining down around us.

Nico had his gun out instantly, firing back as shadows moved outside. More shots rang out, the echo of them making it impossible to tell how many there were.

"Where's Nate?" I shouted, my pulse pounding.

"Here!" came his voice, closer than I expected. I turned in time to see him crouched behind the counter, his own weapon drawn. "They're flanking the lot!"

Another shot rang out, and this time, I saw the impact.

Nico staggered.

It was like the world slowed down.

His body jerked back as the bullet tore into his chest. He stumbled against the car just outside, gripping his side, his gun slipping slightly in his grasp. He managed to fire off one last shot—then his knees buckled.

"Nico!" Alessandra screamed, breaking from my grip.

I moved fast, lunging after her, but she was already scrambling toward him. I got to Nico first, catching him before he collapsed fully. His breathing was shallow, blood seeping through his fingers where he clutched his wound.

"Nico, stay with me," I said, my voice shaking.

He tried to smirk, but it came out weak. "Been... through worse..."

"No, you haven't."

Alessandra was kneeling beside us, her hands pressing against the wound, but there was too much blood. Too much, too fast.

"Hold on," she whispered, voice raw. "You hold on, please—"

His fingers twitched, barely brushing hers. Then his hand fell still.

Alessandra let out a sound that tore through me.

A sob. Broken.

I barely had time to process before Nate grabbed my shoulder. "We have to move—now!"

I snapped back into reality. Gunfire was still raining down. We were outnumbered. If we didn't leave now, we'd be joining Nico.

I grabbed Alessandra's arm. She didn't move.

"Alessandra, we have to go," I said, trying to keep my voice steady.

She wasn't listening. Her hand was still on Nico's chest, her breathing ragged.

"Alessandra!" I said again, this time rougher. "We need to leave, now."

Slowly, like she was dragging herself back to reality, she looked up at me. Her eyes were wet, but her jaw was clenched tight.

She nodded once.

I didn't give her time to second-guess. I pulled Nico's body into the backseat, my hands slick with blood. He wasn't cold yet. It was all too fresh.

I slammed the door shut.

"Go!" Nate shouted, covering us as we dove into the car.

I tore out of the parking lot, the tires screeching against the pavement, gunfire still echoing behind us.

Alessandra sat beside me, staring straight ahead. Silent.

The city blurred past us, and I knew—this wasn't over.

This was war.

And we had just lost our first soldier.

Chapter 55

Grief and Revelations

Alessandra

The drive back to the estate stretched into forever. The city blurred past in streaks of neon and shadow, but I didn't really see it.

I didn't see anything.

All I saw was Nico, bleeding out in Steven's arms.

Nico, who had been there my whole life.

Nico, who had pulled me out of worse nights than I could count.

Nico, who had died protecting me.

The hum of the tires against the road faded beneath the roar in my head, a mix of grief and rage so suffocating I thought it might crush me.

I had seen death before.

I had caused death before.

I had pulled the trigger and ended my father's life without hesitation. I had buried enemies without a second thought. I had watched men bleed out on cold concrete, and I hadn't broken.

But this—this was different.

I should've seen it coming.

I should've known Vito wouldn't sit still forever.

I should've saved him.

Nico.

Someone I had never imagined a world without.

Steven's hand was tight around mine, his thumb brushing back and forth in slow, steady strokes. He didn't say anything. He didn't try to fill the silence with empty comfort or tell me everything would be okay.

Because it wasn't okay.

It might never be.

By the time we reached the estate, my body felt disconnected from my mind. Like I was floating somewhere outside of myself, watching as Steven led me inside, as the heavy front doors shut behind us, as the world kept moving when it should've stopped.

I barely noticed climbing the stairs, barely noticed the shift in lighting as we entered our bedroom. The only thing I was fully aware of was the empty space where Nico should have been.

Steven guided me toward the bathroom, his movements careful, patient. He turned on the faucet, filling the tub with steaming water, the scent of lavender drifting up as he poured something in.

I slid down the wall, watching him, but not really seeing him.

The reality of Nico's absence sat like a stone in my chest.

He was gone.

And I was still here.

My body trembled with the weight of grief. Steven turned to find me on the floor. Wordlessly he slid next to me and wrapped his arm around my shoulders and pulled me close.

The heat of his presence should have melted the ice in my veins, but it didn't. I had stood over my father's body and felt nothing. I had sent men to their deaths without hesitation. But this—this was grief I didn't know how to hold.

I stared at the opposite wall, unblinking.

Nico was dead.

I should've done more.

I failed him.

Steven's arm tightened around me. "You're shaking."

I hadn't even realized.

"I can't stop seeing it," I whispered.

He didn't ask what I meant. He already knew.

The gunfire.

The blood.

The way Nico's body jerked when the bullet hit.

The way his fingers twitched before they went still.

Steven pressed his lips to my temple. "You don't have to hold it in."

But I did. Because if I let go, I wasn't sure I'd come back.

I pressed harder against him, desperate for something to anchor me. "He was always there, Steven. Always." My voice cracked. "And now he's just... gone."

"I know," he murmured, holding me tighter.

The first tear slipped down my cheek. Then another. And then—

The dam broke.

The sobs came fast and violent, shaking my whole body, tearing from my throat like they had been waiting all night to be free. I clung to him, nails biting into his arm as the grief hit with the force of a tidal wave.

Steven held me through it, rubbing slow circles on my back, murmuring words I barely heard. I wasn't sure how long we stayed like that, me crying into his chest, him grounding me with nothing but his presence.

By the time the storm passed, exhaustion weighed down every part of me. I turned toward him. His eyes burned with love, with grief, with something heavier than I could name.

"I don't know how to keep going after this," I whispered.

"You don't have to do it alone," he said.

"I don't want to keep you at a distance anymore," I confessed. "I love you. I want us—not just in pieces. All of it."

He kissed me then. Not with hunger. Not with desperation. With certainty. With promise.

"I love you too," he whispered back. I felt the truth in my bones.

We stayed on the floor for a long time, the silence wrapping around us, until at last I reached for his hand and laced my fingers through his. Together, we stood, unsteady but united, and walked toward the bedroom.

As we crossed the threshold, a sense of peace settled over me, a peace I hadn't felt in a long time. I turned to face him, my heart pounding with a mix of fear and anticipation. "Steven," I whispered, my voice trembling.

He stepped closer, his presence filling the room like a storm. His lips found mine in a kiss that was slow and deep, a promise wrapped in passion. For a long moment, we simply breathed together, foreheads pressed close, holding on as though the world might end if we let go.

"I would do anything for you. I would give up everything for you. I love you," he murmured, and I believed him. I always would.

That night, nothing else mattered—not the war outside, not the lies, not the shadows waiting for us at dawn. There was only us, clinging to the fragile truth we'd finally spoken aloud. For the first time in what felt like forever, I felt safe. Whole.

"Thank you," I whispered, my voice heavy with exhaustion and emotion. "For everything."

He pressed a kiss to the top of my head, his arms tightening around me. "Always," he whispered back, his voice filled with love. "I'm with you, Alessandra. Always."

As I drifted off to sleep, I knew that no matter what happened, no matter what challenges we faced, we would face them together. We had lost so much, but we had also found something in each other that was worth fighting for.

Chapter 56

Memorials and Manipulation

Alessandra

The day of Nico's funeral was gray and overcast, as if even the heavens were mourning his loss.

The estate was filled with mourners—men and women from all corners of the Cosa Nostra, all there to pay their respects to a man who had been a fixture in their world for decades.

I stood at the front of the room, my expression carefully controlled as I accepted their condolences. Some were genuine. Others were calculated, offered not out of grief, but obligation. In our world, even death was political.

Nico deserved better than this.

He had been more than just my consigliere. He had been a mentor, a protector. A piece of my past that I had foolishly believed would always be there.

Now he was gone.

And I was still here.

A hand on my back grounded me. Steven. Silent and steady beside me, offering his presence as a shield, a tether. I leaned into it slightly, but my body remained rigid. If I let myself soften, if I let myself grieve openly, I wasn't sure I would be able to stop.

A few feet away, Salvatore stood with his arms crossed, his eyes scanning the room with the practiced vigilance of a man who had seen too much bloodshed. I caught his gaze, and in it, I saw my own reflection—rage barely concealed beneath mourning black.

We were all thinking the same thing.

This wasn't over.

The man responsible was still breathing.

I forced myself to focus as the last of the mourners passed, each touch of their hands on mine feeling distant, detached. The weight of the day pressed down on me, suffocating. I longed for solitude, for the moment I could finally allow myself to feel the loss, to break beneath it.

But there was no time for that.

Not yet.

Not when Vito Valenti was still circling like the vulture he was.

Steven's voice cut through my thoughts. Low, controlled. "Alessandra, someone's approaching."

I knew before I turned.

Vito.

His presence felt like a sickness infecting the air, a slow, creeping rot that settled into the bones.

Dressed in a sharp black suit, he moved through the crowd with calculated ease, his expression appropriately somber, his movements respectful. But I knew better than to trust appearances.

Vito was a viper wrapped in silk.

And today, he had slithered into my home.

Salvatore tensed, his hand moving subtly to the inside of his jacket. I barely shook my head. Not here. Not now.

Vito reached us, offering a small nod before speaking.

"Alessandra," he said, his voice smooth as ever. "My deepest condolences. Nico was a good man. A loyal man."

I let the words hang in the air for a beat before responding. "He was."

He shifted his gaze to Steven, and I felt rather than saw the way my husband's shoulders squared beneath the scrutiny.

Vito smiled, thin and unreadable. "And you must be the husband I've heard so much about. Steven, isn't it?"

Steven didn't waver. "That's right."

Vito's eyes narrowed slightly. Studying. Calculating. I could practically hear the gears turning in his head, weighing Steven in his mind.

Then, casually, as if commenting on the weather—"I've been hearing a lot about you lately. Seems you've been quite busy."

Steven's jaw clenched, but he didn't take the bait.

I did.

"Is there something you want, Vito?" I asked, my voice clipped. "Or are you just here to disrupt my mourning?"

He feigned a look of offense. "Alessandra, please. I would never disrespect the dead. I came to offer my help."

Help.

I already knew where this was going.

Still, I played along. "Help with what, exactly?"

Vito exhaled slowly, like he was some benevolent man forced to explain something obvious. "I know you've been under a lot of pressure lately. The FBI breathing down your neck, the weight of the Navarra empire on your shoulders. It's a lot for one woman to handle."

His voice softened, almost pitying. "I thought I might be able to take some of that burden off your hands."

The air in the room shifted.

I stiffened. "And what would that cost me?"

He tilted his head slightly, feigning innocence. "Cost? Why, Alessandra, I'm simply offering to take those troublesome territories off your hands. You've got enough on your plate without having to worry about managing all that real estate. Think of it as a gesture of goodwill."

I felt the way Steven tensed beside me.

Felt the heat of his anger.

Felt my own fury rise beneath my skin.

Nico's body wasn't even cold, and this bastard was already circling like a predator, trying to take what was mine.

He thought I was weak.

He thought Nico's death had broken me.

He was wrong.

I forced a slow breath, keeping my expression carefully neutral. "You can keep your goodwill, Vito." My voice was like ice. "Those territories are staying with the Navarras. And if you think you can use Nico's death as leverage, you're more of a fool than I thought."

For the first time, his mask slipped.

Just for a second.

The polite indifference wavered. A flicker of irritation. Of anger. Of something ugly lurking beneath his carefully constructed exterior.

Then—just as quickly—it was gone.

His smile returned, sharp and insincere. "Very well," he murmured. "But remember, Alessandra, I offered you a way out."

His gaze flicked to Steven. "Don't come crying to me when you find yourselves trapped with no escape."

The words crawled down my spine.

I didn't react. Didn't flinch.

I just watched as he turned, walking back through the room, disappearing into the sea of mourners.

Only when he was out of sight did I let my fists unclench.

Steven shifted beside me. "He's going to make a move soon."

I exhaled through my nose. "I know."

He hesitated. Then, quietly—"Are you okay?"

I turned to him, meeting his gaze. "Not yet."

He nodded, understanding more than I could ever put into words.

I looked back at the crowd, my mind already moving ahead, already planning.

Vito had made his move.

Now it was my turn.

And this time, I wasn't just defending what was mine.

I was going to destroy him.

Chapter 57

Connecting Dots

Steven

The day after Nico's funeral, the world felt wrong. The grief sat heavy in my chest, but I couldn't let it slow me down. We didn't have that luxury.

Not with Vito tightening his grip.

Not with Doug still out there, running scared.

I had let him off too easy the first time. I wouldn't make that mistake again.

Doug had published a story designed to burn down the Navarra family, and Vito had made sure he was holding the match. That much I knew. But I needed details—who gave him the information, what promises were made, and how deep he was in.

And if Doug had more to lose than just his career?

Even better.

I called him just after noon. "Doug. It's Steven. We need to talk."

A hesitation. Then, "Steven—look, man, if this is about the article—"

"It is," I cut in. "Where are you?"

Doug exhaled sharply, like he'd been hoping to avoid this conversation altogether. "Deli by the office."

"I'm on my way."

He was already at a table when I walked in, hunched over a coffee cup, his knee bouncing under the table. His eyes darted toward me as I approached. Nervous. Good.

I sat across from him, not bothering with small talk.

"Are you ready to tell me why you really ran my story under your name?" I asked, keeping my tone even.

Doug stiffened. "It wasn't your story," he muttered, but the way he said it lacked conviction.

I leaned forward. "It was my research, my notes, my investigation. You took it, Doug. And now I need to know why."

Doug shifted uncomfortably. "Look, I didn't steal anything, alright? The story was dead in the water. You ghosted. Your editor handed it off, figured I could do something with it."

"That right?" I said, tilting my head slightly. "Because I'm having a hard time believing you just happened to dust off my work and drop it at the exact moment Vito Valenti needed someone to set fire to the Navarra name."

Doug's throat bobbed as he swallowed. His hands clenched around his coffee cup. "Steven—"

"Who gave it to you?" I interrupted. "Who told you to run it?"

Doug's knee was bouncing faster now, his fingers tightening. "I told you, it came from the editor."

I stared at him, letting the silence stretch. Then I leaned in, lowering my voice.

"No, Doug. Someone made sure you ran it. Someone made sure it hit at the worst possible time for the Navarras. And you were either too greedy or too stupid to ask why."

His jaw twitched. He didn't like that.

Good.

"Was it Vito?" I pressed, my voice dropping lower, sharper.

Doug's eyes darted around the deli. He was unraveling.

"Steven, you don't get it," he said, his voice barely above a whisper. "I didn't have a choice."

I scoffed. "There's always a choice, Doug."

"No, there's not," he snapped. "You don't say no to a guy like Vito Valenti. You don't tell him you're not interested in a career-making story. You don't just walk away."

His breathing was shallow now. He was spiraling, panicking. I needed to push him further.

I leaned back in my seat, my tone almost casual. "And what happens when Vito's done with you? You think he'll just let you walk?"

Doug's face paled.

Yeah. He'd thought about that.

I nodded slowly. "You're in the deep end, Doug. You don't even see the bottom."

He rubbed a hand over his face, looking exhausted. "Steven... what do I do?"

I let that sit between us for a second. Let him feel how little control he had left.

Then I spoke.

"You cut ties. No more favors. No more stories. You disappear from his radar."

Doug let out a shaky breath. "I can't just—"

"Yes, you can," I said. "And you will. Because if you don't, Vito won't be your biggest problem."

I didn't blink. Didn't break eye contact.

Doug swallowed hard.

"...Okay," he muttered. "I get it."

No, he didn't. Not yet.

But he would.

He nodded, eyes flicking up at me, still wide with fear.

Then, just as I turned to leave, he spoke.

"He's planning something," Doug blurted out, voice tight.

I froze, then slowly turned back. "What did you say?"

Doug licked his lips, looking like he already regretted saying anything. But the fear in his eyes wasn't just for himself anymore.

"He said things are about to change," Doug muttered. "That the Navarras were living on borrowed time. And that when the dust settles, he's going to be the one left standing."

My pulse hammered against my ribs.

Vito wasn't just causing chaos. He wasn't just undermining Alessandra.

He was preparing to take everything.

I yanked out my phone the second I stepped outside, dialing Alessandra. She answered immediately.

"Steven?"

"I just talked to Doug," I said, keeping my voice low. "Vito's definitely behind the story. He's using Doug to stir the pot. But that's not the worst part."

A pause. Then, "Go on."

I exhaled. "Doug said Vito told him that things are about to change. That the Navarras were living on borrowed time."

Silence.

Then—Alessandra's voice, measured but tense. "Did he say when?"

"No," I admitted. "Just that when the dust settles, Vito's going to be the one left standing."

Another pause, this one heavier. Then, her voice sharpened. "Then we don't have much time."

"We need to figure out his timeline," I said. "And his next move."

"I'll talk to Salvatore," she said. "See what intel we can pull together."

I took a breath, nodding. "I'll be home soon."

She hesitated. Then, softer—"I love you."

"I love you, too," I told her.

I ended the call and slipped the phone back into my pocket.

Vito had been playing a long game. But now, so were we.

Chapter 58

Betrayal

Steven

I was scanning my emails when my phone buzzed with a message from Doug.

> Need to talk. Urgent. Meet at the old factory. Alone.

The old factory was a place I had taken sources before—people who didn't want to be seen talking to a journalist. It was isolated, abandoned, a perfect place for a conversation that needed to stay off the radar.

Or for an ambush.

I sat in my parked car, fingers tapping against the steering wheel as I weighed my options. Doug was desperate—I had seen it in his eyes last time we talked. But desperation made people unpredictable. He could be trying to fix his mistakes. Or he could be setting me up.

I considered calling Alessandra, or Nate, but if Doug really did have something to say, bringing in backup might spook him. I needed him to talk. And if this was a trap? I'd handle it.

I typed out a reply.

On my way.

The drive felt longer than it should have. My mind raced through all the ways this meeting could go wrong. Doug's message had set off alarm bells, but if there was any chance of getting something useful out of him, I had to take it.

I parked my car a block away, slipping through the shadows until I reached the entrance. The factory was a hulking, dilapidated building—its windows shattered, walls covered in graffiti, and the smell of decay thick in the air. It was the perfect place for secrets, and for traps.

I pushed open the rusted door, stepping into the cavernous space inside. Dust motes floated in the weak shafts of light streaming through the broken windows. The place was as empty and desolate as I remembered, except for the man pacing near the center of the room.

Doug.

He looked worse than the last time I'd seen him—dark circles under his eyes, his hair disheveled, and a nervous energy that practically radiated off him. He jumped when he saw me, then quickly composed himself, trying to play it cool.

"Steven," he greeted me, his voice tense.

"Doug," I replied, keeping my distance. "What's so urgent?"

He ran a hand through his hair, his eyes darting around the room as if expecting someone to jump out of the shadows. "Look, man, I'm in over my head here. I didn't want any part of this, but... I didn't have a choice."

The unease in my gut tightened into a knot. "What do you mean?"

Doug hesitated, and for a moment, I thought he might bolt. He swallowed hard, looking like he was about to be sick.

A sense of dread washed over me, but before I could respond, the door behind me creaked open, and the sound of heavy footsteps echoed through the factory. I turned just in time to see a group of men—Vito's enforcers—emerged from the shadows, guns drawn and aimed at my chest.

"Doug, what is this?" I hissed, stepping back instinctively.

Doug's face twisted in guilt and fear. "I'm sorry, Steven. I didn't want to do this, but he... he promised he'd let me go if I delivered you."

My blood ran cold. "You've made a huge mistake, Doug."

But Doug didn't respond, too afraid to meet my eyes as the enforcers closed in. One of them grabbed my arm, yanking it behind my back and forcing me to my knees. Another kicked my legs out from under me, and I hit the ground hard, pain shooting through my ribs.

Vito's men quickly restrained me, tying my hands and shoving a gag into my mouth. I struggled against them, but it was no use. They were too strong, too well-trained.

As they dragged me toward the door, Doug stood frozen, watching with wide eyes. "Steven... I'm sorry," he whispered, but his words felt hollow.

I tried to shout, to warn him that Vito wouldn't keep his promise, but the gag muffled my voice.

One of the men grabbed my hair, yanking my head back so I was forced to look at him. "Enough talking."

The last thing I saw before being shoved into the back of a van was Doug's pale, terrified face.

Then—darkness.

A sharp, brutal impact.

And everything faded.

The world came back in pieces.

A dull ache in my skull.

The distant hum of voices.

The sting of a fresh cut across my cheek.

I cracked my eyes open, my vision blurry, my head pounding. The air was thick with mildew and something metallic—blood.

My blood.

A dim light flickered above me, casting long, jagged shadows across the room. I was tied to a chair, my wrists bound, my body aching.

And then—

A voice.

Smooth. Amused.

"Well, well."

Vito Valenti stepped into view, adjusting the cuffs of his suit jacket like this was some kind of business meeting.

"Look who finally decided to wake up."

I swallowed the coppery taste in my mouth and forced myself to meet his gaze.

Vito smiled. "You're a tough guy, I'll give you that." He reached into his pocket, pulling out a knife. "But tough only gets you so far."

He crouched in front of me, the blade glinting as he dragged it lightly down my cheek. Just enough pressure to draw a thin, stinging line of blood.

I clenched my jaw, refusing to flinch.

Vito sighed. "See, Steven, I have a problem. Your wife—the lovely Donna—she doesn't seem to understand how things work." He twirled the knife lazily between his fingers. "She's been trying so hard to hold on, but we both know she's running out of time."

I glared at him.

He grinned. "Oh, don't worry. I'm not going to kill you. That'd be too easy. No, I need you alive."

The knife pressed just beneath my jaw, and for the first time, I saw it in his eyes.

Enjoyment.

Control.

Power.

He leaned in close, his voice dropping to a whisper.

"I need her to break."

The words sent a cold chill through me.

He wasn't going to kill me.

He was going to use me.

Vito smiled again, tapping the flat of the knife against my cheek before standing. "Get comfortable," he said, turning toward the door. "You're not going anywhere."

The door slammed shut, and I was alone.

Bleeding.

Bound.

And knowing, with absolute certainty—

That Alessandra would never stop until she burned this entire empire to the ground.

Chapter 59

This is War

Alessandra

The world had been unsteady since Nico died, but now it felt like it was tilting violently beneath me, threatening to throw me into the abyss.

Steven was missing.

And I knew exactly who had him.

I stood in my bedroom, my fingers curled around the edge of the dresser, gripping the wood so tightly my knuckles ached. The room was dark except for the glow of the bedside lamp, its soft light doing nothing to chase away the storm brewing inside me.

I had been waiting for my phone to ring for hours, but I already knew—Steven wasn't going to walk through that door. Not unless I dragged him back myself.

My pulse was slow, steady, controlled—but beneath that, a fire was burning, scorching away everything except the singular thought that pulsed in my veins like a war drum:

Vito took him.

Vito took him.

Vito took him.

A sharp knock on the door broke the silence.

I turned, my face already schooled into something unreadable. Salvatore stepped inside, his expression grim. "We have confirmation." His voice was flat, but his eyes burned with the same fury I felt. "Doug led him into a trap. Vito's men took him."

The air in the room seemed to shift, pulling tight around me like a noose.

For one long, fragile moment, I felt something crack inside me.

And then—

It hardened.

The grief. The fear. The doubt.

All of it turned to steel.

I straightened, smoothing my hands down the silk of my blouse, the movement slow, deliberate. My heart was a steady, measured beat in my chest.

"Where?" I asked.

Salvatore hesitated, just for a second. "A warehouse outside the city. He's keeping it quiet, but our contacts say he's planning something."

Of course, he was.

Vito didn't just want to kill Steven.

He wanted to use him.

To send me a message. To break me.

I turned toward the closet, pushing past the gowns and heels, reaching for what I really needed. The cold weight of my gun settled into my palm, its presence grounding me. I checked the magazine—full—before securing it at my hip.

Then, I reached for the knife.

The one my father had given me. The one I had used to slit a man's throat when I was twenty-one. The one that reminded me who I was.

Steven had seen the softness in me, had helped me find it again.

But tonight, there was no softness left.

Only sharpened edges.

I turned back to Salvatore. "Call the captains. We meet in twenty minutes."

The men were already gathered by the time I entered the study. They stood when I walked in, their eyes filled with expectation, with tension, with something that bordered on doubt.

Nico's absence was a phantom in the room.

But I was still here.

And tonight, I would remind them who I was.

I took my seat at the head of the table, fingers drumming once against the wood before I spoke.

"Steven is in Vito's hands." My voice was calm. Controlled. "We're getting him back."

Silence.

Then, one of the captains—Angelo, the youngest of them—spoke. "With respect, Donna... Vito has been setting this up for weeks. He wouldn't take your husband unless he was prepared for retaliation."

I tilted my head slightly. "Are you suggesting we don't retaliate?"

Angelo hesitated. "I'm saying he's expecting it. And if we walk into a trap—"

"We are walking into a trap." I leaned forward, letting the weight of my words sink into them. "But the difference between us and Vito is that he thinks we'll fight like prey."

I let that sit.

Then I smiled. Cold. Sharp.

"We are not prey."

That was all it took. The hesitation in the room dissolved, replaced by something sharper.

Resolve.

Loyalty.

Vengeance.

Salvatore stood. "The Donna is right. Vito thinks he's in control. That means he's underestimating us."

The captains murmured their agreement, their doubt hardening into purpose.

"We go in fast, we go in clean," I continued. "We take back what's ours. And when it's over, we burn Vito's empire to the ground."

No one argued.

Because they knew.

This wasn't just about Steven.

I was strapping a knife to my thigh when my phone rang.

I didn't even look at the screen before answering.

"Alessandra," Nate's voice came through, tight with something between frustration and concern. "Tell me you're not about to do something insane."

I let out a humorless laugh. "Define insane."

"Your men have been moving for the past hour. You're mobilizing for a fight."

I didn't confirm it. I didn't have to.

"Where's Steven?" he demanded.

"In Vito's hands."

A heavy pause.

Then—"Alessandra, listen to me. If you go in guns blazing, you're giving the Feds everything they need to shut you down."

I let out a slow exhale, pinching the bridge of my nose. "Steven is being held hostage, Nate. If you're calling to tell me to stand down, don't waste your breath."

He cursed under his breath. "Seriously, Alessandra."

I softened—just for a second. "I'm getting him back, Nate."

A pause.

Then—his voice, quieter. "Do you even have a plan?"

I smiled, sharp as a blade.

"Oh, I have several."

He exhaled roughly. "I can't help you."

I expected that.

But then—

"But I can keep certain people out of your way for a few hours."

I blinked.

A gift.

Not much. But enough.

"I'll take it," I murmured.

There was a beat of silence. Then, softer—

"Bring him home, Alessandra."

The night was thick with silence as we pulled up to the warehouse. The air smelled like rust and gasoline, heavy with the promise of blood.

I stepped out of the car, Salvatore beside me, the weight of my gun steady against my hip.

I exhaled.

Vito had made a mistake.

He thought he had taken something from me.

But he had only given me one more reason to end him.

I lifted my chin, voice steady as I gave the order.

"We go in quiet. We come out with Steven." My eyes darkened. "And we leave nothing standing."

The men nodded.

I took one last breath.

Then—

We moved.

Straight into the fire.

Chapter 60

Just Survive

Alessandra

The air smelled like rust and mildew.

Gunfire cracked through the night, sharp bursts echoing off the metal walls of the warehouse. We moved like shadows, quick and merciless, cutting down Vito's men with the precision of people who had been fighting wars long before tonight.

But I didn't care about the fight.

I only cared about him.

Salvatore was at my side, his movements as controlled as ever, but I could feel his urgency. He knew as well as I did—every second counted.

I wasn't letting Vito take anything else from me.

We pushed through another hallway, my boots slick with blood I didn't have time to acknowledge. My breathing was even, my hands steady, but inside—inside, I was coming undone.

Then we reached the door.

Heavy. Reinforced. Locked from the inside.

Salvatore exchanged a glance with me, already knowing. No words needed.

One. Two.

He slammed his weight into it. The wood groaned.

Again.

A sickening crack.

The door buckled.

I was through before the splinters settled, my gun raised—

And then I saw him.

Steven.

Tied to a chair, his head slumped forward, a fresh cut bleeding down the side of his face. The dim light cast harsh shadows over his body, highlighting every bruise, every mark.

My vision blurred at the edges, but I didn't let myself stop moving.

"Steven!" My voice cracked.

He stirred, groggy, his head rolling slightly before his eyes opened—blue, hazy with pain but alive.

His gaze locked onto mine, and for a second—just a second—relief flickered there.

"Alessandra..." His voice was hoarse, barely audible.

I didn't realize I was shaking until my hands fumbled with the ropes at his wrists. My knife wasn't cutting fast enough. Every second that passed felt like an eternity.

He winced as I finally pulled the last restraint free, and when he tried to stand, his knees buckled.

I caught him.

He collapsed into me, his weight sending me stumbling back a step.

He was trembling. His breathing was ragged, uneven. His body sagged against mine, and I tightened my grip, trying to hold him up, hold him together.

Salvatore stepped closer. "We need to move."

Steven barely lifted his head. "M'fine," he mumbled, but he wasn't. His limbs weren't working properly.

"Steven, look at me," I said, gripping his jaw. His skin was clammy. His pupils blown. "What did they do to you?"

"Don't know." His words slurred slightly, and that terrified me more than the blood.

I clenched my jaw. Drugged. Vito hadn't just wanted to beat him —he wanted to break him.

I pressed my forehead against his for the briefest moment. "I've got you," I whispered.

Then I pulled back and shoved a pistol into his hand. "You're going to walk out of here with me, understand?"

His grip was weak, but he nodded. "With you."

We moved quickly, but Steven's steps were heavy. He leaned on me more than he should have, his breath labored. I kept my arm around his waist, keeping him steady.

Then—footsteps.

Salvatore tensed ahead of us. "They're coming."

Steven tightened his grip on the gun, blinking hard like he was trying to force himself to wake up.

We pressed against the wall as shadows stretched along the corridor.

Salvatore didn't wait.

The second Vito's men came into view, he fired.

The hallway erupted in violence.

Steven jerked at the sound, but he stayed standing. Barely. I turned, firing down the opposite side of the hall as more men flooded in.

Gunfire roared.

Steven fired, his shot going wide before he gritted his teeth and forced his body to obey. His second shot hit its mark, sending a man staggering back.

But he was losing time. His body was failing him.

Then—his legs gave out.

He collapsed, and I barely caught him before his head hit the floor.

Shit.

I dropped to my knees beside him, my hand on his cheek, tilting his face toward me. "Steven."

His eyelids were fluttering.

No, no, no.

He was not passing out.

I shook him roughly. "Stay with me."

A shuddering breath. His fingers twitched.

But he was slipping.

My panic turned to pure rage.

I wasn't losing him.

Not like this.

I gritted my teeth, pressing my back against the wall as another barrage of gunfire ripped through the hall.

Steven was slipping. His knees had buckled once already, and I knew he wouldn't stay on his feet much longer. His breathing was ragged, his grip on the gun in his hand growing looser by the second.

We need to move. Now.

"Salvatore!" I barked. "We have to get him out of here!"

Salvatore turned, took one look at Steven swaying, barely conscious, and didn't hesitate.

He shoved his gun into my hands. "Cover me."

I raised it instantly, squeezing the trigger the second another one of Vito's men rounded the corner. He dropped before he had a chance to fire, but I didn't have time to celebrate the shot.

Salvatore moved fast. He hooked Steven's arm over his shoulders and hauled him up, bearing most of his weight. Steven groaned, trying to stay upright, trying to fight, but his legs weren't cooperating.

"I've got him," Salvatore grunted. "You focus on getting us out."

I nodded, falling into step beside them. My heart pounded as we pushed toward the exit. The cold night air hit like a slap as we burst through the warehouse doors—

Only to be met with more of Vito's men.

Gunfire erupted again.

I dropped to one knee, taking aim, squeezing off a shot that sent one of them spinning to the ground.

Salvatore dragged Steven forward, shoving through the chaos as I covered them.

We were so close.

Then—more shots.

I didn't see where they came from, but I felt Steven jerk against Salvatore, heard his sharp intake of breath.

Adrenaline surged through me.

Salvatore cursed under his breath. "He's hit but still up—keep going!"

No. No, no, no.

Steven stumbled but stayed upright, his grip tightening on Salvatore. I saw the fresh blood soaking through his shirt, dark and spreading fast. If he fell now, he wasn't getting back up.

I moved fast, throwing the back door of the car open just as they reached it.

"Inside," I ordered.

Salvatore shoved Steven in first. He collapsed against the seat, his body done. I followed, slamming the door shut behind me.

Salvatore was in the driver's seat an instant later.

And then we were gone.

The estate was quiet when we arrived. Too quiet. The kind of quiet that pressed against my ribs like a warning.

Salvatore and I got Steven inside as fast as we could. He was barely conscious, his breathing ragged, his weight heavier by the second.

The doctor was waiting in the bedroom, already rolling up his sleeves. His eyes flicked to Steven's blood-soaked shirt.

"How bad?" I demanded.

"Get him down," the doctor said instead, all efficiency as he grabbed his bag.

Salvatore and I eased Steven onto the bed. He let out a low, pained groan, but his eyes barely fluttered.

Too weak. Too out of it.

The doctor yanked open Steven's shirt. The bullet wound was high in his shoulder, still bleeding sluggishly. The bruises and cuts littering his body made my stomach churn.

Drugged. Beaten. Shot.

I was going to kill Vito.

"I need fluids to counter whatever they gave him," the doctor muttered. "And I need to get the bullet out now."

Steven's body gave out then. His eyes slipped shut.

I stopped breathing.

"Steven—"

"He's stable," the doctor said quickly. "For now. But I need space to work."

Salvatore gripped my shoulder. "Let him do his job."

I didn't move. Not at first. My legs felt locked, my fists still clenched at my sides. But I couldn't just stand there while Steven was bleeding out in front of me.

Finally, I forced myself to let go of his hand.

"I'll be right outside," I said.

Steven didn't hear me.

But Vito would. When I came for him, he would know it. And I was going to destroy him.

Chapter 61

Strategic Advantage

Steven

The mornings had become a ritual.

It wasn't peaceful—not really. Not with the weight of everything looming over us. But for a few minutes each day, we tried.

The dining room was quiet except for the faint clink of silverware and the soft hum of conversation from the kitchen staff. Alessandra sat across from me, dressed in one of my button-downs over sleep shorts, her hair still a little messy from sleep. For a moment, she looked more like my wife than the Donna of a criminal empire.

She sipped her coffee, studying me over the rim of her cup. She did that a lot now. Checking. Making sure I was really here. That I hadn't disappeared into the dark places my mind kept trying to drag me.

I let her.

"I was thinking we could take the boat out this weekend," I said, keeping my voice even. "Get out of the city for a bit."

Alessandra arched an eyebrow, setting her mug down. "You want to take a vacation in the middle of a war?"

"A break," I corrected, cutting into my eggs. "A few hours on the water wouldn't kill us."

Her lips twitched, almost smiling. "I don't know. I think Vito might disagree."

I shrugged. "We won't invite him."

She huffed a quiet laugh, shaking her head. It wasn't much, but it was enough. Enough to remind me that not everything had to be about blood and strategy.

But then the moment ended.

The doors to the dining room opened, and Antonio stepped inside.

Alessandra's eyes snapped up immediately, any trace of softness disappearing as she straightened in her chair.

"Antonio," she greeted, setting her coffee down. "What is it?"

He approached quickly, his posture rigid, the set of his jaw tense. "Donna. Mr. Porter."

I exhaled slowly, already knowing whatever came next wasn't good.

Antonio didn't waste time. "Vito has been making moves," he said, his voice low and urgent. "Since the night Steven was rescued, he's been reaching out to the other families, trying to rally support."

Alessandra's lips pressed into a thin line, but she didn't look surprised. "We knew this was coming."

I nodded in agreement. We'd learned about Vito's attempts weeks ago from one of the families who had been loyal to Nico. But what we didn't know was whether or not he had succeeded in gaining their support.

Antonio hesitated. That pause told me everything.

I leaned forward, gripping my coffee cup a little tighter. "How many families have agreed to hear him out?"

"Three that we know of," Antonio admitted. "Maybe more. He's promising them a share of Navarra territories if they help take you down."

A sharp silence settled over the room.

Alessandra was the first to break it. "That's bold," she murmured, more to herself than to us. "Even for him."

I watched her carefully. She wasn't just angry. She was calculating.

She looked at Antonio. "And?"

He shifted slightly, his fingers flexing at his sides. "Some of our men have been approached."

My stomach dropped.

Antonio continued quickly. "But they didn't switch sides."

Alessandra's brows lifted slightly, intrigued. "Go on."

"They're feeding us intel from inside his camp."

I let out a slow breath, my mind already working through the implications. That meant we had eyes on Vito's operation—on his meetings, his movements. It was a dangerous game, but one that could finally give us an edge.

But I also knew what Alessandra was about to say before she even opened her mouth.

"I didn't authorize that," she said flatly.

Antonio dipped his head slightly in acknowledgment. "No, Donna. But the opportunity presented itself. These men didn't turn on us; they turned against him. They came to us after the first meeting, wanting to stay loyal."

Alessandra leaned back in her chair, considering.

I could see the war in her eyes. This kind of play was risky—too many things could go wrong. If Vito sniffed out the double agents, they wouldn't just be killed. They'd be made examples of. And if the information was unreliable, or worse, misleading, we'd be walking into a trap.

But... if it worked?

This could change everything.

I met her gaze, letting her see the same thoughts running through my mind.

Finally, she turned back to Antonio. "How do we know they aren't playing both sides?"

Antonio didn't flinch. "We've tested them. Sent them with false information, seen what made it back to Vito. The leaks only run one way."

She exhaled slowly, tapping her fingers against the table in thought.

I knew she was thinking about Nico—how he would have handled this. He had been cautious, deliberate, never one to trust easily.

But she wasn't just thinking about Nico. She was thinking about me.

Because the last time she'd hesitated, I had been taken.

"We use it," she finally said, her voice cool, detached. "But we control the narrative. No unnecessary risks."

Antonio nodded. "Understood."

"Salvatore needs to be briefed. I want a list of every meeting Vito has had with these families, every location, every name. If he's planning an attack, I want to know where and when before he makes his move."

"Yes, Donna," Antonio said before heading out.

The room was quiet again.

I exhaled and ran a hand through my hair. "That was a risk."

She looked at me. "You don't approve?"

I smiled faintly. "Did I say that?"

Alessandra studied me, then sighed, moving toward me. When she reached my chair, she placed a hand on my face, stroking it gently. "We're running out of time, Steven."

I covered her hand with mine. "I know."

She sighed, then leaned down slightly, pressing a kiss to my forehead. A soft, fleeting thing.

But enough.

Enough to remind me that no matter how much the world tried to tear us apart, we were still here.

Still fighting.

And we would fight until the bitter end.

Because Vito had already taken too much from us.

And we weren't going to let him take anything else.

Chapter 62

Inevitability

Alessandra

It had been nearly three months since Steven's abduction, and in that time, we had fortified, planned, and anticipated every possible way Vito might retaliate. The estate was more secure than it had ever been—security had doubled, surveillance had tripled, and alliances had been scrutinized down to the last detail.

And yet, despite everything, I felt like we were waiting for a storm that refused to break.

Salvatore entered my study without knocking, his expression unreadable but his presence alone enough to confirm what I already knew: there was news. Bad news.

"Doug Stapleton is dead," he said, his voice flat. "Found last night."

I barely blinked. The words didn't shock me. Doug had always been a loose thread, and Vito didn't leave those hanging for long.

"Cause?" I asked, even though I didn't need an answer.

"Two to the back of the head," Salvatore confirmed. "His body was dumped in an alley downtown."

A long silence stretched between us. Doug had been many things —an opportunist, a coward, and a liability—but above all, he had been useful. If nothing else, his death proved what we had already suspected. Vito was cleaning house, tying up loose ends. That meant he was preparing for something. Something big.

Salvatore shifted slightly. "It's a message, Donna. He's letting us know he's done playing."

I inhaled deeply, forcing calm into my voice. "Then we move before he does."

Salvatore gave a slight nod, already expecting the order. "We've been tracking his communications. Our men inside say he's still courting the other families, but the response has been mixed. Some are hesitant to get involved, especially with the losses he's already taken."

"Good," I said, but my tone was distant. Because it wasn't enough.

Hesitancy wasn't loyalty. If Vito gave them a better reason to join him—a promise of power, money, control—they would take it. We had to be smarter, faster.

I tapped my fingers against the desk, thinking. "What about his infrastructure? His supply chains, his enforcers—any signs of where he's making his next move?"

"Not yet," Salvatore admitted. "But we've been pulling pieces together. He's been moving cash in strange ways—short-term payoffs, bonuses for key men in his organization. He's consolidating."

A cold knot formed in my stomach. He's buying loyalty.

"Any shifts in leadership?" I asked.

Salvatore's expression darkened. "Yes. And that's the other reason I came to you." He hesitated, and that alone told me I wasn't going to like what he was about to say. "Vito's making overtures to men who were loyal to Nico."

I went still.

Betrayal in this life was inevitable, but the idea of men who had once served alongside Nico—who had once stood in my corner—now considering Vito's offer? That cut deep.

Steven walked in then, his gaze flicking between the two of us. He had the uncanny ability to read a room in seconds, and the tension in this one was thick. "What's going on?"

I looked at him. "Vito is getting bolder. He's not just rallying support—he's making moves on men we once trusted."

Steven's jaw tightened. He crossed his arms, his entire body tensing like he was ready for a fight right then and there. "And how many are listening?"

Salvatore hesitated. "Enough to be a problem."

Steven muttered a curse under his breath, running a hand through his hair. "Then we need to send a message of our own."

I nodded slowly. "Not just a message. A warning."

A silence stretched between us before I continued. "We don't wait for him to make the next move. We act first. Show these men that siding with him isn't an option. That they don't get to hesitate."

Salvatore gave me a knowing look. "You're thinking preemptive strikes."

"Yes," I said without hesitation. "We start cutting off his resources. Not just his supply lines, but his people. If he's consolidating power, then we take it from him piece by piece."

Steven studied me carefully. "You're talking about targeting multiple families."

"Yes."

A long silence. Then Steven exhaled slowly. "Alright," he said. "Then let's plan it right."

I met his gaze and nodded. Because this time, we weren't just going to defend ourselves.

We were going to finish this.

Chapter 63

The Weight of a Name

Alessandra

I could have walked away a long time ago.

That thought had lingered in my mind more than once—especially in the quiet moments with Steven, when the war outside these walls felt like it might finally end.

We could leave. Disappear. Let someone else take the reins of the Navarra empire while we carved out a life somewhere untouched by this world.

But I wouldn't.

Not because I wanted power. Not because I craved control.

Because if I left, the Navarra name would remain exactly what my father made it—a legacy of blood and corruption, whispered in fear and cursed in death.

And that? That was something I couldn't allow.

I wasn't fighting to keep the Navarra family on top. I was fighting to end it, to burn the rot out of its foundation so that when I finally did walk away, there wouldn't be anything left to pull us back in.

Steven understood that.

He never tried to convince me otherwise, never asked me to step aside and let someone else take over.

But I knew he thought about it.

I saw it in the way he looked at me when he thought I wasn't paying attention, in the way he held me a little tighter at night.

Because he wanted me safe. Because he wanted to believe there was a future beyond this.

And for the first time in a long time, I wanted that too.

A future where we weren't looking over our shoulders. Where we weren't defined by the weight of our pasts.

Where he wasn't Steven Porter and I wasn't Alessandra Navarra.

Because my name had put a target on his back. And his name? It could never truly be his again, not with the way it had been dragged into this war.

One day, we would leave it all behind. One day, we would decide on a name that was ours, not his, not mine—ours.

But not yet.

Not until Vito Valenti was dead.

The week following Antonio's intel was a slow, deliberate march toward war. I didn't rush. I didn't act on emotion. I planned. I mobilized. And when I struck, I would make sure no one doubted who was in control.

Vito had spent the last few months pulling other families into his orbit, using their greed and ambition to fuel his war. He thought sheer numbers would tip the balance in his favor. That was his mistake. Numbers meant nothing if morale was shattered, if fear outweighed loyalty.

I was going to make sure every family considering Vito's offer saw exactly what it cost.

So I studied them.

I had Salvatore work with our remaining loyal captains,

compiling a list of families who had either already aligned with Vito or were still deciding. Some were minor players looking to grab whatever scraps they could, while others had been close allies to the Navarras before my father's death. Their betrayal stung, but I wasn't naive enough to be surprised.

Betrayal was a currency in our world.

They had made their choice. Now, they would pay the price.

It started with the Santinos.

A mid-sized family, eager to prove their worth to Vito, they had been supplying him with weapons and manpower. They were also careless.

Two of their men were found floating in the Hudson, their bodies riddled with bullets and their mouths stuffed with severed fingers—theirs. The message was clear: talk too much, pledge your loyalty to the wrong man, and you lose more than just your life.

The Santinos responded exactly as I expected.

Paranoia spread like wildfire. They stopped all shipments to Vito, convinced they had a leak in their ranks.

They did.

The next day, their underboss was gunned down in broad daylight outside his mistress's apartment. Two shots to the head, two to the chest—quick, clean, efficient. The woman he'd been with fled the city within hours.

By the time the Santinos realized they were being systematically dismantled, it was too late.

They pulled back. Cut ties with Vito.

One down.

The DeLucas were harder to reach. They were smart, insulated, their hierarchy tight. But their weakness? Their money.

For decades, they had relied on a few key legitimate businesses to launder their cash—an import/export company, a chain of restaurants, a high-end real estate group.

I burned it all to the ground.

Figuratively, at least.

The city's financial crimes division suddenly found itself flooded with anonymous reports detailing tax fraud, shell companies, and offshore accounts linked to the DeLucas. Search warrants were issued. Assets frozen. Several high-ranking members were arrested.

In one week, I turned a thriving criminal enterprise into a bleeding carcass.

Vito had promised them power, but all they had now were empty accounts and legal battles.

They, too, cut ties.

The Marchesis were different.

Loyal to my father for years, they had only sided with Vito because they thought I was weak. That I wouldn't have the stomach to do what needed to be done.

I reminded them who I was.

Their eldest son, their heir, was found beaten and broken in his own home. Alive, but barely. My men left him breathing on purpose.

I wanted him to be able to tell his father what had happened.

To tell him that he had underestimated me.

To tell him that if he didn't sever ties with Vito immediately, his son's survival would be the last mercy I ever showed.

By morning, the Marchesis had publicly denounced Vito.

In one week, I cut three of Vito's strongest allies out from under him.

By the time the dust settled, every family still considering his offer saw the truth: siding with him meant suffering.

Some would hold out, of course. Some would stay loyal to him out of fear or pride. But others? They would hesitate.

And hesitation was all I needed.

The reports came in that night. Vito had called an emergency meeting. He was furious, demanding answers, scrambling to hold onto his coalition.

But there was another consequence.

Our double agents—every man we had planted inside his organization—were now in danger.

He would start hunting them.

I had anticipated that.

By dawn, they were recalled, every last one of them quietly disappearing back into our ranks before Vito could root them out.

The doors had officially closed.

This wasn't a war between families anymore.

It was just him and me.

Steven found me in my office the next morning.

He didn't ask what I had done. He already knew.

He stood in the doorway, arms crossed, watching me. "He'll retaliate."

I met his gaze without hesitation. "I'm counting on it."

His expression was unreadable for a long moment. Then, he stepped inside, coming around the desk until he was in front of me.

He reached out, brushing his fingers along my jaw. "You didn't sleep last night."

"I had things to take care of," I admitted.

His touch was warm, grounding. "Alessandra..."

"I won't let him take anything else from us," I whispered. "I won't."

Steven nodded. He understood. He always did.

"We'll be ready," he said, his voice sure.

I leaned into his touch, just for a moment. "Yes," I murmured. "We will."

Vito had made his move.

I'd made mine.

Chapter 64

Watching and Waiting

Alessandra

It had been quiet. Too quiet.

For the past two weeks, Vito hadn't moved. No retaliations. No counterstrikes. No desperate plays to rebuild what I had torn down. It was unnatural. Uncharacteristic. And it meant only one thing—he was planning something.

We were prepared for that.

I didn't let my guard down. My captains didn't let their men get comfortable. I wasn't arrogant enough to believe that three major blows were enough to cripple him completely. Vito Valenti was a survivor, a cockroach that could scuttle away when you thought you had him cornered.

But now? Now, there was nowhere left to run.

Steven and I were mid-conversation when Salvatore walked into my office.

The estate had been operating at full alert, men posted at every entrance, rotating shifts watching for even the slightest movement outside our walls. Still, Antonio moved with urgency, his expression carved from stone.

Steven clocked it first, lowering his coffee. "Tell me."

Salvatore nodded once, glancing at me before speaking. "Vito's coming."

Everything inside me went still.

Steven sat up straighter. "When?"

Salvatore hesitated.

I set my own mug down and leveled him with a look. "Tell me."

"Tonight," he said. "Late. He's bringing everything he has left. I don't know how he got so many men together so quickly, but the word is he's desperate. He knows you've been bleeding him out. He knows he won't last much longer if he doesn't hit back now."

I exhaled through my nose, my mind already sorting through contingencies.

Steven cursed under his breath. "Are we sure?"

Salvatore nodded. "Absolutely. One of the last agents we pulled out left behind a contact, someone deep in Vito's inner circle. They reached out this morning—this is it. Vito's throwing everything at us."

I leaned back in my chair, fingers drumming against the table.

I had been waiting for this.

I had wanted this.

Vito's biggest flaw had always been his belief that brute force would win him wars. That he could outgun, outmuscle, and outnumber anyone who stood in his way. And maybe that had been true once.

But not anymore.

I had spent months dismantling his network, breaking his alliances, turning his own men against him. And now, he was walking into this fight with more enemies than he realized.

Steven turned to me, watching, waiting.

I met his gaze. "We end this tonight."

He nodded. "Then let's get ready."

Chapter 65

No Matter What

Steven

The sense of unease had settled into my bones, heavy and unshakable. I felt it in the silence of the halls, in the way every man stationed at his post held himself just a little tighter, more alert. The estate had become a fortress, and yet, for all our preparation, it still didn't feel like enough.

Vito wasn't just coming for territory anymore. He was coming for blood.

I moved through the house, checking in with the men, making sure they knew their roles. It was second nature by now—knowing the weak spots, reinforcing them, anticipating every possible move. But my mind wasn't on the logistics.

It was on her.

Alessandra carried herself with the same quiet strength she always had, but I could see the weight of it pressing down on her. This wasn't just another battle for control; this was personal. Nico's death, my abduction—Vito had taken too much from her already, and now he was forcing her into a war that neither of us wanted but both of us knew was inevitable.

I stopped near one of the windows, looking out over the grounds. The estate was eerily still, the night thick with tension. I pulled out my phone, staring at the screen for a beat before dialing.

Nate answered on the first ring. "Steven." His voice was steady, but there was something under the surface. Something tight. "How's everything on your end?"

I'd called him almost immediately after the conversation with Salvatore.

"We're ready," I said, though the words felt flimsy. No one was ever truly ready for war. "But I need to know you're there, that when it starts, we're not alone."

There was a pause, then a quiet exhale. "You know I'm here," he said, though there was something unspoken in his tone. "But you also know what I can and can't do."

I closed my eyes for a second. Nate's hands were tied in ways mine weren't. He could only do so much without burning his entire career to the ground. I hated that it had to be this way, but I understood.

"Just... be ready," I said.

Another silence. Then, softer, "Steven... take care of yourself. And take care of her."

I swallowed hard. "I will."

We ended the call, and I stood there for a long moment, gripping the phone so tightly my knuckles ached.

Tomorrow, everything would change.

That evening, I found Alessandra in our room. She was by the window, the dim light casting long shadows against her skin. Her arms were crossed, but not out of defiance. It was a rare show of vulnerability—like she was holding herself together by sheer force of will.

She must have heard me come in because she turned, a small, tired smile pulling at her lips. "Hey."

I crossed the space between us, resting my hands on her waist. "Hey."

She leaned into me, just enough that I could feel the tension still locked in her muscles.

"How are you holding up?" I asked softly.

"I'm ready." She exhaled slowly, her fingers gripping the front of my shirt. "But that doesn't mean I like what's coming."

I cupped her face, my thumb tracing the edge of her cheekbone. "We'll get through this."

She let out a quiet laugh, but there was no humor in it. "You don't know that."

No, I didn't.

The truth sat heavy between us. The Navarra family had been at war before, but not like this. This wasn't just about control—it was about survival.

"I'm not losing you," she said, the words quiet but absolute.

"You won't," I replied, even though I knew it was a promise I had no right to make. But if this was the end, if tomorrow everything went to hell, I wasn't going to waste tonight.

She didn't argue, just pressed her forehead to my chest, her breath warm against my skin. I wrapped my arms around her, holding her as tightly as I could, like I could fuse us together if I tried hard enough. Her body molded against mine, every curve fitting perfectly against me as if we were made for each other.

But it wasn't enough. Not tonight.

I dipped my head, capturing her lips in a kiss that was raw and unrelenting. There was no softness, no hesitation—just the need to hold her as if the world might end tomorrow.

"We need to forget," I murmured against her lips, my voice rough with everything I couldn't say. "Just for tonight."

She nodded, her eyes shining with the same hunger and ache that burned through me. "Then make me forget," she whispered.

I pulled her closer, clinging to her like she was the only thing keeping me standing. The war, the loss, the fear—all of it faded until there was nothing but her.

We held on to each other like it might be the last time.

And if it was, we weren't going to let go.

"I love you," she whispered against my lips.

"I love you too," I replied roughly.

Tomorrow loomed over us like a storm cloud, but for tonight—for just this moment—all that mattered was us.

And if this was the end, at least we'd go down together.

That night, we lay in bed, tangled together in the dark. Neither of us could sleep.

Her fingers traced slow patterns over my skin, not in a way that was meant to seduce, but in a way that made me think she was trying to memorize me—every scar, every inch. Like she was afraid this might be the last time she got to do it.

I caught her wrist, pressing a kiss to her palm. "I love you." I wasn't sure I could say it enough.

She turned her head against the pillow, looking at me in the dim light. "I love you, too."

I didn't say anything else.

Neither did she.

Because what else was there to say?

We had until sunrise.

After that, we would be at war.

Chapter 66

At the Ready

Alessandra

The night was dark, thick with the kind of silence that always came before bloodshed.

For weeks, we had been waiting for Vito to strike. His reach had been damaged after Steven's rescue, his alliances weakened. But he wasn't done. Not yet.

And neither were we.

I stood in my office, staring at the map spread across my desk. Markings of escape routes, supply caches, and controlled demolition points were scribbled across the blueprints of the estate. This wasn't just a fight—it was an ending.

A knock at the door pulled me from my thoughts.

"Come in," I called.

Salvatore stepped inside, his expression unreadable, but I knew the weight he carried. He had been a loyal enforcer, Nico's right hand, and now... he would take my place.

"You're sure about this?" he asked, his voice quiet but firm.

I nodded. "Steven and I can't fight this war from the inside anymore. If we stay, we're targets. If we go, we have a chance to finish this—permanently."

Salvatore exhaled sharply, crossing his arms. "And you expect me to clean up the mess?"

I met his gaze, unwavering. "I expect you to lead. The men trust you. More than that—they need you. Vito won't stop until he's dead or in control. If you step up, if you give them something to rally behind, we have a chance of keeping the business from falling into his hands."

His jaw tightened, his loyalty warring with his instinct for survival. "And if I refuse?"

"You won't," I said simply.

Silence. Then—he sighed, dragging a hand down his face. "You're a pain in the ass, you know that?"

A small smile touched my lips. "I've heard."

He shook his head, but there was something resigned in his expression. "If I do this, I want something guaranteed."

I nodded. "Name it."

"When it's over—when Vito is nothing but a memory—I get to walk away. No debts. No favors. No unfinished business."

I considered his words. He had given everything to this family, sacrificed more than I ever had. If he wanted an out, he deserved it.

"You have my word. Because when this is over, there shouldn't be anything to walk away from," I said.

Salvatore studied me for a long moment before nodding. "Alright. Let's burn this place to the ground."

For weeks, we had waited for Vito to strike. His reach had been damaged after Steven's rescue, his alliances weakened. But he wasn't out. Not yet. And now, after months of planning, of playing this war in the shadows, he was making his final move.

We had prepared for this. Every man was in position, the estate fortified like a fortress. I had run the numbers, predicted the angles, mapped every possible breach point. And yet, standing here now, the weight of what was coming pressed against my ribs, making it hard to breathe.

Because no matter how much we prepared—war was war.

I adjusted the holster at my hip, rolling my shoulders to shake off the tension. Steven was in the house, stationed with Salvatore in the command room. He had wanted to be out here, on the front lines, but I wouldn't allow it. Not after what he had been through. Not when I still woke in the middle of the night, reaching for him just to make sure he was still breathing.

"Stay sharp," Salvatore muttered, his eyes scanning the darkness. "They'll be here soon."

I nodded, my grip on the gun tightening as I listened to the silence, waiting for the first sign of trouble. My heart was pounding in my chest, adrenaline coursing through my veins, but I forced myself to stay calm. I had to be ready.

And then, the night exploded. Gunfire erupted from all sides, shattering the silence and sending shockwaves through the estate. Vito's men poured in, their figures barely visible in the darkness as they fired with ruthless precision.

"Get down!" Salvatore shouted, pushing me behind a column as bullets whizzed past us, the sound deafening in the night.

I crouched low, returning fire, but it was clear we were outnumbered. Vito had brought everything he had, and despite our preparations, we were being overwhelmed. I could hear the shouts of our men, the sounds of bodies hitting the ground, and the acrid smell of gunpowder filled the air.

"We need to fall back!" I shouted to Salvatore, but before he could respond, an explosion rocked the estate, throwing us both to the ground.

I hit the ground hard, the wind knocked out of me as I struggled to get my bearings. My ears were ringing, my vision blurred, but I forced myself to crawl to my feet, desperate to find Steven.

"Alessandra!" Salvatore's voice cut through the chaos, snapping me back to the present. I turned to see him helping one of our men to his feet, both of them dazed and battered from the first explosion. "We need to move!"

I nodded, starting toward him, but before I could reach Salvatore, a second explosion tore through the night, far more powerful than the first. The shockwave hit with brutal force, sending Salvatore and the men around him flying. I stumbled, barely keeping my footing as debris rained down.

My heart pounded as I scanned the area, desperate to find Steven. The estate was a war zone, with flames roaring and the shouts of our men echoing through the night. And then I saw him—Steven, struggling to stand amidst the chaos, his face set in grim determination despite the obvious pain.

Relief surged through me, but it was short-lived. A third explosion ripped through the courtyard, and I watched in horror as Steven was thrown to the ground, his body slamming hard against the unforgiving earth. He didn't move.

"Steven!" I screamed, the sound ripping from my throat as I raced toward him. I dropped to my knees beside him, panic clawing at my chest. He was breathing, but it was shallow, and his eyes fluttered open as I cradled his head in my lap.

"I'm... okay," he rasped, his voice barely audible over the roar of the flames.

"We have to get out of here," I said, trying to stay calm as tears blurred my vision. "We have to go now."

Salvatore, dazed but alive, was struggling to get back on his feet a few yards away. But I knew we didn't have time to wait for him to recover. The situation was spiraling out of control, and every second we lingered was a second closer to death.

Steven groaned as I helped him to his feet, his body trembling from the shock. "Where... where do we go?"

"We stick to the plan," I whispered, gripping his hand tightly. "Just us."

Salvatore, still recovering from the blast, was too disoriented to notice as I guided Steven away from the wreckage. We moved quickly, using the chaos and smoke as cover as we slipped through a side path, away from the main courtyard. The spot where we'd stashed the car earlier was close, but it felt like miles as we navigated through the destruction.

The estate was collapsing behind us, the flames devouring everything in their path. But we couldn't look back. There was only forward.

We reached the secluded spot where the car was hidden, away from any prying eyes. I opened the door and helped Steven inside, his movements sluggish but determined. My hands shook as I started the engine, the weight of what we were leaving behind pressing down on me like a leaden blanket.

As we sped away from the inferno, I glanced at Steven. His face was pale, a thin line of blood trailing from a cut on his forehead, but his eyes were sharp, focused.

"We made it," he murmured, his voice weak but steady. "We got out."

"Barely," I muttered, my grip tightening on the steering wheel as the city lights blurred past us.

His hand found mine, squeezing it gently.

We had escaped, but the fight was just beginning. The estate was in ruins, and the men we had left behind... I couldn't think about that now. Not when Steven was beside me, alive but fragile.

We drove into the night, leaving behind the ashes of our old life, with only the uncertainty of what the future would hold.

Chapter 67

Ghosts

Steven

We drove through the night, leaving behind the chaos and devastation that had once been our home. Alessandra had driven at first, her knuckles white on the steering wheel, the tension in her body radiating through the small car. When I finally woke up, the darkness outside was beginning to lighten, the first hints of dawn breaking through the trees.

"Let me take over," I said, my voice rough with exhaustion. Alessandra didn't argue, simply pulling over to the side of the road and sliding out of the driver's seat. She moved like a machine, precise and deliberate, but I could see the weariness in her eyes, the toll of the night etched into every line of her face.

I took the wheel, and she curled up in the passenger seat, her head resting against the window. As I drove, the adrenaline that had kept us going began to fade, replaced by a bone-deep exhaustion that settled into my muscles. But I pushed through it, focused on getting us to safety.

We had agreed on Cedar Key, a small coastal town far enough

from the city to offer anonymity but close enough to keep us connected to the outside world if needed. It was a place neither of us had any ties to, a place where we could disappear.

As we finally pulled into the driveway of a modest coastal home, the sun was beginning to rise, casting a soft glow over the sleepy town. The house was small, unassuming—exactly what we needed. Nate had sent us here, to a decommissioned FBI safe house that had never made it onto any official records. It was perfect for our purposes, a place to lay low and regroup.

Alessandra stirred as I parked the car, blinking against the early morning light. Her eyes met mine, and for a moment, we just looked at each other, the weight of everything we had been through settling between us.

"We're here," I said quietly, reaching over to brush a strand of hair from her face. She nodded, but the tension in her body didn't ease.

We climbed out of the car and made our way inside. The house was sparsely furnished, just the basics—a couch, a small kitchen, a single bedroom with a bed that looked like it hadn't been slept in for years. It was a far cry from the luxury we were used to, but that didn't matter now. We weren't here for comfort.

Once inside, Alessandra collapsed onto the couch, her body sinking into the worn cushions. I sat beside her, watching as she stared blankly ahead, her expression unreadable. The silence between us was heavy, filled with the weight of everything we had lost.

"Alessandra," I said softly, reaching out to take her hand. She didn't pull away, but she didn't respond either. The grief and shock were still fresh, the reality of our situation pressing down on us like a vise.

"We'll get through this," I whispered, though the words felt inadequate. We had no plan, no resources, and our enemies believed us to be dead. It was a thin advantage, but it was all we had.

She finally looked at me, her eyes glassy with unshed tears.

"What now, Steven?" she asked, her voice barely above a whisper. "What do we do now?"

I pulled her into my arms, holding her close as she buried her face in my chest. "We disappear," I said, my voice firm despite the uncertainty gnawing at me. "We let the world think we're dead. And when the time is right, we finish what we started."

She didn't respond, but she didn't pull away either. I knew how hard this was for her—the idea of abandoning the fight, of letting Vito think he had won. But we had no other choice. Survival meant disappearing completely, becoming ghosts in the world we once ruled.

We spent the rest of the day erasing any trace of our identities—burning our old IDs, destroying anything that could lead Vito to us. Every step felt like a small death, a piece of our old lives disappearing into the flames, but it was necessary. We couldn't afford to leave any trace behind.

That night, as we lay in bed, holding each other close, the exhaustion finally began to overtake us. The adrenaline that had kept us going was gone, replaced by a bone-deep weariness. But as I held Alessandra in my arms, I felt a sense of calm wash over me. We had survived the night, and we had each other. For now, that was enough.

"I love you," I whispered, pressing a kiss to her forehead.

"I love you too," Alessandra replied, her voice filled with a quiet strength.

As we drifted off to sleep, the weight of what lay ahead loomed large. For now, though, I held the only future that mattered to me in my arms.

About the Author

I write romance for readers who crave a little drama, suspense, and a little simmer in their happily-ever-afters. With brooding heroes, fierce heroines, and dangerous desires, my stories explore love that burns hot—and sometimes leaves a scar. If you're looking for passion behind closed doors, you've found the right author.

I'm a southern girl at heart, fluent in sweet tea and the art of saying 'bless your heart' when the situation calls for it.

Made in the USA
Coppell, TX
15 June 2026

81372100R00177